WINTER WISHES IN HOPE COVE

HOPE COVE BOOK 7

HANNAH ELLIS

Published by Hannah Ellis
www.authorhannahellis.com
Postfach 900309, 81503 München
Germany

WINTER WISHES IN HOPE COVE

CHAPTER 1

It was the view that Lizzie had first fallen in love with. Seaside Cottage was wonderful, but it was the moment of stepping through the crumbly wooden door in the tall hedge at the end of the garden that had taken her breath away.

The view had left her speechless the first time she'd seen it. Now, more than four years later, the rugged Devon coastline still had the power to stop her in her tracks.

"Did you forget something?" Max asked, turning to see why she'd paused.

"No. Just admiring the view." Most of the time, she was too busy shepherding two toddlers and her loyal old springer spaniel to enjoy it. "It never gets old."

"Just like me," he quipped.

She spluttered a laugh. "Your hairline would suggest otherwise."

"Hey!" He ran his hand through his hair. "I'm in my prime, I'll have you know."

"We'll have to start thinking about how to celebrate your fortieth before long."

"I'm not forty for two years!" Max ran his teeth along his bottom lip. "You really love teasing me, don't you?"

"Only about your age. And only because you're so sensitive about it."

"I'd like to remind you that you're older than me."

She nodded. "Only by a year. And I look great for my age."

Taking a step towards her, he slipped an arm around her waist. "What are you implying about me?"

"Nothing." She laughed at how easy it was to wind him up. "I think you look great. For your age!"

"You're mean." He tickled her until she squirmed to get away from him. "Are we going? We'll be stumbling along in the dark if we don't get a move on."

It had been Lizzie's idea to walk along the coastal path rather than along the road. She always chose that way if daylight permitted.

Pausing, she glanced up at the house. "Are you sure the girls will be okay with Dotty?"

"We're only going to the pub. And the girls are fast asleep."

"We should probably have asked Emily and Jack to come over instead of leaving them with a woman in her seventies."

"Dotty offered," Max said. "She likes to feel useful. Can we just go? I'm hungry. We're wasting date night, hanging around at the back of the house."

"We're not wasting anything. First, I was enjoying the view. Then I was enjoying teasing you. So far date night's going brilliantly."

He rolled his eyes. "Let's go."

Taking his hand, she pulled him away from the path and down the couple of uneven steps to the beach.

"This is the wrong way," he pointed out.

"It's so beautiful." Lizzie looked out to the horizon as the last rays of sunlight shimmered on the water. "I want to have a paddle."

"Your feet will freeze off."

"It's not that cold." Actually, there was a nip in the air, but considering it was October that was to be expected.

"You're in a strange mood," Max said while she took her shoes and socks off, hanging onto his arm for support.

"Humour me." She gave him a quick kiss before hurrying to the water's edge. The cold water made her gasp as it rolled over her toes. After a moment she got used to it and rolled up her trouser legs to venture a little deeper. "You should come with me," she called to Max.

He sat on the sand further up the beach and only shook his head as he watched her in amusement.

"It's wonderful," she told him, but he still didn't move.

After a few minutes of walking in the waves, her toes began to go numb and she walked back up the beach to Max. He had a stick in his hand and had written *I love Lizzie* in the sand.

"You're so romantic," she said, sitting heavily beside him. "Keep on like this and you might get lucky tonight."

He smiled lazily and gave her a lingering look that she couldn't quite read.

"You're quiet," she remarked. "Everything okay?"

"Everything's great. Apart from the fact I'm about to starve to death."

"Is that a subtle hint for me to hurry up and put my shoes and socks back on?"

"It wasn't supposed to be subtle."

After brushing as much sand as possible from her feet, she pulled her socks on and pushed her feet into her shoes. "I might regret putting my feet in the water. I'm going to have damp socks all evening. Then I'll end up with sand in the bed tonight."

"There's always sand in the bed," Max said. "There's sand everywhere. I thought you said it's good exfoliation."

"I have to find a way to put a positive spin on it or it'd drive me crazy." She held out her hand for Max to pull her up and they set off again.

"Are you really worried about Dotty looking after the girls?" Max asked when she glanced up at the house.

"No." Their neighbour wasn't exactly sprightly, but the girls were asleep, and they'd told Dotty she should call if they woke up. "Having Dotty to babysit makes me miss Scarlett. And that's something I never imagined myself saying."

Scarlett was the niece of the local cafe owner and had done a lot of babysitting for them over the past six months. Unfortunately, she'd moved away the previous month to attend university in Exeter. It was only an hour away and she'd said she was happy to come back on weekends to babysit, but they didn't feel they could ask her to drive all that way just so that they could go for dinner at the local pub.

"The girls will miss her too," Max said. "University should be good for her though. Not just the degree, but socially."

Lizzie wasn't so sure; Scarlett was one of the most socially awkward people she'd ever met, and she wondered whether the university environment might be too much for her.

"I messaged her a few times," Lizzie said. "But she only ever sends me a few words in reply."

"Probably because she only ever used us for money. It's going to be a much cheaper night out with Dotty babysitting."

"Scarlett didn't only babysit. She used to hang out a lot, even when we weren't paying her."

"Yeah. Like when she wanted you to edit her books for free."

Lizzie had to admit Max might have a point. She liked to

think that Scarlett saw them as friends, but it was always hard to tell what was going on in her head.

"It's nice to be out anyway," she said, as she walked hand in hand with Max. "What made you desperate for a night out? Hard week at work?"

He shot her a sidelong glance, his eyes sparkling at her teasing. After cutting down to working part-time, he currently only worked on Monday and Tuesdays. The rest of the week he was in charge of childcare and housekeeping.

"I think you're a great house-husband," Lizzie said, giving his hand a squeeze. Beneath the light-hearted jibes, she really did appreciate him working part-time. It had taken a lot of pressure off her and meant she could concentrate on her freelance editing business without worrying that the twins were being neglected.

"I wasn't desperate for a night out," Max said. "I just like to spend time with my beautiful wife. If I'd have known how much teasing there'd be, I'd have opted for a takeaway and an early night."

She leaned briefly into him as they walked. "I only tease you because I love you so much."

"And because it's fun," he said.

"Yes. I do find it very enjoyable."

He gave a gentle laugh and they continued on in silence. Soon, the path curved with the coastline and began the descent to the pretty little bay at Hope Cove. The daylight was fading fast, but the streetlights cast a gentle glow across the beach. Gusty winds lifted a fine spray from the water, forming a mist which reached up to low-hanging grey clouds. Even when the weather wasn't at its best, Lizzie still loved the view. Fishing boats sat tilted on the sand, and seagulls hopped between them, their incessant cries drifting on the wind.

When they reached the pub, the warmth of the room

enveloped Lizzie and she rubbed her arms to warm herself further. She smiled at the owner of the local cafe as they approached the bar. Verity was a lovely, gentle soul and had been one of the first friends Lizzie had made when she moved to the village.

"Have you found yourselves a new babysitter?" Verity asked, while Max ordered drinks.

"Dotty offered to stay with the girls for the evening." Lizzie bent to stroke the chocolate Labrador nuzzling at her legs. His owner, Bill, stood beside Verity at the bar. "I was just saying we miss having Scarlett around. You must miss her too."

"I do," Verity said. "Have you heard much from her?"

"Not really. Just the odd message but she doesn't say much."

Verity shook her head and clicked her tongue. "I'm worried about her."

"Isn't she having a good time?" Lizzie asked, secretly hoping Scarlett hated university and would move back to the village and be available for babysitting at the drop of a hat.

"I've no idea," Verity said. "She doesn't say much, only that it's fine. I'm sure she sees me as her fuddy-duddy old aunt, so I was hoping she might have confided in you or Emily. She's very fond of you both."

"I don't think that's how she thinks of you. But she hasn't said anything to me about uni either."

Bill smiled at Lizzie then instructed the dog to lie down with a firm nod of the head. "If Scarlett says she's fine, I'm sure she is," he said kindly.

"She's at an impressionable age," Verity said. "I'm worried she's got in with a bad crowd."

"What makes you say that?" Max asked.

Verity's cheeks were flushed and her brow creased in concern. "It's probably nothing, but she's living with a new friend. She won't let me visit, and she won't answer my questions. Before she went away she was worried about money. She even thought she couldn't afford to go to uni for a while. Now she suddenly has money. I don't know where it came from."

Max smiled. "Scarlett's always good at figuring out a way to get what she wants. I wouldn't worry. She's a student and wants her independence."

"I hope that's all it is." Verity touched Lizzie's arm. "Will you let me know if you hear from her?"

"Of course." Lizzie smiled at her and Bill, then followed Max to a booth at the far side of the room.

"I'll give you two minutes to decide what you want to eat," he said as he passed her a menu. "Then I'm going to the bar to order, and if you haven't decided I'll choose for you."

"You get very grumpy when you're hungry," she said, then told him what she wanted without looking at the menu.

When he returned from ordering food, he slipped onto the seat beside her, draping an arm around her shoulders and kissing her cheek.

"You're very affectionate this evening," she remarked.

"Am I?" His gaze drifted across the pub with the faraway look that he often had recently.

"What's going on with you?" Lizzie asked.

He snapped from his trance. "Nothing, why? Do you have a problem with me being affectionate?"

"No. I didn't mean that. You just seem as though you have a lot on your mind."

Lizzie suspected she knew exactly what was bothering him. She'd been bracing for a conversation where he told her he was fed up with only working part-time and wanted to increase his hours. His days spent doing housework and looking after the girls probably weren't very fulfilling. Max was like her – he'd always thrived on his work. Even when he'd switched careers from law to property management, he'd still worked long hours.

"The only thing on my mind," he said, "is spending a relaxed evening with my gorgeous wife."

She was prevented from commenting on how cheesy he sounded by the butterflies that fluttered in her stomach. His leg pressed against hers as he leaned closer, and she felt like a teenager as they shared a tender kiss.

"That was actually a lie," he said as he pulled away. "You're not the only thing on my mind."

"What else?" she asked, feeling slightly light-headed.

"Food. I'm starving."

Playfully, Lizzie shoved at his arm. She was sure there was a lot more going on in his head, but she was also happy to delay the conversation. Finally, she was perfectly content with their family life and really didn't want things to change.

CHAPTER 2

Story time at the bookshop had always been Tara's favourite part of the job, and it had only become more enjoyable with time. She was proud of the sense of community she and James had cultivated. They knew so many of the local children and parents that it was difficult to go anywhere in Newton Abbot without stopping for a chat.

She'd been enjoying her morning coffee in the quiet shop when the door opened, jingling the bell above. Maya and Phoebe toddled in and made a beeline for the beanbags in the children's section.

"They missed you last week," Max said, wandering in after them with a bunch of flowers in one hand and a wrapped gift in the other. Tara had been friends with Max since they were kids, and she'd been touched when he'd rearranged the girls' schedule so they could come to story time on Thursday mornings. They had the whole day with their daddy and all three of them seemed to enjoy coming to the bookshop.

"I was a bit busy last week," she said sheepishly.

"So I hear. I wasn't entirely surprised, to be honest.

Anyway, I'm happy for you. Congratulations!" He smiled warmly as he handed over the flowers and present.

"Thank you." She set them on the counter and hugged Max. "I was worried eloping might have meant we missed out on wedding presents, but we're doing okay so far."

"What was it like getting married at Gretna Green?"

"Really lovely." She beamed thinking of it. "We met this Scottish couple who were getting married on the same day. They were great fun."

"I'm glad you had a good time." The door at the back of the shop opened and James walked in. "Congratulations!" Max said, reaching to shake his hand.

"Thanks." James scooped Phoebe up when she barrelled into his legs. "How are you doing, you little rascal?" She grinned at him and wriggled to be let down again.

"So you were here last week?" Tara asked Max.

"Yes. Your mum and Amber had everything under control."

"I was worrying about Mum the whole time we were away," Tara said. Not that it was anything new; her mum's episodes of depression meant that Tara had spent most of her life worrying about her. "It seems as though she enjoyed looking after the shop, though."

Max nodded. "Debbie was great with the kids. It all seemed to go very smoothly from where I was sitting."

"See," James said. "We'll be able to go away more often."

"Maybe." Tara ignored the hint of smugness in James's voice. He'd insisted that Debbie would be fine looking after the shop and had even thought it might be good for her. Tara hadn't been quite as confident but was happy to be wrong on this occasion.

As a crowd of lively customers drifted in over the next fifteen minutes, Tara and James milled around, tickling small children and chatting with their grown-up counterparts.

Tara had just taken her seat in front of the children when a blonde-haired four-year-old called Archie came over to her.

"Can we have the hungry caterpillar today?" he asked.

Tara glanced at the pile of books in her lap. "I didn't pick that one for today."

"It's my favourite. I like it when we wriggle like caterpillars."

"It's good to read different books. Not the same ones every week."

"But it's my very favourite." He stuck his bottom lip out dramatically. "And I like it when we pretend to turn into butterflies at the end and everyone flies around the room."

Rosie, who was sitting cross-legged at the front, wriggled on her bottom. "I like being a butterfly too."

"Did you have it last week?" Tara asked. "When I wasn't here?"

Archie looked thoughtful for a moment, then shook his head firmly. "No." Beside him Rosie giggled, giving away the fact that he was lying.

"Are you sure?" Tara looked him straight in the eyes.

His face cracked into a grin and he laughed loudly. When Tara caught Max's eye, he shrugged and tried his best to look innocent.

"Fine." Tara gave Archie a playful poke in his tummy. "Go and fetch the caterpillar book."

Archie moved to the box of well-loved children's books that were set aside for story times and found it straight away. "That nice lady read it last week," he said when he handed it to Tara.

"I thought she might have done. That nice lady is my mummy, you know?"

"She's very good at reading stories."

"Glad to hear it," Tara said, then scanned the eager faces on the carpet in front of her. "Now, do we have any hungry caterpillars here this morning?" Amid giggles, the children dropped onto their tummies and squirmed around as she began the story.

An hour went by in a flash and Tara was waving kids goodbye before she knew it. Some parents hung around to chat and browse the shop while the kids looked through the books and played with a box of battered toys.

Tara's best friend, Amber, had arrived late with her little boy, Kieron, so Tara didn't get a chance to greet her properly until things died down. By that time, only Max remained, chatting away to James while the girls played on the carpet.

"Congratulations!" Amber said, wrapping Tara in a hug. "I left your present with the rest of them."

Tara glanced at the collection of gift bags and presents by the counter. "I can't believe so many people bought us gifts."

"I think we've got quite a good supply of wine and champagne," James said, joining the conversation.

"I don't know why you're surprised," Amber said. "You're the hub of the community. Everyone around here loves you." She moved to settle a dispute over a toy between Kieron and Phoebe. "I got really upset the other day because I realised that this time next year Kieron will be in school and we won't be able to come to story time any more."

Tara also didn't like the thought of not having them there. "You'll just graduate to the after-school story time on Tuesdays instead."

"It's not the same," Amber said. "I love my Thursday mornings." She intercepted Kieron as he was about to hit Phoebe over the head with a book. "I'll have to take him home. He's refusing naps, but he turns into a monster at this time of day. I try to get him to have some quiet time at least."

She held a hand out to him, gently telling him it was time to go. "Do you want to come to the pub on Friday night?" she asked Tara. "I want to hear all about the wedding and have a proper look through the photos with you. Preferably without this one around so I can concentrate." She indicated Kieron with a tip of her chin as they started towards the door.

"Friday sounds good," Tara said. At one time, they didn't even need to plan it – Friday night in the Bluebell Inn was just part of their routine, but these days it wasn't such a regular occurrence. "I'll see if Josie and Sam want to come too."

"Great. See you!" Amber called from the door.

"We should get going," Max said, when Tara wandered back to the children's corner.

"What's your plan for the afternoon?" she asked him.

"The usual routine: late lunch at Verity's cafe, then a run around the beach and back home to chill out in front of the TV until Lizzie finishes work."

"That sounds good," Tara said. "Did you ever figure out a way to keep the girls awake in the car so they nap at home?"

Max tidied up the toys around the girls, dropping them back into the box. "No. I made a new plan. They have a snack in the car and I drive the long way home so they fall asleep. Then I park up on the drive and recline my seat for my own nap until they wake up."

"So Thursdays are pretty nice?" James said.

"I love Thursdays." Max looked thoughtful. "I also enjoy Wednesdays and Fridays when they're in nursery in the morning and I get some peace. Mondays and Tuesdays are good too, when they're in nursery all day and I get to go to work."

"It sounds like you've got it all sussed out," Tara said.

Max smiled. "I'm not sure about that."

"You make it look very easy," James said.

"It's definitely not easy." Max lifted Maya on to his arm, then offered Phoebe his hand. "I can't complain, though."

"I'll help you put the girls in the car." James coaxed the

toy from Phoebe and picked her up. Immediately, she leaned towards the bookshelf, reaching for a book with a cuddly toy attached to the front cover. "You want a book, do you?" James said. "You'd have to ask your daddy nicely."

Max sighed. "This free story time costs me a fortune."

"It's books," Tara said. "They're educational."

"We'll take that book." Max groaned when Maya lurched towards the bookshelf. "I guess we'll need two."

Tara looked through the shelves for a book for Maya, while Max pulled his wallet out and handed her his credit card.

"You could always learn to say no to them," Tara pointed out as she took the card to the till.

"I don't have a problem saying no to them," he replied. "It's the twenty-minute screaming fit I'll have to endure that I have a problem with. And it's not like you can spoil kids with books, is it?"

"Definitely not," James said. "And I say that completely impartially as the owner of a bookshop."

"When Lizzie gives me an earful, I'm blaming you two."

Tara handed him his card back and walked to the door with them. "Why don't you and Lizzie come to the Bluebell Inn on Friday night too?"

"Maybe." He kissed Tara's cheek at the door. "I'll speak to Lizzie and let you know. Congratulations again."

Tara wandered to the back of the shop and was browsing through the wedding presents when James returned.

"People were really generous," she said. "I wasn't expecting gifts. Not from customers."

"A lot of them feel like friends." He picked up a box and gave it a gentle shake. "Too big for a photo frame … I guess vase."

"I say random ornament … open it up."

He pulled the wrapping off then lifted the flaps on the box. "Candle," he said. "We were both wrong."

"That's pretty." Tara peered at the large glass candle-holder. "We should move these upstairs. We'll look a bit strange opening presents if customers come in."

James began picking up boxes and bags until his arms were full. After holding the door for him, Tara went to the counter and retrieved her phone from the shelf under the till. She was re-reading a message when James came back.

"What's wrong?"

Her head snapped up. "Nothing. I got a message from Nat." Her half-sister messaged her regularly these days. They'd practically been estranged until about six months ago when Tara had reconnected with her dad and his family. Tara and James had been to London to see them, and they'd met a couple of times at convenient locations between London and Devon.

Getting to know her half-siblings had been slightly unsettling for Tara. At fifteen, Ben was your stereotypical moody teenager who didn't seem overly interested in the appearance of his older sister in his life. Natalie, on the other hand, had welcomed Tara with open arms and decided they should be best friends – at least judging by the number of messages she sent.

"What did she say?" James asked.

"She says congratulations again on the wedding." Tara's eyes scanned the message. "She's *sooo* excited for us. Then there are about twenty emojis. And she asked if she can come and stay with us at the weekend."

"This weekend?"

"Yeah. She wants to bring us a wedding present, and she's desperate to see the bookshop. Dad offered to drive her down on Friday afternoon." Tara took a deep breath, unnerved by the idea of having her half-sister encroaching on the life that she'd spent so long keeping her dad and his family away from.

"That's fine, isn't it?" James said. "It's a good excuse to clean up the spare bedroom."

"Yes," Tara said without enthusiasm. "Except we'll be working all day on Saturday so she'll be bored."

"I can manage on my own. You could take her out somewhere."

"We also said we'd help Mum on Sunday. She wants you to put her new wardrobe together for her and take away the old one."

"I can do that alone. Or we can take Nat with us."

"To Mum's house? I don't think so."

"Why not?"

"It'd be awkward for Mum. I don't want to make her uncomfortable."

"She might be okay with it. Ask her."

"I can't," Tara insisted. "It'll cause issues."

"But maybe she'd be fine with it."

"Of course she wouldn't be. She's emotionally unstable and she's still in love with my dad. How's she going to feel about spending time with one of Dad's children from his other wife?"

"I don't know. And you won't know unless you ask her."

"There's no way I'm asking her." Tara groaned as another message came through on her phone. "It's Nat again. *Please say yes. Really want to hang out with my favourite sister!* Followed by a winky face and then about a hundred more emojis."

"I think there's a bit of hero worship going on there. You can't disappoint her."

Tara sighed. "I guess we can see Mum later on Sunday after Nat's left. What about Friday night, though? We're supposed to meet everyone in the pub."

"She's seventeen. We can take her with us, can't we? It's probably more fun for her than sitting around here with us. We'll look cool, taking her to the pub."

"Yeah, because the Bluebell Inn is such a happening place for teenagers!"

"Oh stop being so miserable." James nuzzled her neck until she laughed and pushed him away. "Tell her she can come and you can't wait to see her. And add a load of smiley faces so she knows you mean it."

Reluctantly, Tara tapped out a reply. The thought of introducing her sister to her friends and showing her where she lived didn't exactly fill her with joy, but she supposed it was only for one weekend.

CHAPTER 3

Emily sat on the window seat in the bedroom, staring out across the garden to the rolling waves of the sea. A few boats bobbed a little way out and a sailing boat moved steadily along the horizon. In her lap was the notebook in which she'd been scribbling notes for her next book: a historical romance weaved around the smuggling trade in Hope Cove in the early 1900s. She'd drifted into a daydream where the scenes of her planned novel played out in her head like a film.

At the sound of the front door opening, she snapped out of the trance and called hello in reply to Jack. Her foot had gone numb from where she'd been sitting with it underneath her, and she hobbled down the stairs.

"What's wrong?" Jack asked.

"My leg went dead." She stopped and wriggled her toes, circling her ankle to get the blood flowing back to it. "How was work?" She had to think for a moment to remember the day. On Mondays and Tuesdays he worked at the local pub, and the rest of the week he worked as a property manager – a job-share arrangement with Max. It was Wednesday so it was the property management stuff. He seemed to prefer that. There was more variety to his days. Not that he ever complained about working in the pub. The social side of it suited him well.

"Work was good. How long until dinner?" His eyes flashed with anticipation. "I've been looking forward to your casserole all day."

"I said I'd make casserole, didn't I?" She'd fully intended to, but time had got away from her. "I can start on it now. It'll take an hour or so. Sorry," she said at the disappointment in his eyes.

"That's fine. Maybe I'll just whip us up something quick."

"I really was going to cook." Usually it was Jack who cooked, but she'd promised him that morning that she'd make dinner. "I didn't notice the time."

"It doesn't matter. I can make pasta."

"I'm sorry." She wrapped her arms around him and snuggled into his chest. "I'm a terrible girlfriend, but I promise I'm going to raise my game when I'm your wife."

"So I can expect dinner on the table every evening when we're married?" he asked mockingly.

"I wouldn't go that far. I'm trying to get lots of work done now so I can completely relax on our honeymoon." They were on a tight budget so they weren't going anywhere fancy but would have a few days back in Oxford to see family and friends – something that they never seemed to find time to do – and then they'd have a few nights in London where they'd play tourists, visiting the sights and going to a show.

"I'm not sure I believe you're not going to work while we're away."

"I promise I'm not. And I want to try and cut down on work generally."

"You say that often," Jack said. "And I'm not sure why

when the books are selling and it's all going so well. You only say you're going to cut down because you think I want you to, but I don't mind doing all the cooking. It's only because you said you were going to cook that I was thinking about it."

"You're very good to me, you know?" She kissed him, then pulled away and headed for the kitchen. "I'll throw some pasta in if you want something quick. I'll try again for the casserole tomorrow."

"It's not a big deal. Don't worry about it." He sat at the kitchen table while she pulled out a saucepan and filled it with water.

"I got a message from Tara earlier," Emily said. "Inviting us to the Bluebell Inn on Friday night to celebrate their wedding."

"It's so cool that they eloped."

"Do you wish we were doing the same?" she asked.

"No. I like a party. I can't wait actually."

"Glad to hear it," she said, turning the hob to its full heat. "I can't believe it's only a week and a half away. The last six months have flown by."

"What time are our mums arriving on Saturday?"

Both of their mums were coming over for Emily's hen party. The two of them got on well and would drive down together and stay for a night.

"Around lunchtime, I think. Did you decide when you're driving to Oxford? Friday night or Saturday morning?"

"Probably Saturday."

"You don't sound very enthusiastic about your stag night."

"I'm not. I can't be bothered. Living in a village must have changed me because I'd much rather have drinks in the Bluebell Inn with Sam and Max than have a pub crawl around Oxford with the old football crew."

Emily sat opposite Jack while she waited for the water to boil. "If you leave on Saturday morning we can go to the Bluebell with everyone on Friday night."

"That sounds like a good plan. Drinks with everyone will be fun. Have you spoken to Josie? Do you know how she's doing?"

"She's fine. Hopefully she'll be there on Friday night. I wanted to meet up with her this week, but she fobbed me off. I think she's sick of hearing me talk about the wedding."

"She's eight months pregnant. And she's massive. I'm sure she just can't be bothered to move."

"I offered to go to her place so she wouldn't have to move."

"I wouldn't read too much into it," Jack said.

"It makes me sad how we've drifted apart. I've tried to be supportive around the pregnancy, but it's like she doesn't want me around. If it wasn't for Lizzie I wouldn't even have a maid of honour."

"So that's still annoying you?" Jack asked with a small smile. "The only reason Josie turned you down is because she doesn't want to stand at the front of the church in a bridesmaid's dress when she's eight months pregnant."

Rationally, Emily knew that was the reason, but she was still hurt that Josie had said no when she'd asked her to be her maid of honour. Usually, Josie would throw herself into everything. Emily had almost expected she'd enjoy showing off her baby bump in front of everyone. She'd always liked to be the centre of attention.

"It's great that Lizzie's been so supportive," Jack said. "She seems really excited about the wedding whenever I speak to her."

"Yes, she's been great." She'd been dress shopping with Emily when Josie hadn't felt up to it. Emily wasn't sure how she'd have managed without Lizzie's friendship over the past months. They met up for lunch once or twice a week for a break from the solitude of being self-employed and working from home.

As the water began to boil on the stove, Emily went to put the pasta in, then searched the cupboard for a jar of sauce. It wasn't exactly gourmet cuisine, but Jack had known from the outset that he wasn't getting a domestic goddess for a wife.

CHAPTER 4

Tara was about to close the shop on Friday afternoon when the bell above the door tinkled and her dad and half-sister walked in.

Nat's eyes were wide as she took in the shop.

"This place is gorgeous," she cooed as she embraced Tara. "The window displays are stunning. I bet no one can walk past without coming in. You're so lucky. Is it really half yours?"

"Well, we're married now. We share everything." Tara was also officially part owner of the bookshop. The paperwork had been finalised and her name was on the deeds.

"It's great to finally see the place after hearing so much about it," her dad said as Tara hugged him. "Congratulations on the wedding." He passed her a gift bag.

"Mum and I chose the present," Nat said happily. "It's from a pottery shop near our house. They hand-paint everything. All their stuff is gorgeous."

"Thank you." Tara stepped around them to switch the sign on the door to closed and lock the door. "James is upstairs. Shall we go up?"

"In a minute," Nat said. "I need to have a proper look around first." As she set off along the rows of bookshelves, Tara walked to the back of the shop with David.

"It really is great," he said.

"We've put a lot of work into it."

"It's paid off," he said, before they descended into silence. They hadn't spent much time together since Tara was a little girl, and there were moments when he felt like a stranger.

"I love it!" Nat crooned as she looked around the children's corner. "It's so cute. I bet kids love coming here."

"They do," Tara said proudly. "We have story time twice a week. It's my favourite time. Author visits are also great. Any time that we have groups in is fun."

"You're so lucky to be surrounded by books all day," Nat said. "I'm a bookworm too. We have that in common."

"It's a recent thing for me," Tara replied, slightly distracted by Nat's glossy dark hair which fell around her shoulders in a similar style to her own. "When I was your age, I hardly read at all. I thought only geeks read so I stayed away from books. Working in a bookshop converted me."

"You must have had an interest before you started working here?" Nat said, bounding over to her. "How can you get a job in a bookshop if you don't like books?"

Tara hid her mouth behind her hand as she mock whispered, "I lied."

"Really?" Nat's eyes sparkled with silent laughter.

"Yes. But if I'm going to tell you this story we should go upstairs and involve James. He likes to tell his side of it."

"I definitely want to hear this," Nat said as Tara opened the door at the back of the shop, which led to a flight of stairs and the flat above.

"Are you staying for dinner?" Tara asked her dad. "You can stay the night if you don't mind sleeping on the couch."

"No," Nat said quickly. "He's going home again tonight. I need some parent-free time."

David smiled at Tara as she directed them up the stairs. "Have you got anything special planned for the weekend?"

"Not really," Tara replied. "We're going to meet some friends in the pub tonight."

"Brilliant!" Nat said. "Will your friend Amber be there? And Josie? I can't wait to meet them."

Tara told her they would. She barely remembered mentioning her friends to Nat, but apparently her sister had a good memory.

"You know Nat's underage?" her dad said.

"Yes." Tara paused at the top of the stairs. "I wasn't planning on getting her drunk. They sell non-alcoholic drinks in the pub too – coke, lemonade … vodka." She winked at Nat before opening the door to the flat.

"Ha-ha," her dad said dryly.

"All my friends drink anyway," Nat said.

David frowned. "Doesn't mean you can."

Tara held the door for them. One thing she found difficult about reconnecting with her dad was seeing him interact with her half brother and sister. Especially his relationship with Nat. Their closeness reminded Tara of how she'd been with him when she was a little girl, before their family had fallen apart. Back then, Tara had idolised him.

"Something smells amazing!" Nat said, giving James a big hug.

"I made lasagne," he replied, looking slightly surprised by the affectionate greeting.

"I love lasagne," she said. "I think it might be my favourite food. Did I tell you that or was it a lucky guess?"

"Lucky guess." James moved to shake David's hand. "There's loads of food," he said. "We presumed you'd eat with us."

"I'd love to," David said. "Thanks."

"The couch is comfy if you want to stay," James offered.

"Don't you encourage him too." Nat sighed dramatically. "He's not staying the night."

"I could get offended," David said, raising an eyebrow.

Nat waltzed over and put her arms around his waist. "It's nothing personal, I just want to hang out with Tara."

"I know." He rubbed her back.

"Who wants a drink?" Tara asked, feeling slightly uncomfortable. The fact that Nat had a good relationship with their dad shouldn't be a surprise. He'd been a permanent fixture in *her* life.

The whole reason Tara was making an effort to be in touch with him was so that she could build a better relationship with him too. It would take time, that was all.

"Who's hungry?" James asked, pulling the lasagne from the oven while Tara poured the drinks.

Dinner was eaten to the soundtrack of Nat's nonstop chatter. She was studying for her A-levels and told them all about school, her teachers and friends and favourite subjects.

"I should get going," David said, shortly after they'd finished eating. "Have you got everything you need?" he asked Nat.

She stood when he did. "Yes. I'm only here for a weekend. There's not much that I need."

"What about money?" he asked, pulling his wallet out.

She took the two twenty-pound notes he handed to her. "You're the best."

"Do whatever Tara and James tell you to," he said.

"Dad! I'm seventeen, not a kid."

"I realise that. You tell me every five minutes." He kissed the top of her head. "I love you."

"I realise that," she said mockingly. "You tell me every five minutes."

Rolling his eyes, David moved to Tara and kissed her cheek. "Thank you for having her to stay. She's been really excited about it."

"Happy to have her," James said, when Tara seemed to lose the power of speech. She wasn't sure she shared the sentiment and had the feeling the weekend might not be the most relaxing.

"Call if there are any problems," David said as he walked to the door. "Have a great time. I'll be back on Sunday afternoon."

It struck Tara how much of his weekend would be spent sitting in the car. The drive to their place took three hours if there was no traffic. And there was never no traffic.

"There's a train from Newton Abbot," she said. "Nat could get the train and save you the journey."

"That's a good idea," Nat said.

Dad shook his head. "She's never taken a train on her own before."

"I'd make sure she got the right one," Tara said. "And you could meet her at the station at the other end."

"I don't mind the drive." He looked to Tara. "And it's nice for me to see you."

Tara's lip stretched to a tight smile. "See you on Sunday then."

CHAPTER 5

Lizzie cleaned the kitchen after dinner on Friday while listening to Max chase the girls around the living room.

"You better not be swinging them around," she called, knowing his tendency to throw them in the air and hang them upside down by their feet. "They just ate!"

"They're attacking me!" he shouted amid giggles. "You need to come and rescue me."

Lizzie walked into the hallway, wiping her hands on a tea towel as she went. In the living room doorway, she leaned on the doorframe and watched Max writhing on the floor while the girls climbed all over him. He mock cried when Phoebe kneed him in the stomach. The girls found it hysterical and jumped on him even more while he curled up in a ball and covered his head.

"Save me!" he called, glancing out at Lizzie. "I'm outnumbered."

Lizzie looked on in amusement, then grimaced at the line of snot running from Maya's nose and reached for a tissue. As soon as Maya saw Lizzie coming towards her, she buried her face in Max's shoulder, wiping snot all over his sleeve.

"You're disgusting!" he cried, peeling her off him and holding her up in the air with his arms outstretched. "Absolutely disgusting." Her giggles reverberated around the room, then faded at the sound of a loud rapping at the door.

Their visitor let themself in and the girls ran excitedly to the door at the familiar voice.

Max pushed himself up from the floor. "Were we expecting Scarlett?"

"No." Lizzie stepped into the hallway to see Scarlett crouched down to the girls, embracing them both at once. Her copper-brown hair hung loosely to the middle of her back. The low-maintenance blunt cut looked a little scruffy but suited her well. When she stood up, the girls took a hand each and pulled her towards the living room. Tilly had wandered in from the kitchen but padded back to her dog bed when she saw who it was.

"Hi," Lizzie said, touching Scarlett's arm when she avoided eye-contact.

"Hi," she replied, following the girls to their toy box and sitting down with them.

"We didn't know you were coming," Max said.

"Because I didn't tell you." Scarlett was always fairly direct, but seemed irritated today.

"How's uni?" Lizzie asked.

"It's fine."

"How's your housemate?" Max asked.

"All right." She looked up at Lizzie and frowned as she changed the subject. "I heard what happened last week."

"What do you mean?" Lizzie perched on the edge of the armchair.

"I told you if you need me to babysit on the weekends you should call me and I can come back. But Verity told me you asked Dotty to babysit."

"We were only going to the pub for a couple of hours,"

Lizzie said. "We didn't want you to drive all the way from Exeter for that."

"It's not even that far. And Verity gave me her car, so I may as well make use of it. I might start coming back here every weekend."

"You shouldn't do that," Max said. "You'll miss out on the uni experience if you're not there on the weekends. Make sure you get involved in the social side of it."

"I'd rather come back here."

"What about your housemate?" Lizzie asked. "She'll probably be annoyed if you're never there on the weekends."

Scarlett took a toy horse that Phoebe passed to her. "I don't like my housemate so that doesn't matter."

"Have you fallen out with her?" Lizzie wasn't overly surprised; she couldn't imagine Scarlett was easy to live with. But it didn't bode well if they weren't getting on just a few weeks after moving in together.

"We ignore each other," Scarlett said. "It's not a problem. Anyway, I can babysit from now on so don't ask Dotty again. You'll have to pay me extra for petrol, though."

Max raised an eyebrow. "It's much cheaper when Dotty babysits."

"You get what you pay for," Scarlett said. "And I don't think you should put a price on your children's welfare."

"The girls were fine with Dotty," Max said.

Scarlett rolled her eyes. "She's about a hundred years old. If the kids wake up would she even hear them crying? And can she manage the stairs to get to them?"

"Scarlett!" Lizzie hissed. "Dotty's seventy. She's not exactly an invalid."

"Whatever. Are you going out or what?"

"When?" Lizzie asked.

"Now. I came to babysit not hang out with you." She looked at Max and her gaze fell to his shoulder. "You should get changed. You're a grown man – use a tissue not your sleeve."

"I didn't—" Max stopped abruptly, realising she was joking. Lizzie was always impressed by her ability to keep a straight face when she teased.

"We'll go for a drink I suppose," Lizzie said.

"We could drive over to Averton," Max suggested. "Join Tara and James's wedding celebration."

Lizzie gave a nod of approval. They'd told Tara they wouldn't make it due to a lack of babysitter, but it would be nice to join. "You're not driving back to Exeter tonight are you?" she asked Scarlett. "You're staying at Verity's place?"

"Yes. It's not going to be Verity's place for much longer, though. She's moving this weekend. That was another reason for me to come back. I said I'd help her move."

"Verity's moving?" Lizzie asked in surprise. Verity lived in a flat above her little cafe, and Lizzie had no clue she'd been planning on moving.

"They decided it makes more sense."

Max's brow creased and Lizzie was glad it wasn't just her who was confused. "Who's *they*, and what did they decide?"

"Verity and Bill. They decided it makes more sense to live together, so Verity's moving into his house."

Lizzie looked to Max and then Scarlett. "I'm confused. When you say Bill, you mean …?"

"Labrador Bill," she said, helping the girls line up the toy animals.

"Labrador Bill?" Max said slowly.

"Bill who has the Labrador called Perry. I like to call him Labrador Bill. Not that there are any other Bills in the village that I know of. But everyone knows the dog."

"Why would Verity move in with Bill?" Lizzie asked.

"Why did you move in with Max?" Scarlett's tone implied that she thought Lizzie was a bit thick.

Max's jaw hung open and he stared at Scarlett. "Verity and Bill are together?" he finally asked.

"Didn't you know that?"

"I see them together a lot, but I just thought they were friends."

"No." Scarlett shook her head. "Lovers."

Max slapped his hands to his face, covering his eyes and then shaking his head as though trying to remove the mental image. "Isn't Bill a lot older than Verity?"

Scarlett shrugged. "Ten years."

"Not that much of an age gap then," Max mused.

"No. About the same as you two, isn't it?"

Lizzie stifled a laugh at the look of horror on Max's face. She couldn't catch Scarlett's eye, but she was fairly sure she was winding him up.

"We're the same age," he snapped.

"Oh," Scarlett said innocently. "I always thought you were older than Lizzie."

"No," he grumbled.

"Why don't you get changed?" Lizzie stood and tipped her chin at Max. "Do you want us to put the girls to bed before we go?" she asked Scarlett.

"No. I know what I'm doing."

Five minutes later, Lizzie followed Max out of the house. He turned to look at her on the front path.

"Did she seriously think I was ten years older than you? And does she think you look young for your age, or does she think I'm approaching fifty?"

"I think she was having fun at your expense," Lizzie said, stopping by the car.

"That's really rude!"

"Oh, Max!" She leaned into him affectionately. "If you look closely you can see the glimmer in her eyes when she's joking."

"She always looks straight-faced to me. Do you think she was joking about Verity and Bill too?"

"No. I think that's true."

"Good luck to them, I guess. I wonder what Verity plans to do with her flat."

"I asked Scarlett while you were getting changed. She says she's trying to convince Verity to rent the flat to her."

"How could Scarlett afford to rent the flat? And why would she need it when she's living in Exeter?"

"She wouldn't say," Lizzie said. "Just told me she was working on a plan for something awesome and she'd let me know more soon."

"She's always plotting something. It doesn't sound as though uni's going too well."

"I suppose it was inevitable that she'd struggle with the social side."

Max opened the car door for her. "Hopefully she'll settle in better with time."

"I'm secretly happy she's so keen to come back and babysit," Lizzie said as she got in the car. "She's really grown on me."

They continued to chat as they made the half-hour drive to Averton. The Bluebell Inn was fairly quiet for a Friday night. They were the first of their group to arrive and saved the long table at the side of the room. Max sat close beside Lizzie, his leg touching hers.

She turned slightly to face him and ran a hand through his hair when he drifted into a daydream. "Are you okay?" she asked.

"Yes."

"What are you thinking about that's making you look so serious?"

He rubbed at the side of his face, then opened his mouth and closed it again. "I've been thinking of doing some decorating," he finally said. "The living room could do with painting, and maybe the hall too. The walls are filthy."

"Yeah," Lizzie said slowly. "Because we have two small children who seem to constantly have dirty hands and like to kick the walls. I'm not sure there's much point in redecorating at the moment."

"I suppose so," he agreed.

"At least now we don't care about them leaving dirty fingerprints everywhere. It would drive you crazy if the walls were newly painted."

"That's true. Maybe I'll leave it."

Lizzie frowned. "Are you bored of being at home so much?" As much as she hated the thought of their family life being disrupted, if he wanted to go back to working more hours she couldn't really begrudge him that.

"No." He reached for his pint. "I like it."

The response came quickly and he sounded genuine. That didn't make a lot of sense, though: if he was thinking of redecorating, he *must* be bored.

"Tara and James are here," Max said, putting an end to the conversation.

CHAPTER 6

On the drive over to Averton, Nat had hounded Tara with questions about the area, and about her life. By the time they reached the pub she was in desperate need of a glass of wine.

"Do you come in here a lot?" Nat asked as they stood by the bar.

The landlord, Andy, gave a gentle laugh as he poured their drinks. "Tara's one of my best customers. She's kept me in profit for the last ten years."

Tara rolled her eyes. "This is Andy, my favourite barman. Shame about his sense of humour."

"It's really nice to meet you. I'm Nat, Tara's sister."

"Nice to meet you too." Andy set their drinks on the bar. "I didn't know you had a sister," he said to Tara.

"Half-sister," she replied, then scanned the room. "Max and Lizzie are already here." She raised a hand to wave and moved to join them.

Tara felt a pang of irritation when Nat proudly announced that she was her sister when introduced to Max and Lizzie. It was irrational to be annoyed by it; it was true, after all.

"I didn't know you had a visitor this weekend," Lizzie said. "Are you bringing Nat to the hen party?"

Tara swore loudly. "I completely forgot," she said in a panic. "I can't believe I forgot."

"What did you forget?" Jack asked, appearing beside them.

Tara forced a smile as she looked up at him and Emily. "I forgot to message you," she said to Emily, scooting along the bench to make space. "I meant to message and ask if it's okay to bring Nat to the hen party. You don't mind, do you?"

"Of course not." Emily removed her coat as she sat down. "The more the merrier."

Josie arrived with Sam, and while everyone was greeting them and making a fuss of Josie's bump, Amber arrived too.

"You should have brought Paul," Tara said. "Then we'd have the whole gang. It's not very often we're all out together."

"I didn't even think about it," Amber said. "Just left him to look after Kieron as usual. Hi!" she said, looking at Nat. "I'm Amber. I've been looking forward to meeting you."

Tara had spoken to Amber the previous day, telling her about the impending visit and how nervous she was about spending an entire weekend with Nat. Ever the calming presence, Amber had reassured her it would be fine.

"I've been looking forward to meeting you too," Nat said, beaming from ear to ear. "Tara's told me all about you."

Frowning, Tara slipped her hand into James's. She was fairly sure she hadn't said much to Nat about Amber at all.

"How are you feeling?" she asked Josie.

"Like a whale. I thought I'd be one of those women who got a dainty bump and a glowing complexion, but every inch of me seems to have swelled up. I feel fat and uncomfortable." She massaged the top of the bump. "I swear she's going to break my ribs if she keeps pushing her foot into them. She's been kicking like crazy today."

"Can I feel?" Tara asked, then leaned across James when Josie nodded.

"Here …" Josie moved Tara's hand and pushed it against her taut belly.

"Oh my God!" Tara said. "That's amazing." She beamed at James in delight.

"Can I have a turn?" he asked hesitantly.

"Go for it." Josie leaned back in the chair as they poked her. Tara moved James's hand to the right place and kept hers there too.

"Oh, wow!" He laughed.

"I want to feel," Emily said, walking around the table.

Tara and James retreated as the rest of the group took it in turns to feel the baby kicking.

"You've still got a few weeks, haven't you?" Tara asked.

"Another month. But there's no way I can possibly get any bigger."

"Are you still going to make it to the hen night?" Emily asked, returning to her chair.

"Yes." Josie smiled but looked exhausted. "There's no way I'd miss it."

"Are you sure it's okay for me to come?" Nat asked.

"Yes," Emily said. "It'll be good to have you there."

"I've never been to a hen party before." Nat lowered her voice. "I'm underage so I can't drink alcohol."

"It's not that kind of hen party," Emily said with amusement. "It'll be very tame. We're just hanging out at my house."

"Our seventy-year-old neighbour is coming," Lizzie said. "She's likely to bring her knitting. It's definitely not going to be a wild night."

"If you're sure." Nat looked to Tara. "Do you think I should check with Mum and Dad?"

"No." Tara suddenly found it hilarious that they were related. They couldn't be more different. "If you stay with me, you live by my rules, and I say it's fine. I might even let you have a glass of wine."

"Dad would totally freak out."

Tara stared at her, trying to figure out if she was serious. When Tara was seventeen she'd been completely wild and did whatever the heck she wanted. "Not if he doesn't find out," she said.

Amber moved closer to Nat, asking her about her A-levels and the subjects she was taking.

"Is it the stag night tomorrow night too?" Max asked Jack.

"Yeah. Go-karting in the afternoon and then a pub crawl in the evening. You can still change your mind and join if you want?" He looked from Max to James and Sam.

"I haven't got anyone to look after the shop," James said. Tara resisted the urge to jump in and say she'd take care of it, knowing that James wasn't actually keen to go on Jack's stag night.

Sam looked questioningly at Josie.

"I've already said you should go," she told him. "I'll be fine. I'm going to be out tomorrow night anyway. I might stay at Emily's or Lizzie's."

He looked torn. "I dunno."

"I promise I won't go into labour while you're not here." Josie patted his leg. "We've still got another month to wait. You may as well have a night out while you can."

Sam grimaced. "I was actually quite happy using you as an excuse. I'm not sure I can keep up with Jack and his mates on a night out."

"You should come," Jack encouraged him. "My uncle will

be out with us, and Emily's Mum's boyfriend. You won't be the oldest." Max and Sam were ten years older than Jack, and he enjoyed teasing them about it.

"Thanks. You just made me feel even older." Sam blew out a breath. "Sod it. I'll go if Max will."

"Max has to stay with the girls so I can go to the hen night," Lizzie pointed out.

"Can't you get a babysitter?" Jack asked.

Lizzie shook her head. "Everyone will be at the hen party."

"We could move the hen party to your place," Josie suggested. "Then you don't need a babysitter."

"I suppose we could," Lizzie mused. "If that's okay with Emily?"

Emily shrugged. "I guess that's fine."

"Are you sure?" Max asked, glaring at Emily. "If you'd rather have it at your place just say and I'll stay and babysit."

Lizzie gave his arm a playful slap. "You should go with Jack. It'll be fun."

"I can already feel the hangover," Max said, rubbing at his temples.

"Come on…" Jack coaxed. "It'll be a laugh."

"Go on then," Max agreed.

"We can drive to Oxford together," Jack said. "We can all stay at my mum's place."

"I'm looking forward to it actually," Sam said, then looked to Josie. "Promise you won't go into labour."

"I promise. But four weeks from now I'm going to be wishing I did. I honestly don't know how I can cope with another month of this."

"I can't wait," Lizzie said. "Four weeks and I get a tiny baby to cuddle."

"Have you brought wedding photos to show me?" Amber said to Tara, redirecting the conversation.

"I sent you all the ones we took. And I emailed you the professional ones yesterday."

"Haven't you printed them out? I thought you'd have an album to show me."

"No. I might get around to that one day. I was just planning on printing out a couple of the best ones for now to put in frames."

Amber pouted. "I wanted you to go through them with me."

"I can," Tara said, pulling her phone out, then resting her arm on the table as she swiped through them.

Amber told her to slow down, then took the phone from her before passing it around for everyone to see.

"So this is just a random couple you met and made friends with?" Sam asked, as he and Josie looked through the photos.

"Yes. They're from the Isle of Skye and they were so lovely." Tara's eyes lit up and she turned to Emily. "The guy had read your books."

"No way!" Emily said, her eyes widening.

"Yes. It was hilarious listening to James and Nick discuss the Oxford Castle series. They both claimed it was the historical facts that they loved. Neither of them would admit it was the romance."

"There are definitely a lot of fascinating facts in those books," Sam mused.

"It's really pathetic that none of you can own up to enjoying romance," Tara said.

James took a sip of his pint and said nothing. Sam was also playing it cool and subtly asked Jack for a game of pool to get out of the conversation.

After they'd played one game, Josie gave in to the yawning and told Sam she needed to go home to bed. The rest of them chatted over another couple of drinks before they dispersed in their separate directions. Tara found it fairly amusing how tame their nights out had become. Not that she minded. She supposed it was a sign that they were all happy and settled.

"It was so cool to meet all your friends," Nat said from the back seat as they drove home.

"I feel awful," Tara said to James. "I completely forgot about Emily's hen party." She'd rearranged her plans with her mum on Sunday, but the hen night had slipped her mind.

"I don't think she realised," James said reassuringly.

"I hope not." Tara sank back into the seat. "She can be a bit sensitive about stuff like that."

"About her friends forgetting her hen party?" James said. "I think that's quite understandable."

"You've had a lot going on with the wedding," Nat said, patting Tara's shoulder. "I'm sure she'd realise that. I bet you're a great friend really."

Tara inched away. She wasn't keen on physical contact with people she didn't know well, and even though Nat was her sister, she was a virtual stranger in Tara's eyes. She also found her quite exhausting to be around and was glad to get into bed that night for a break from the constant chatter.

"What's that look for?" James asked as they snuggled down together.

"It was an interesting day."

"You wanted to get to know your dad and siblings better. It's a good thing, isn't it?"

"Yes." It was part of her plan to deal with her issues and move on from them. That and talking about everything from her past with a professional. Her weekly appointments with a counsellor had stopped for the time being, but Tara had found them helpful in sorting through her emotions.

Unfortunately, the reality of spending more time with her dad and half siblings wasn't proving to be as easy as she'd have liked. Not only was she finding getting to know her siblings difficult, but she'd also found herself lying to her mum when she'd rearranged their plans on Sunday. She'd neglected to offer her mum much in the way of an explanation, so she told herself it was hardly a lie at all.

"What's the problem?" James asked.

Tara screwed her nose up, not sure whether she should voice the thought that niggled at her the most. She'd probably sound like a horrible person.

"Tell me," James said.

She blew out a breath. "Nat's kind of annoying."

James only laughed and cuddled her tighter.

~

The headlights on the dark winding roads were hypnotic as Jack and Emily drove home from the pub. Emily's mind replayed the conversations from the evening. It was a curse of hers, mentally chewing over conversations when she should let them go and move on. She knew she had a tendency to take things the wrong way and get upset over trivial comments. With the intention of sparing Jack the negativity, she stayed silent for the drive.

"It's so clean and tidy in here," she remarked as they walked into the house. The living room was spotless, and she found herself irrationally annoyed by the fact.

"That shouldn't be a surprise to you," Jack said. "It was you who cleaned."

She kicked her shoes off and made a beeline for the couch. "I spent all day cleaning in preparation for the hen party. That was a waste of time."

"Not really." Jack sat beside her, running an arm along the back of the couch behind her. "Now we have a nice clean house and no one will come and mess it up tomorrow."

"It's annoying how they just changed the location without consulting with me first. It is my hen party."

He raised an eyebrow. "They asked you if it was okay."

"Yes, but I could hardly say no in front of everyone."

"Does it matter if it's at Lizzie's house and not here?"

"No." She realised she was being petulant, but she always had the impression that no one was actually very interested in her hen night and were only coming out of a sense of obligation. "I think Tara forgot all about the party, you know."

"No she didn't. She forgot to ask you if it was okay for her sister to come. That's all."

"That's what she said, but I think the real reason she didn't ask me if Nat could come was that Tara had forgotten about it. And I wouldn't be surprised if Josie cancels at the last minute."

"To be fair," Jack said, "you can't really blame her if she does. She looks so uncomfortable. She's definitely not one of those pregnant women who glow. I thought she looked ill."

Emily had to agree; Josie really didn't look great. "I always thought that when I got married, Josie would be excited and enthusiastic. I'm disappointed that she's not more interested."

"She is interested." Jack pulled Emily to him and she nestled against his chest. "She's just got a lot going on. Try not to read too much into it. You'll have a great night tomorrow, and in a week we'll be getting married."

"You're right, as always. I wish I didn't over-think everything so much."

"I really think it's good that the hen party will be at Lizzie's house. Less stress for you. I'm happy that Max and Sam are coming to Oxford with me too."

"Yes, that's good. I'll feel better knowing you have some responsible adults with you."

He laughed. "They'll probably try and keep up with the rest of the lads and end up in a worse state than anyone."

"You might be right," she said, amused. Talking to Jack made her feel better, as it always did. She touched his cheek and kissed him tenderly. "I love that you're always so rational. Does it annoy you that I'm so neurotic?"

"I don't think you're neurotic," he said, then flashed a cheeky smile. "Although that's probably my rational brain telling me the right thing to say."

"It was definitely the right thing to say. Completely incorrect, but the right thing to say."

"I actually like that you're slightly neurotic. Life would be boring if we were both completely rational."

"I never said you were *completely* rational."

"Obviously not or I wouldn't be marrying you!"

She gave him a playful shove and stood up. "Let's go to bed," she said, offering him her hand. "Tomorrow's probably going to be a long day."

CHAPTER 7

After a good night's sleep, Tara woke feeling much more positive. It was going to take a while to get used to having her sister involved in her life, but spending more time together would surely help the process.

"What do you want to do today?" she asked, when Nat emerged from the bedroom.

Tara and James had been up for an hour and were drinking coffee in the kitchen.

"We don't have to do anything special," Nat said. "I'm happy to hang out here and in the shop. I'd actually love to spend the day hanging around the bookshop. I could curl up in one of those beanbags and read for the day. You'll have to recommend some good books."

James immediately went to the living room and plucked a book from the bookcase. "You should read this."

"You'll like it," Tara said. "Emily wrote it. She's the one whose hen party it is tonight."

"That's so cool." Nat beamed as she turned the book over to read the back cover.

"It's the first in a series," James said. "I guarantee you'll be hooked."

"I'm going to start it this morning," Nat said.

"Are you sure you don't want to go out somewhere?" Tara asked. "We could go shopping or go for a drive and out for lunch?"

"I'm really happy here," Nat said.

Tara would probably have preferred to go out. It felt a little strange to have Nat hanging around. Having something to do might have made it easier.

There was a steady trickle of customers to the shop that morning. Tara was about to suggest taking Nat out for lunch when the door opened and her mum walked in. A shiver ran across Tara's neck, and she silently cursed herself for not being honest with Debbie about the reason they'd needed to rearrange lunch on Sunday. It had felt easier not to mention Nat's visit, but that had meant landing herself in an uncomfortable situation now.

James greeted her cheerfully and gave her a big hug.

"I had a hairdressing job nearby," she said, "so I thought I'd call in on the way home. I'm excited about looking after the place again when you're at Emily's wedding. I really enjoyed it last time." She kissed Tara's cheek.

"You were a big hit," Tara said. "The kids at story time were very complimentary."

"That's nice. It's such a lovely group." She smiled over Tara's shoulder as Nat wriggled out of the beanbag.

"Hi!" Nat said. "You must be Debbie. I've heard a lot about you."

Tara wished the ground would open up and swallow her when her mum cast her a questioning glance. "This is Nat," she said, hoping that would be enough of an introduction. She wasn't sure she could bear to use the word sister in front of her mum. And saying she was Dad's other kid just sounded rude.

"Oh." Debbie's hand shot to her mouth then fell to rest at her chest. "You're Natalie. Goodness, of course you are. David's shown me photos of you."

"Everyone calls me Nat. Except Dad."

"Yes. Sorry." Debbie looked at Tara and then back at Nat. "You two look alike. How funny? I couldn't see it in photos, but in person the resemblance is clear."

"Do you think so?" Nat asked eagerly. "We've got the same colour hair, but I didn't know if we really looked alike or not."

"Definitely," Debbie said, appearing incredibly calm at the situation, which must be awkward for her. "I didn't realise you were visiting."

"It was a last-minute thing," Nat said. "I begged Tara to let me come and stay. I wanted to hear about the wedding. And I've never seen the bookshop before."

"It's wonderful, isn't it?" Debbie said.

"Yes! And I met all Tara's friends last night. It's so brilliant that I got to meet you too."

While Nat beamed at Debbie, they fell into a slightly uncomfortable silence.

"Do you want a cuppa, Debbie?" James asked.

"No. I've got some jobs to do this afternoon. I was only stopping in for a quick hello." She looked to Tara. "Have you got something nice planned with Nat tomorrow? That's why you couldn't make lunch?" There was no hint of bitterness or accusation, just curiosity.

"We haven't got anything planned, have we?" Nat said before Tara could get a word in. "We could all have lunch together?"

"I suppose we could." Tara searched her mum's features, getting ready to help her out with an excuse.

"Why don't you come to my house?" Debbie suggested. "I'll cook, like we originally planned."

Tara barely managed to hide her surprise. "That would be lovely," she said. "If you're sure it's not too much for you?"

"No. That's great. I better go and get the shopping done now then. I'll see you tomorrow."

Tara gave her a quick hug before she left.

"Isn't it weird?" Nat said as the door closed behind Debbie. "We're sisters, but we don't really know each other's mothers."

"It's a bit strange," Tara agreed vaguely, wandering over to the till and hoping Nat would go back to her book.

No such luck. Nat's gaze followed Tara. "My best friend, Winnie, say it's weird when people ask how many siblings I have and I say three. She says I shouldn't count you, since we barely know each other. And she says it's ridiculous to count Reuben because he died before I was even born."

Tara froze at the mention of her baby brother, who'd died when Tara was only six.

"He was still my brother," Nat continued. "Dad told me all about him. I've got photos of him in my room. And you too." She smiled at Tara, then returned to sit in the green beanbag.

Tara's entire body had tensed. She flinched when James put a hand on her arm, not realising he was beside her.

"I'm going to see if we've got something for lunch," she said, moving away from him. "I can make sandwiches."

In the little kitchen at the back of the shop, she gripped the counter and took a deep breath. When James's hands landed at her hips, she leaned back, pressing her back into his chest.

"Is it me or is she weird?" she whispered.

"She's a little over-enthusiastic," James said, his breath

tickling her cheek. “I’m sure she means well. I think she’s just eager to please. And she might be nervous.”

“I don’t like how she talks about Reuben like that. It’s so strange.”

“Because you don’t talk about him,” James said softly. “If she’s grown up with your dad talking about him, maybe it’s normal for her. And she’s right; he was her brother too.”

“She’s nothing to do with Reuben.” Tara had to force the words out as her throat tightened. “I wished she’d never come here. It all feels too much.”

“It’s bound to take some time to get used to her.” James slipped his arms around her waist and rested his chin on her shoulder. “Once you get to know each other it will be easier.”

“I only wanted to sort things out with Dad. Now I get stuck with more family members than I want. I would have been perfectly fine with just having you and Mum in my life. I have your family too, and they’re much easier to deal with than my family.”

“My parents live in France and we hardly see them,” James pointed out. “That makes them pretty easy to deal with. My sister can be annoying.”

“Yes. But Kate is really sweet. When you say she’s annoying, you say it with affection. And her annoying traits are fretting that you’re not eating properly and always giving you food to take home. That’s not actually very annoying at all.”

“True. But I really think Nat is nervous. She seems desperate for you two to get on well. Once she relaxes she probably won’t be so intense.”

“I hope so,” Tara said. “I have the feeling things are going to end up really awkward. How can I tell her to back off without offending her?”

“You don’t need to. She’ll be gone again tomorrow afternoon.”

The bell rang in the shop and James went back through to serve the customer while Tara went upstairs and made sandwiches for the three of them.

Nat's mention of Reuben left her feeling unsettled all afternoon. Maybe James had a point, though. The fact that Tara almost never spoke about him meant that any mention of him left her rattled. All the grief and emotions she'd kept buried came to the surface. It was exactly those emotions that she was supposed to be facing up to by seeing the counsellor and trying to rebuild her relationship with her dad. Somehow, she'd expected the process to be easier. For one thing, she hadn't anticipated that her half-sister would be so keen to insert herself into her life.

Hopefully James was right and it would just take time for them to get used to each other.

CHAPTER 8

Since Max had cut down on his working hours, Lizzie had been able to get into a steady routine during the week and was able to take the weekends off. On Saturday morning, the four of them ate breakfast, then took the dog for a walk along the gusty beach.

"Are you sure you don't mind me leaving you with the girls?" Max asked when they were back in the warmth of the cottage. The girls were happily playing in the living room while Lizzie sliced fruit for them in the kitchen.

"Of course not. I bet you'll have a good time in Oxford." When he didn't reply, she turned to find him watching her intently. "What's going on with you?" she asked, tilting her head.

"Nothing."

"Liar!" She went to him and laid her hands on his shoulders. "You look as though something's bothering you and it's starting to worry me. If you really want to go back to working full-time, you can say so. I like you being at home more, but not if it's making you miserable."

Surprise flashed in his eyes. "That's not the problem. I definitely don't want to go back to working more."

"Really?" Lizzie grazed her fingertips over the skin at the back of his neck, glad that her work routine wasn't about to be disrupted. "There's something on your mind, though, isn't there?"

He glanced away from her for a moment before looking her right in the eyes. "I'd like us to have another baby."

Caught off guard, Lizzie let out a gentle laugh. She searched his face and her smile fell away. "You're not joking?"

Slowly, he shook his head.

Lizzie's hands fell to Max's shoulders before she moved away from him. "Don't you like the two we've got?" she asked, trying to keep the atmosphere light while she gathered her thoughts.

"I like them a lot," Max said, moving to sit at the table. "Which is partly why I'd like to have another."

Lizzie's mind was in overdrive as she tried to figure out what to say. "I was just starting to think we have our lives back under control. I really like where we are now." She enjoyed the kids at this age, starting to be a little more independent and also lots of fun to be around as their personalities developed.

Max looked at her sadly. "I have the feeling that if we wait too long, things will keep getting easier and we'll never want to go back to the beginning."

"That's true." The trouble was, Lizzie already had that feeling. Could she really cope with the sleepless nights and the colic and crying and never getting a moment's peace? The thought of it made her anxious.

Max drummed his fingers on the table. "The chances of us having twins again are pretty slim, and having one baby will probably seem like a breeze. I like the idea of being able to enjoy the newborn phase without it being such utter chaos."

"What makes you think it wouldn't be chaos?" she asked, taking a seat beside him.

"Optimism?" He smiled briefly. "I just think we'd be better prepared the second time around. We'd know what we were doing, and it wouldn't be so fraught. That first year with the twins is a blur of sleep deprivation and hating each other."

"Did you hate me?" she asked.

"No. But you hated me!"

"I kind of did," Lizzie acknowledged. She also hated thinking back to the time when the twins were tiny. It was like looking back at someone else – a crazy person.

"You don't want to do it again, do you?" Max asked.

"I'm a bit surprised by the conversation." That was as honest as she wanted to be. "I'll have to think about it."

"Okay."

With a rush of guilt, and the feeling that she'd do anything for Max, she entwined her fingers with his. "I'm not saying no."

"I know." He pulled her hand to his lips and kissed her knuckles. "I need to throw some things in a bag. Jack will be here to pick me up soon."

"It's nice that you're going with him," Lizzie said.

"Yeah. I think it'll be a good laugh. It'll probably do Sam good to get away for a night. Is Josie staying here tonight?"

"Yes." Lizzie had a message from her that morning to say she was going to get a lift over with Amber and would stay the night. Lizzie had agreed she'd drive her home the following day. "I'm a bit worried about her. She insists she's fine, but she's obviously having a rough time. I don't know if it's normal pregnancy stuff or what? I know she was really stressed at the start of the pregnancy because of the miscarriages, but she seems really down whenever I see her."

"Sam said she's tired all the time and doesn't feel great. I think it's normal pregnancy complaints. I'm sure there's nothing to worry about. And she's not got long left now."

Lizzie hoped he was right. She'd be relieved when the baby arrived safely. "I suppose I was lucky to be one of those women who enjoyed being pregnant. I assume everyone will be the same."

"I think you were happier when you were pregnant than I've ever known you." Max squeezed her leg and gave her a flirty smile. "Wouldn't you love to be pregnant again?"

She rolled her eyes. "Didn't you say you need to pack?"

"Love you," he said, and gave her a quick peck on the cheek before heading upstairs.

The day ended up being surprisingly chilled out. Lizzie got most of the tidying done while the girls napped, then Scarlett appeared and took them for a walk in the buggy while Emily came to put a few decorations up along with her mum and Jack's mum. Verity was providing the catering, and Emily brought an array of drinks, so it wasn't much work for Lizzie at all. She was just putting the girls to bed early in the evening when people started to arrive.

She could hear Josie and Amber, along with Tara. Presumably her sister was with her too. The voices drifting up the stairs meant that it took the girls a little longer to fall asleep than usual, and Lizzie waited in the room with them until they'd both drifted off.

By the time she went downstairs, the living room was a bustle of people. Dotty had just arrived, along with Tammy, a local woman who Lizzie had become friends with through Dotty's knitting club. When Emily had moved to Hope Cove, Lizzie had encouraged her to join the knitting club too. She hadn't needed much encouragement and even took part in the knitting side of it, whereas Lizzie went for the coffee, cake and good company.

She'd just greeted everyone in the room when she heard the front door open and then Scarlett's voice calling out that the food had arrived.

"You can take it into the kitchen," Lizzie said, stepping into the hallway to find Verity and Scarlett carrying platters of food.

Emily followed them into the kitchen. "This looks fantastic."

"I'll get the rest from the car," Scarlett said, and left again.

"There's more?" Emily asked, as she and Lizzie peered at the selection of sandwiches and savoury snacks.

"There's another platter of sweet things," Verity said, "and some nibbles. I prefer to make too much than too little."

They were taking the cling film off the platters when Scarlett arrived with the rest of the food. She set the platter on the kitchen counter and handed a bag to Verity.

Tara appeared at the door and smiled at Scarlett. "Could I borrow you for a few minutes?" she said. "I want to introduce you to Nat. You're about the same age, and I'm worried she'll think I've brought her to a party full of old people. Dotty's currently talking to her about knitting patterns."

"Who's Nat?" Scarlett asked.

"My little sister," Tara said, her voice sounding suddenly strained.

Scarlett frowned. "I didn't know you had a sister."

"Half-sister," Tara said. "We don't know each other well, but she's come to stay with me for the weekend."

"Okay. I'll talk to her. At least then she'll think you've got one cool friend." Scarlett's eyes sparkled with mischief as she left the kitchen.

"She makes me laugh," Lizzie said, pinching a mini sausage roll from the platter on the kitchen table.

Verity paused in unpacking snacks from the shopping bag. "Has she spoken to either of you about uni?"

"She didn't say much to me when I asked," Emily said. "Just that it was fine, and that she might need me to help her with some of her assignments."

"She asked me if I'd proofread them for her too," Lizzie said. It had been the same when Scarlett had been studying for her A-levels earlier in the year. She'd constantly been asking Lizzie and Emily for help. She found writing assignments a struggle due to her dyslexia. Prior to that, she'd roped them in to help with the series of novels she was writing, so they were quite used to the requests.

"I'm not worried about the academic side." Verity's features tensed. "She'll get through that on sheer determination."

"What's the problem then?" Lizzie asked. "She's probably not going to be very social, but that's just her nature."

Verity glanced at the door. "I don't know how she's managing for money," she said quietly, then shook her head. "I probably shouldn't say anything. Bill thinks I'm worrying about nothing."

"What's the issue with money?" Emily asked, when the silence felt awkward.

"At first she thought she couldn't afford uni at all," Verity said in hushed tones. "And then her plan was to go to uni but keep living with me and work in the cafe at the weekends to pay for her tuition. She said she might even have to get another job in the evenings. Then all of a sudden she said she'd figured out a way to afford accommodation in Exeter. And now she says she'll only work some weekends because she needs to study."

"I assumed she'd taken a student loan," Emily said.

"That was the problem all along," Verity whispered. "She's not eligible for one."

Lizzie shook her head in confusion. "I thought everyone was eligible for a student loan."

"Only if you're deemed to *need* a loan," Verity said, looking troubled.

"Surely Scarlett needs a loan," Emily said.

Verity checked the doorway again. "The assessment is based on your parents' income. Scarlett's parents can afford to pay for her to go to uni, they just refuse."

"That's crazy," Lizzie said, not sure whether she was referring to the loan system or parents who refused to pay for their child's education.

"They think it's a waste of money," Verity said. "According to them, Scarlett would be suited to a job in a shop or restaurant."

"Scarlett's got loads of potential." Lizzie smiled lightly. "Not that there's anything wrong with working in a shop or restaurant, but Scarlett's so creative. It'd bore her."

"I know that. Her parents don't seem to be able to look past her dyslexia."

"That's sad," Emily said. "I always knew Scarlett had it tough, but she rarely speaks about her parents. I wasn't sure exactly what the situation was."

"When Scarlett realised they weren't going to pay for uni for her, she came to stay with me. She'd been working hard to get the A-levels she needed, but she pretty much gave up then. It was only you two encouraging her with her writing and helping her study that seemed to perk her up. That's why I thought she might have spoken to you about uni. I really don't know where she's getting money from."

"Are you sure her parents didn't change their minds and pay for her?" Lizzie asked.

"Scarlett would have said so. Besides, I spoke to her mum

and they seem to be under the impression that I'm helping her. I didn't like to say otherwise so I just kept quiet on the subject."

"Max is always saying how cunning she is," Lizzie said. "If she needed money, she no doubt cooked up some scheme to get some."

"That's what worries me," Verity said. "What kind of scheme? I'm concerned this new friend that she's living with is a bad influence. She could've got Scarlett involved in selling drugs or something."

Emily shook her head. "She's too sensible for that."

"I hope you're right. If the opportunity comes up, could you try and ask her questions? See if you can find anything out to put my mind at ease?"

"We can try," Lizzie answered. "You know what she's like, though. She's very good at keeping her cards close to her chest."

Tara walked in, interrupting them. She looked at Lizzie. "Would you mind if I put myself in charge of serving drinks?"

"Oh my goodness." Lizzie put a hand to her mouth. "I forgot to offer anyone drinks. I'm a terrible host."

"I'm very happy to take on the job," Tara said, opening the fridge. "I think I'll start everyone on Prosecco."

When Verity picked a couple of bowls of nibbles and took them to the living room, Emily followed her, murmuring about being sociable.

A moment later, Amber appeared in the doorway. "Do you need any help in here?"

"You can help pass drinks out," Tara said.

"It's nice that your sister's come for a visit," Lizzie said as Tara filled glasses with Prosecco.

"I'm not so sure about that," Tara said under her breath.

"Isn't it going well?" Amber asked.

Tara put a hand on her hip while she waited for the froth to dissipate in the glasses. "Does she seem really immature to you?"

"How old is she?" Lizzie asked.

"Seventeen."

Lizzie was surprised. "I'd have said younger."

"She said she's never been to a hen party, but when I was talking to her earlier I got the impression she doesn't go to parties in general. I don't think she's ever tasted alcohol. She's never been on a train alone … she just seems so innocent."

"Oh dear." Amber groaned. "You're going to corrupt her, aren't you?"

"Probably," Tara said through a laugh. "Not intentionally. It's funny to think there's only a year or so between her and Scarlett. Scarlett seems so worldly and streetwise."

"I'm not sure that's a good thing." Lizzie contemplated how unsupportive Scarlett's parents were. "Scarlett's that way by necessity."

Tara continued filling the glasses. "It's weird having a sibling who feels like a stranger."

"It'll probably just take a bit of time to get used to each other," Amber said, rubbing Tara's arm.

"That's what James says. Anyway, let's get some alcohol in people and get the party going."

Lizzie picked up a couple of glasses and went through to the living room. She almost laughed at the look on Nat's face when Tara thrust a glass of Prosecco at her. Tentatively, she took a sip, then turned to Scarlett, who was in full flow of conversation beside her.

"It sounds really good," Nat said. "I don't know what I want to study yet. I'm definitely going to university next year, though. I'd like to move away, but my parents would prefer I keep living at home."

"You have to do what you want," Scarlett told her. "Don't worry about what anyone else says. If it was up to my parents, I wouldn't be at uni at all. I'm only there because Emily told me I could do whatever I set my mind to."

Emily was hovering at the fireplace beside Lizzie and leaned to whisper in her ear. "If she's selling drugs it's my fault, isn't it?"

"Definitely!" Lizzie agreed, then realised she was still holding two glasses of fizz and passed one to Tammy, who was sitting beside Josie on the couch.

"I think I'm going to go up to bed," Josie said.

"Already?" Lizzie asked.

Tara was passing around drinks and jumped in on the conversation. "If you disappear now, you'll miss the party games I brought."

Lizzie chuckled. "Are they similar to the ones you organised for Josie's hen night?"

"Pretty similar," she said, amusement flashing in her eyes.

"They're the exact same ones, aren't they?" Josie asked.

"Yes!" Tara grinned. "But pinning the junk on the hunk was so much fun last time, I thought we should do it again."

"Are you okay?" Emily asked, as Josie heaved herself off the couch.

"Yes." She swallowed hard. "I've got heartburn and I can't get comfy. I just want to go to bed. Sorry."

"It's fine," Emily said, following her to the door. "Do you need anything?"

Josie insisted she was fine and told Emily to enjoy her party.

"She's not exactly a great advert for pregnancy, is she?" Emily murmured to Lizzie.

"No. I said the same to Max this morning. I'll go up and check on her in a bit." Lizzie gave her arm a squeeze. By the look on Emily's face, it was clear she was missing having her best friend being the life and soul of the party.

Thankfully, they had Tara to keep everyone amused as she cajoled them into silly games and made sure everyone's glass was topped up.

CHAPTER 9

Alcohol could definitely be to blame, but Tara also thought it was having Nat with them that made her feel queasy when they arrived at her mum's house for lunch. Using her key, Tara opened the door, then shouted hello as they walked in.

Debbie was in the kitchen but walked through to the living room to join them. "I've gone all out and baked an apple pie for dessert," she said as she hugged them each in turn. "There's a chicken roasting and the veg is prepared."

"That sounds great," Tara said. The house looked clean and tidy too. A sure sign that her mum was on an even keel emotionally. She'd been that way for a while now, so Tara was on high alert for the inevitable crash. The cycle was always the same.

"How was the hen party?" Debbie asked as they seated themselves around the room. "I was worried you'd both be too hungover to get out of bed."

"I just had one glass of wine," Nat said. "I had a really good time."

"That was sensible of you," Debbie said.

Tara rested her hand on James's leg. "I wasn't quite as sensible."

"Someone's got to be the life and soul of the party," James said.

"That's what I thought." Tara grinned. "And no one else was volunteering for the job."

Debbie plumped the cushion behind her to get comfy. "I'm glad you had a fun night anyway."

"It was great talking to Scarlett about university," Nat said. "She says she's going to start her own publishing house one day. I wish I knew what I wanted to do with my life."

"You've got plenty of time to figure it out," Debbie said.

"I suppose so." Nat's eyes scanned the room before stopping at the row of framed photos on the sideboard. "We've got that photo at our house too."

Debbie's brow furrowed. "Which one?"

"The one of Reuben laughing. Dad says it's his favourite photo of him. It's hanging in our hallway with the other family photos."

"That's nice." Debbie's eyes misted over and she looked a little lost for words.

"Dad said Tara was playing peekaboo with him to make him laugh."

"Yes," Debbie said. "Tara could always make him laugh."

"Do you have any more photos of him?" Nat asked. "Dad's got some, but not very many."

Debbie moved to the cupboard and pulled out her shoebox full of photos. She gave it to Nat, then perched on the arm of the couch beside her.

"What was he like?" Nat asked, picking a handful of photos out of the box.

Debbie pursed her lips and looked thoughtful. "He was a sweet little thing. Of course. All babies are. He was quite a good sleeper and didn't cry very much. He liked to be cuddled and loved it when we stroked his cheek."

"I'm going to put the kettle on," Tara said, standing abruptly. In the kitchen she busied herself filling the kettle, then slumped into a chair at the kitchen table.

James followed her in a moment later, taking her hand and pulling her out of her seat.

"Don't be too nice to me," she said. "If you're too nice I'll start crying."

"Okay." He folded his arms around her and she relaxed against his chest. "You realise you've not snapped at her once? That's a win."

"She's here for a few more hours. Let's not jinx it!"

"You only need to get through lunch. By the time we get home, David will be coming to pick her up."

"In future, I'm going to stick to meeting her for an afternoon or for dinner and preferably with Dad around. A whole weekend's too much." She sighed and rested her forehead on James's shoulder. "Am I a horrible person?"

"No. If having her to stay is too much for you, it's probably better to be honest about it."

"She'd be offended," Tara said. "But it's a long way to come for a weekend, so it's not as though it will be a regular occurrence. I'll just need to be ready with an excuse if she asks to come again."

"Maybe talk to your dad about it. He might be able to put her off if he knows it's too much for you at the moment."

"I'd also like to meet up with Dad sometime without her around."

When she'd met up with him six months ago and told him she wanted them to try to have a relationship, it had just been the two of them. The few times she'd met him since then he'd always brought Nat. Ben had only come along once, and Tara had got the impression he was there under duress.

"Tell him that," James said.

"I'd feel as though I was being whiney and demanding."

"I'm sure your dad would understand. Nat too."

"Maybe." Not for the first time, Tara wished she'd never started on her mission to sort things out with her dad. She was sure she'd be happier without so much family drama in her life. "Let's just get today over with. I'll be able to think more clearly when she's gone."

As they drank coffee in the living room, Nat and Debbie continued to pore over the box of old photos. Debbie happily told stories about those few months when they'd had Reuben in their lives. The more she talked, the more Debbie seemed to remember. Tara quietly listened to stories from her childhood that she'd never heard before. Gradually, the conversation became easier to listen to, and the stabs of grief reduced until she was smiling at the story of her six-year-old self almost pushing Reuben's pram into a bush because she wasn't tall enough to see where she was going. There'd been a blue knitted blanket covering her baby brother. The memory came back to Tara vividly. Her parents had hovered at either side of her, trying to discreetly help her steer while she insisted she could do it alone.

"I've been wittering away," Debbie said, breaking Tara's thoughts. "The chicken must be almost done. I'm going to finish getting lunch ready."

"Do you need any help?" James asked, then followed Debbie to the kitchen when she said she could probably find him a job.

"It's weird seeing Dad in these photos." Nat's gaze was on a photo of the four of them. "He had a whole other life. A different family."

Tara wasn't sure what to say. It was the reason why she'd cut contact with her dad for so long – she couldn't bear the fact that he had another family. She'd felt so rejected that she'd refused to see him for almost ten years. They'd spoken on the phone from time to time, and he'd emailed her regularly, but she'd been too angry with him to spend time with him.

"Let's go and see if they need help with lunch," Tara suggested, taking the shoebox from Nat's lap and returning it to the cupboard.

They ate in the kitchen, everyone suitably hungry and murmuring about how good the food was as they tucked in.

"Is Emily excited about the wedding?" Debbie asked.

"I think so." Tara nodded as she chewed. "It's always hard to tell with Emily."

"Are you still happy to look after the shop for the day?" James asked.

"Yes," Debbie said, slightly hesitantly.

"If you'd rather not, we can close the shop," Tara said in a rush. "It's not a problem."

"It's fine. Only that I had Amber and Josie calling in to help me before. Everyone will be at the wedding this time. I'm sure I'll manage, though."

"I don't want it to cause you any stress," Tara said. "We'll close for the day."

"Don't do that." Debbie took a deep breath and sat up straighter. "I enjoyed it last time. I'm sure I'll be fine."

"We won't be far away," James said. "You can always call us if you have any problems."

"Maybe I could help," Nat suggested, drawing everyone's attention. "I could come and visit again next weekend. Then I could help Debbie in the shop while you're at the wedding. I don't know anything about working in a shop, but it would be company for you, and moral support." She looked eagerly at Debbie.

"That might be nice," Debbie said, while Tara's whole

body tensed. She hadn't expected she'd need to have an excuse ready for Nat quite so soon.

"It's a long way to come," Tara said. "Dad probably won't want to spend the whole weekend driving you around again."

"You said there's a train. I could get the train. It'll be fun. I'd really like to help with the bookshop."

"Are you sure you don't mind?" Debbie asked. "You've probably got better things to do with your weekend."

"I'd love to come." She looked to Tara. "Please say I can!"

She had no excuses. "I guess it's fine, if it's okay with your mum and dad."

"They won't mind. I'm so excited."

Tara felt James's leg press against hers under the table. She forced a smile and focused on her food.

~

David was waiting in his car outside the shop when they arrived back.

"Sorry." Tara smiled at him. "Have you been waiting long?"

"No, not really." He gave Nat a hug. "Did you have a good time?"

"The best. We were at the pub on Friday, then we went to a hen party last night. It was so much fun meeting Tara's friends."

David raised an eyebrow. "A hen party?"

"A very tame one." Tara opened the door to the shop and led the way up to the flat.

"It sounds like you've been busy," David said.

Up in the flat, Tara put a pot of coffee on while Nat went to collect her things.

"How's your mum?" David asked, standing in the middle of the kitchen.

"Fine," Tara said, slightly annoyed when James moved around her to get mugs out. She'd been happy at having something to do. "We were just over there actually."

"At Debbie's house?"

"Yes. She cooked lunch for us." Tara leaned against the counter, not sure what to do with herself now that James had taken over the coffee-making.

"Nat went to Debbie's house with you?"

Tara felt a tinge of relief at not being the only person to think it was an odd situation. "Yes. Mum called into the shop yesterday, so they met then. We were supposed to have lunch with her so she invited Nat too."

"Right." He pressed his lips together.

"Debbie's so nice," Nat said, joining the conversation as she walked into the kitchen. "She's going to be looking after the shop next weekend when Tara and James are at a wedding. I said I could come and help her. Is that okay?"

"Next weekend?" David asked, taken aback.

"Yes. I'm not doing anything. And it'll be fun to help Debbie in the shop."

David gave a small shake of the head as though he couldn't quite get his head around the conversation. "Does Debbie often look after the shop?" he asked Tara.

"No. She did it a few weeks ago when we got married. It went really well so she volunteered to do it again."

"Except last time she had Tara's friends to help her," Nat put in. "This time she'll be alone so I thought it would be fun to help her out. Can I?"

"We'll have to talk to your mum about it. But it's probably not very practical. You've got studying to do, and it's a long drive."

"I can get the train. Then I can study on the way. I bet I can study in the bookshop too if it's not busy."

"Let's talk about it later." David clearly wasn't keen on the idea, which made Tara feel better. If he was the one to say no, it would be easier for Tara.

James handed out coffees and put milk and sugar out on the table. Thankfully, David and Nat didn't linger once they'd had a drink. Tara felt a wave of relief when they'd left.

"It wasn't that bad," James said, when she flopped onto the couch.

"If it wasn't that bad, why am I so relieved that she's gone? And why am I so happy that Dad didn't seem to like the idea of her coming again next week?"

"Because it's a stressful situation." He lifted her legs and took a seat on the couch. "It'll get easier."

"I don't want it to get easier," she said grumpily. "I just want them to go away and not come back. It's not worth the stress."

"Do you really believe that?"

She blew out a breath. "No. Probably not." Her phone buzzed in her pocket, and she pulled it out to read a message from Nat, telling her that she was definitely going to persuade her parents to let her come again next weekend. She said she was coming no matter what and she couldn't wait to see Tara again.

As she relayed the message to James, Tara manoeuvred herself to lie her head in his lap. She wished she'd been more assertive and said no when Nat had suggested helping with the shop. It would probably have hurt Nat's feelings, but it would have been better for Tara.

When had she got so soft that she was concerned about hurting people's feelings?

CHAPTER 10

Emily was the first to wake up on Sunday. Her mum and Jack's mum slept on while she made herself a cup of coffee then stood by the kitchen window watching small birds fly between the tree and the bushes.

"You're up early," her mum said, startling her.

"Ten o'clock isn't early. And it wasn't exactly a late night." She went to pour a coffee for her mum. "Is there any sign of Angie?"

"She's still fast asleep. I could hear her snoring from the landing. She can't even be quiet when she's sleeping."

Jack's mum could be a little overbearing, but Emily generally got on well with her. "She seemed to enjoy herself last night."

"Yes. She definitely drank her fair share of Prosecco. Tara's a lot of fun, isn't she?"

"I was really glad she was there," Emily said, passing her mum a coffee and sitting at the table with her. "She livened things up. At one time it would have been a competition between her and Josie over who could be the most outgoing, but that's hard to believe now."

"Poor Josie. She looked worn out. She's had it tough for the whole pregnancy, hasn't she?"

"Yes. Not that she talks to me about it." Emily tapped a fingernail against the side of the mug. "I feel as though she's moved on to another part of her life and has left me behind. I can't imagine things will change once she has the baby. She'll probably join a load of mum and baby groups and make friends with other mums."

"Maybe. But she'll still be your best friend. The two of you often go through these phases, but you come through them managing to stay friends. Remember the time she caught you in bed with her boyfriend? If your friendship can survive that, it can survive anything."

"Mum!" Emily almost spat out her coffee. "That's not what happened! Josie and Jack had already split up. And I wasn't in bed with him." She shook her head as her mum gave her a teasing smile. To be fair, the situation had been pretty awful, and for a while she'd thought their friendship wouldn't survive. "Anyway, I'm not saying Josie and I aren't friends any more. I'm just a bit sad that she never has time for me."

"I don't think you should take it personally," her mum said, laying a hand on her forearm.

"That's what Jack says. And I'm trying not to. I miss her, though." She looked sadly at her mum. "Also, I can't shake the feeling that she's not going to make it to the wedding."

"Unless she's in labour, I'm certain she'll be there."

"I hope so." Emily glanced at her phone. "I haven't heard anything from Jack yet. Have you heard from Martin? Did he survive the night?"

"I haven't heard from him this morning. He messaged me last night to say he was having a good time."

"It's nice that he went with them."

"He was touched to be invited."

Emily smiled. "Jack's always very inclusive. He doesn't like to leave anyone out. And he gets on well with Martin."

"Jack gets on well with everyone." Her mum paused, taking a sip of her coffee. "Martin and I have been talking about moving in together."

"Really?" Emily didn't manage to hide her surprise.

"Do you think it's too soon?"

Emily probably could have done with more caffeine in her system for this conversation. "I don't know."

"Sorry. I shouldn't have brought it up. I didn't mean to sound as though I was looking for your approval." Her eyebrows twitched together. "Although that was exactly what I was doing."

"You don't need my approval."

"I'd like it, though," she said.

"Well, then you have it. I like Martin. And I just want you to be happy." She smiled. "Are you hungry? I'm going to have toast."

"I'll get it," her mum said, standing.

Angie padded in a few minutes later. "Look at you two making me look lazy," she said loudly. "What a great night it was, though. I had a brilliant time. Have you heard from Jack?" she asked Emily.

"No. I presume he's still asleep."

"He'll need his sleep. It'll be a busy week for you both, no doubt."

"Actually, everything's organised, so I don't think there's much left to do."

The wedding would be a low-key affair in a small chapel in rural Devon, which they'd discovered through Emily's book research. She had become acquainted with the vicar of the parish after she'd discovered the graves of a couple who'd exchanged love letters in the 1900s. She'd since written a book based on the couple, so the quaint little chapel had a special place in her heart and had been the obvious choice of venue for the wedding. It would be followed by a reception at the community hall in Hope Cove.

"Call Jack," Angie said, as she lowered herself onto a chair. "We'll feel better knowing he's okay, won't we? I hope he's not too hungover. Tell him not to drive if he is. Be firm with him. He always needs a firm hand."

"Do you want to call him?" Emily asked.

"No. He'll tell me off for nagging him. You do it."

Emily exchanged a look with her mum and stifled a laugh. "I'll check what time they're setting off," she said, reaching for her phone.

Surprisingly, Jack was already awake when she called. They were getting ready to head home. After much discussion, Angie and her mum decided not to wait to see him but to set off back to Oxford.

"You look very sprightly," Emily said when Jack arrived back early in the afternoon. "At least for someone who was on their stag night last night."

He dropped his overnight bag at the foot of the stairs and swept her into a hug. "I missed you."

"Did you have a good night?" she asked.

"Yes." He relaxed his hold on her. "Pretty civilised but it was really good. I think everyone enjoyed it."

She kissed him, then followed him to the couch.

"Have we got much planned this week?" he asked her casually.

"I don't think so. Just the usual."

"What about next weekend?"

She affected a mock thoughtful look. "I can't think of anything."

Laughing, he pulled her onto his lap. "I'll be honest, I'm

not sure I like you joking about this. You are going to turn up?"

"Turn up where?"

He glared at her. "Stop it, now!"

"Oh, the wedding?" she said teasingly. "Yeah. I'll be there. I've got a new dress and everything."

CHAPTER 11

Tara felt as though she had just blinked and it was Friday again. Just like the previous week, David and Nat arrived as Tara was about to close up the shop. They both hugged her, Nat clinging a moment too long and making Tara uncomfortable. *Great.* She'd only walked in the door and already Tara was on edge.

"Where's James?" Nat asked. Only then did Tara notice that Nat wasn't as upbeat as she'd previously been. Last time she'd been there, she'd practically been bouncing around. She'd definitely lost her bounce this time. Maybe that would make things easier.

"Upstairs," Tara replied. "He has his web design business, so he leaves me to the shop when it's quiet and gets on with that."

"Sounds like he's always busy," David said.

"Generally we don't need two people in the bookshop, so the extra work is good. He likes to be occupied."

The pair of them followed Tara upstairs. James was in the middle of a phone call when they walked into the flat. He was sitting at the kitchen table with his laptop in front of him and the call sounded as though it was with a client. He smiled at David and Nat but picked up his laptop and headed for the bedroom.

"Am I in the way?" David asked. "I wasn't planning on staying for long."

"No. It's fine. James will probably be finished with work soon. We assumed you'd be staying for dinner. It's only pizza and salad if that's okay?"

David checked his watch. "That would be good. If it's no trouble."

"No trouble at all," Tara said cheerfully.

Nat dropped her backpack off her shoulder. "You promised Mum you'd go straight home."

"I know, but an hour doesn't make much difference. And after sitting in the car for so long, it's a relief to move around a bit."

"You should have let me get the train," she said sharply. "Mum wanted me to get the train. I don't know why you had a problem with it."

"I only wanted to make sure you got here safely. It's nice to see Tara too."

The look Nat gave him made her seem like a completely different person to the one who was there the previous week. She seemed to have morphed into a stereotypical stroppy teenager. Worryingly, Tara suspected she'd get on better with this version.

"I'm going to put my things in my room," she said, snatching up her backpack. Her claiming the spare room as her own made Tara's jaw clench, but she decided it was best to let it go.

"Do you want a drink?" Tara asked her dad. After getting them both water, she turned the oven on then moved into the living room.

"It's a lovely flat," David remarked as he stood by the window, looking down at the street.

"We like it."

David's eyes darted around. "Nat's in a bad mood with me. She'll cheer up as soon as I've gone, I'm sure."

"Yeah. She didn't seem very happy. Did something happen?"

"Only the usual drama." He rolled his eyes and moved to take a seat. "Teenagers."

"How's Ben?" Tara said, not sure what else they should talk about.

"He's fine. Barely comes out of his room. As long as he's got his computer games he's content."

"And Gillian's fine with Nat being here?" He gave her an odd look, and she realised it was a strange thing to ask. She just didn't know what to talk to him about. "It must be annoying for you, having to drive all this way. Messes up the weekend for you."

"Nat was adamant she wanted to come. And once she sets her mind to something, there's not much point in arguing. It is always good to see you, though. Even if it's only briefly."

"It's good to see you too," she said quietly, looking towards the kitchen and hoping that Nat or James might appear to act as buffers.

"It sounds as though Debbie's doing well," David said. "I have to say, I was surprised at her volunteering to spend tomorrow with Nat. Is it definitely okay? Sometimes Nat gets carried away. She didn't strong-arm Debbie into it, did she?"

"Mum seems quite happy with the arrangement. I hadn't intended to introduce Nat to Mum. It was only that Mum called in while Nat was here. It's a bit of a strange situation."

David nodded his agreement. "I tried to talk Nat out of coming. I'd hate for her to upset your mum. But she insisted they'd got on great and Debbie was keen for her to come."

Keen was probably a stretch, but she definitely hadn't seemed too bothered by the idea. "It's just for one day," Tara said. "And you said Nat has her studies so it's not as though she can visit too often."

"No. She's desperate to get to know you, but I'd like to try and rein her in a little if possible."

"That would be good," Tara said, then bit her lip as she realised how she sounded.

He looked at her sympathetically. "You didn't want her to come, did you?"

"I did," Tara said in a rush. "I mean, it's fine. She sort of invited herself, but that's okay."

"Sorry. I should've realised that was the case."

"It's not a big deal. I just think if it becomes a regular thing, it might be a bit too much too soon. But I also don't want to upset her."

"I understand," he said.

Tara felt a rush of relief. "I'm still trying to sort my head out. I wanted to patch things up with you, and I didn't really consider the implications of that. Not that I don't want to get to know Nat and Ben better, just that I'm not sure how to do all this."

"I know." He smiled sadly. "I have no idea either. I really want us to have a relationship, but I find it hard to know how. Especially without offending anyone." His gaze flicked across the room as though he was looking for Nat.

At one time, Tara would have been put out by the fact that he seemed more concerned about not offending Nat than he did about building a relationship with Tara. But she could also see how torn he was.

Unsure what else to say, she stood up. "I'll put the pizzas in the oven. Make yourself at home."

After the pizzas were in, she slipped into the bedroom.

James had finished his phone call but was engrossed in his laptop.

"Any chance you can come and save me?" Tara asked quietly.

He ran a hand through his hair. "Sure. What's the problem?"

"I need moral support. It's so weird that he's my dad and I don't know how to be in a room with him."

"You'll figure it out eventually," James said, closing the laptop.

"Until then, can you please come and hold my hand?"

"Yes." He massaged her shoulders as he walked out of the room behind her.

Nat reappeared in a better mood and the atmosphere was lighter. James chatted to David about the project he was working on and his client, who kept changing his mind about things and asking James for endless amounts of tweaks. It was slightly annoying the way they could chat so easily while Tara struggled to hold a conversation with him.

At least Nat was easy in that respect. Conversation was no effort with her – she talked non-stop. Tara started with some strategic yawning at around ten o'clock and complained it'd been a long week of work. She also mentioned having to get up early the following morning to get ready for the wedding. Any excuse to go to bed early and limit the amount of time she had to spend with Nat.

~

Tara's sleep was disturbed, and she felt unsettled as she got ready for the wedding.

"Are you sure you're feeling up to looking after the shop?" she asked her mum when she answered the door to her. "If you're nervous about it, say so. It's fine to close for the day if it's too much for you."

"It's fine," Debbie said in her most soothing voice. "Stop worrying. You look gorgeous, by the way."

"Thank you." Tara had opted for a high-necked maxi dress in a rich maroon. Chiffon sleeves made it great for the cooler weather.

"I wish I had your wardrobe," Nat said, appearing from the living room. "You have such lovely clothes."

"Thanks," Tara said.

"And you really don't need to worry about the shop today. Debbie and I will have everything under control."

That didn't make Tara feel any better. Mainly because it reminded her of how little Nat knew them. If she knew Tara better, she'd know it wasn't the shop she was worried about, but Debbie. She'd spent the majority of her life worrying about her mum and looking out for triggers that would send her spiralling into negative thought cycles and have her back to not being able to leave the house – or some days not even leave her bed. She'd been doing so well recently, but spending a day in the shop with Nat could easily change that.

"Are you ready?" James asked, walking out of their bedroom in his navy suit. He'd worn it for their own wedding a few weeks earlier and looked fantastic in it.

"I should message Lexie sometime," Tara said, as her thoughts drifted to the Scottish couple who'd got married on the same day as them. They'd promised to stay in touch, but Tara wasn't sure it would really happen.

"That was a weird answer to the question," James said with a lazy smile.

"Sorry. Your suit reminded me of our wedding. Which made me think of Lexie and Nick. But yes. I'm ready. Are you?"

He buttoned up his jacket. "I think so."

"We should go then," Tara said. "I want to get good seats in the church."

"Call us if you have any questions," James said as he gave Debbie a kiss on the cheek. "Thanks for looking after the place."

As they walked to the car, James slung an arm around Tara's shoulders. "Stop worrying now. You'll ruin the day if you spend it panicking about your mum."

"I have a bad feeling."

"Well, I think it will all be fine. Let's go with *my* instinct today."

She leaned into him, sighing as she got a waft of his after-shave. "Okay. Your instinct, it is. I'll be very happy for you to be right."

"I promise not to be smug when I am."

"Thanks!" She stood on her toes and kissed his cheek. Taking her by surprise, he grabbed her waist and pulled her close, lowering his face to give her a proper kiss. "I'm feeling more optimistic about the day already," she said when he stepped away and opened the passenger door for her.

It was about a forty-minute drive to the cute little chapel, tucked away in miles of rolling hills. There was no car park so cars were parked on the grass verge beside the drystone wall. They'd arrived reasonably early, but there was already a long row of cars and a trickle of people making their way into the church.

"Max is already here," Tara said as they pulled up behind his car. "I hope he's saved seats for us."

James looked up at the church as they strolled through the churchyard along uneven flagstones. "It's very quaint."

"It's connected to Emily's books. The couple who wrote those old letters that Emily found are buried here I think."

"Slightly creepy."

"I think it's romantic." It was a lovely location regardless of the story behind it. The churchyard was well kept, and a number of the graves had fresh flowers on them. With the sun hanging low in the sky, they'd chosen a good day for a wedding. The haze of cloud looked set to clear up.

Josie called out to them as they were about to go inside. She was wandering between the headstones. "We've taken over a row at the front," she said as she approached them. "Though I'm regretting saving seats for you now. You both look too good. I feel like an elephant wearing a tent. You two looking so gorgeous doesn't help matters."

"Sorry." Tara gave her a hug. "I'd have worn an old sack if I'd realised."

Josie shook her head. "You'd still look stunning in a sack."

"You look great," James said, kissing her cheek. "All glowing and radiant."

"It's very nice of you to lie. Thanks for that."

"I wasn't lying," James insisted.

"Oh, come on! I look terrible. We don't need to pretend otherwise."

"I think you look wonderfully pregnant," Tara said.

"That's closer to the truth. Swap the word wonderfully for massively and you're spot on."

"Are you coming inside?" Tara asked, smiling gently.

"In a minute. I'm trying to stay standing until the last moment. It feels like my insides are being squashed when I sit. The hard seats don't help. You go in. Tell Sam I'm fine. His fussing is driving me crazy."

"We'll see you in there," Tara said, amused.

Inside the church were rows of wooden pews. Sunlight filtered through colourful stained-glass windows, giving warmth to the otherwise stark stone and wood interior. Tara caught sight of Sam straight away. He had one of the twins climbing on him but didn't seem to be paying them much attention. His eyes were fixed on the door.

"Josie's fine," Tara told him as they took seats between him and Max.

"She told me to leave her alone," he said, "but I'm only worried about her."

"I know," Tara replied.

Whichever twin was hanging onto Sam crawled along the pew and stood up on James's lap.

"Hi, Phoebe!" James said. He was always better at telling them apart than Tara was. They weren't identical but they were pretty similar, and when they were dressed the same Tara found it difficult to tell.

"Sorry," Max said. "There's no way they'll sit still for the service. If they get too rowdy I'll have to take them out."

"She's fine," James said as Phoebe prodded his nose repeatedly. Maya sat calmly on Max's knee, looking at a book.

Sam stood up. "I might go and check on Josie."

"We just spoke to her," Tara said. "I told you, she's fine."

His brow creased in a frown. "I'll be back in a minute," he said, then walked out of the church.

Tara caught Jack's eye and gave him a quick wave. He broke away from the conversation with his best man and came over to them.

"How are you feeling?" Tara asked as he kissed her cheek.

"I'm a nervous wreck!" He beamed at Phoebe, who threw herself at him. "Now I'm thinking you had the right idea with eloping. I've been having nightmares all week that Emily doesn't turn up."

Tara looked pointedly at her watch. "She is a bit late …"

"Shut up!" Jack hissed.

"Sorry. Couldn't resist. She's definitely going to turn up. You've got nothing to worry about."

On cue, the vicar came over and told Jack that the bride had arrived. Jack handed Phoebe back to James.

"Wait," Tara said as he began to walk away. When he turned back, she wiped the dusty marks on his jacket left by Phoebe's shoes.

"Thanks." He held his hands out to the sides. "How do I look?"

Tara beamed at him. "Good enough to get married."

CHAPTER 12

The morning of the wedding was lovely and relaxed. Emily had her mum and Lizzie helping her to get ready, and she'd been determined not to dwell on the fact that Josie hadn't joined them as she was supposed to. She'd called first thing, and apologised profusely, but said she wasn't feeling well and wanted to save her energy for the wedding. Emily had psyched herself up for not having her best friend at the ceremony, so she was surprised to see Josie pacing up and down the path in the churchyard when they arrived. Sam was striding by her side, and they looked to be mid-argument.

"I'm so sorry," Josie said, rushing towards Emily as soon as she saw her. There were tears in her eyes and she was deathly pale.

"What's wrong?" Emily asked.

"She's sorry but we're going to miss the wedding," Sam said, catching up to Josie.

"Will you shut up!" Josie hissed at him. "We're not missing the wedding. I'm sorry I couldn't make it this morning," she said, clutching Emily's hand. "I'm a terrible best friend."

"You're not," Emily said automatically. "But are you sure you feel okay?"

"I want to take her to the hospital," Sam said. "But she's refusing."

Josie glared at him. "Because we had a deal. I agreed to stay at home and rest this morning as long as we could definitely come to the wedding."

"There was no deal! I just said that because you were having contractions and still insisting you had to help Emily get ready."

"You've been having contractions?" Lizzie asked with an exasperated sigh.

Tears filled Josie's eyes. "They weren't proper contractions. Just those fake ones. I spoke to the doctor and she agreed I'm fine and I should just take it easy."

"Sam's right," Lizzie said. "You should go and get checked out."

"I'm fine now," Josie complained.

"You're clearly in pain," Sam said.

Emily looked at her sadly. "You do look pale."

"I've looked pale for the last eight months. Pregnancy doesn't agree with me. And I was only uncomfortable on those hard pews. I needed to walk around while we waited. And I wanted to see you before the ceremony. But we're supposed to be talking about you, not me." She squeezed Emily's hand. "You look amazing. Doesn't she look gorgeous?" she snapped at Sam.

He smiled softly. "You really do look beautiful. Jack's a lucky guy. And I'm sorry, but I think I should take Josie to the hospital."

"I think Sam's right," Lizzie said, touching Josie's arm. "Go and get checked out to be on the safe side."

"I'm not missing my best friend's wedding." Her chin

wobbled and she turned to Sam. "New deal – we stay for the ceremony and then I'll do whatever you want. I promise."

His jaw was tense. "Are you sure you're up to it?"

"I'm fine. You're fussing about nothing." She turned and wrapped Emily in an awkward hug. "I love you."

"Love you too," Emily said. "Do you want to walk in with us?"

"No way! I'm not sure I'd even fit down the aisle. We'll sneak in the side door. We've got good seats at the front with Max and James and Tara." She took Sam's arm and waddled away.

Emily's mum had been hovering in the background but stepped forward and offered Emily her arm. "There's never a dull moment with Josie, is there?"

"No," Emily replied. At least Josie had a good reason for causing drama this time. And it didn't matter; all Emily cared about was having her best friend there to watch her get married.

"Are you ready?" Lizzie asked, as they made their way to the main entrance.

Emily took a moment to check her dress and her bouquet, then she nodded at Lizzie. The big old double doors into the church groaned as they opened and a sea of familiar faces stood when the organ sounded. Lizzie walked slowly down the aisle, giving Emily a moment to take it all in before she set off walking beside her mum. She smiled at friends and family as she approached the front of the church, then her eyes locked on Jack. He looked very handsome in his dark suit, and his kind eyes shone with pride.

"Hi," he whispered, taking her hand as she joined him at the front.

The vicar made his welcome address, then asked everyone to be seated while he gave a short talk about marriage. Emily was so excited she could hardly concentrate and beamed every time she turned to look at Jack.

Both of their mums read poems, then Emily and Jack were standing at the front again. When the vicar asked if anyone had any objections, he only left a short pause then smiled at Emily and opened his mouth to continue.

He was interrupted by a shout from the front row before the entire church fell absolutely silent.

"Is everything okay?" the vicar asked, looking at Sam, whose jaw was locked as he grimaced.

"Fine," he said through gritted teeth. "I wasn't objecting. Just had a sudden pain in my arm."

By his pained expression, Emily had a momentary panic that he was having a heart attack before she noticed Josie digging her fingers into his forearm. Even from a distance her knuckles were white from her vice-like grip. Her face was distorted in pain and her eyes were closed. When she opened them, her whole body seemed to relax and she let out an audible breath.

"Are you okay?" Jack asked her slowly.

"Fine," she said with a smile.

He kept his eyes on her. "Are you in labour?"

"No." She shook her head, then nodded. "Well, yes. Probably. But it's fine."

Lizzie sat forward in her seat to look at Josie. "You need to go to the hospital. Now!"

"It's fine," Josie said. "First babies take ages. Carry on." She waved a hand at Jack and Emily.

The vicar looked slightly bewildered. "Should I continue?"

"Yes," Emily said.

"And maybe you could speed things up," Jack suggested.

Emily found it hard not to laugh as they rushed through

the vows. They were about to exchange the rings when there was another yelp from the front row.

"Sorry," James said. He was sitting at the other side of Josie and now had his arm in her grip.

"Just ignore me," Josie said as the contraction passed.

Emily heard Lizzie shooing Max outside to call an ambulance, then they got back to exchanging rings. Once the vicar had pronounced them husband and wife, and Jack had given her a quick kiss, she turned to Josie.

"I think you should leave now!" she said.

"You might be right." Josie was already out of her seat. "Love you both." She blew them a kiss before leaving with Sam.

"I'm going to go and check on her," Lizzie said.

The poor bemused vicar shouted her back, reminding her she was a witness and needed to sign the register. As soon as she'd done that, she disappeared outside.

By the time Jack and Emily walked out into the churchyard, they were just in time to see an ambulance driving away. While everyone congratulated them and showered them in hugs and kisses, Emily couldn't stop thinking about Josie. She sought Lizzie out in the crowd.

"Is Josie okay?" she asked when she managed to get close to her.

"They were definitely proper contractions. Really strong ones too. She told the paramedic she's been having pains since the early hours of the morning."

"Oh my goodness." Emily should have been more surprised than she was. It was fairly typical of Josie to be so single-minded about something that she'd ignore the fact she was in labour just so she didn't miss out on her best friend's wedding. "Do you need to go to the hospital?"

"No. She said she'll call when they get there and she's been checked out. I guess it could still take a while."

Jack appeared beside Emily. "I thought you'd run off on me already. The photographer wants to take some photos in the churchyard."

"Ooh, can we get a picture in front of Edith and William's headstone?"

He tipped his head to one side. "You're kind of weird, you know?"

"I know!" She laughed and leaned to kiss him. "And you just married me."

CHAPTER 13

It was about a half-hour drive from the church back to Hope Cove. Emily was glad of the brief pause in smiling for photographs and endless hugs from friends and family. She sat in the back of the wedding car with Jack, feeling incredibly happy.

Jack leaned back into the headrest and gave her a lazy smile. "Do you know how you sometimes get annoyed that Josie always has to be the centre of attention? And I tell you you're imagining it? I'm starting to think you might have a point."

"I can't believe she came to the wedding in labour!" Emily's whole body shook as she laughed. "She's crazy."

"To be fair, if it weren't for the fact that James and Sam are such wimps, no one would have noticed."

It took a few minutes for Emily to stop giggling. "I suppose she made the day more memorable. I just hope she's okay. Have you got your phone on you? I haven't got mine."

He pulled it from his pocket. "I haven't heard anything from her."

"She was going to call Lizzie when they got to the hospital. Put your phone on loud in case."

They met the photographer in Hope Cove and had some photos taken on the beach before continuing on to the community centre. Their guests were happily drinking champagne and chatting in small groups. Emily and Jack split off to mingle when they arrived, but she headed back to him when she heard his phone ringing.

"I guess it's for you," he said, handing her the phone with Josie's name flashing on the screen.

"I'm so sorry," Josie said as soon as she heard Emily's voice. "I'm a terrible friend."

"You're not. It's fine. I was worried about you, though. Are you okay?"

"I'm fine. I can't believe I made such a scene at your wedding."

"It really doesn't matter," Emily said.

"I'll totally make it up to you. You and Jack can be godparents, and when you see her you'll totally forgive me. She's beautiful."

Emily took a few steps away from the crowd, covering her free ear. "What did you say?"

"I said she's beautiful. Everything about her is perfect."

"You had the baby?" Emily asked as tears filled her eyes.

"You're going to laugh at me so much," Josie said, sounding delighted. "I didn't even make it to the hospital. They had to stop the ambulance and I gave birth in the back of it. No pain relief whatsoever. It was horrific."

"Oh, wow!" Emily searched Jack out of the crowd and beckoned him over. "And everything's okay?" she asked Josie.

"Yes. We're fine. We're at the hospital now. She's absolutely perfect. I'm slightly worried about Sam. He seems to have slipped into a catatonic state, but I'm sure he'll be okay once the shock wears off."

"Congratulations!" Emily said, while Jack looked at her questioningly. "She had the baby," she told him.

"Congratulations to you too," Josie said. "I have to go. Sam's really looking peaky. Oh, is Lizzie there? Put Lizzie on quickly."

Emily walked over to the table where Lizzie and Max were sitting with James and Tara. The twins were in high-chairs, happily chewing away on sandwiches.

"It's Josie," Emily said, thrusting the phone at Lizzie.

"Is everything all right?" Tara asked, taking in Emily's tear-streaked face.

"Everything's fine. She had the baby on the way to the hospital. A healthy little girl."

Lizzie was in tears too by the time she ended the call and handed the phone back. "I want to go and see her," she said, looking to Emily. "You don't mind if I disappear for a while, do you?"

"No. Give her a big hug from me."

"Shall I come?" Max asked.

Lizzie glanced at the girls. "I don't want to take Phoebe and Maya into the hospital."

"Leave them here," Jack said. "They'll be fine."

"We can't ask you to look after them on your wedding day," Lizzie said.

"It's not a problem," Emily agreed. "There are plenty of people to keep an eye on them."

"We'll look after them," James said, moving to the chair beside Phoebe.

"Are you sure?" Lizzie asked.

He nodded. "Of course."

Lizzie kissed the girls on the tops of their heads and told them to be good for James and Tara.

"They'll need a nap soon," Max said. "I'll leave the buggy by the door with their coats and things. Take them for a quick walk and they'll fall asleep easily."

"Okay," James said.

"Thanks," Lizzie and Max called at once, then set off across the room.

~

"I was planning on taking advantage of the free drinks," Tara said as Jack and Emily wandered away to chat to their guests. "I think you've just ruined that plan."

"Max and Lizzie won't be long." James caught a piece of sandwich that Phoebe dropped and handed it back to her. "You'll have plenty of time to get drunk this evening."

Tara sat beside Maya and encouraged her to eat. "Maybe you should get us some food too. We might not get a chance otherwise."

"Good idea," James said and set off for the buffet tables.

Tara appreciated the informal wedding, and it seemed as though all the guests were enjoying the relaxed atmosphere. It meant that no one would notice them slipping away to take the girls for a walk.

"Scarlett keeps giving me funny looks," James said as they coaxed the girls into the buggy.

Tara glanced around and saw Scarlett openly staring at James. "She probably fancies you." She pulled the girls' coats from the top of the buggy and handed one to James. Once they'd managed to get the girls into them, they put their own coats on and set off out of the door.

They hadn't got very far down the road when a voice shouted after them.

"What are you doing?" Scarlett called out.

"Taking the girls for a walk so they have a nap," Tara

said. "We're not kidnapping them or anything. Max and Lizzie went to the hospital to see Josie."

"I didn't think you were kidnapping them." Scarlett stood in front of the buggy, somehow managing to smile at the children while simultaneously looking irritated by James and Tara.

"What's the problem?" James asked, peering over the buggy at the girls.

"Well, they've got the wrong coats on for a start. Phoebe has the purple coat. Maya's is red."

"It doesn't matter, does it?" Tara asked, thinking of the battle it would be to swap them over.

"I suppose not. But it's cold." Scarlett rooted around in the large basket under the buggy and pulled out hats and blankets for them. "And do you really think they're going to fall asleep when they're sitting upright?" She pressed buttons and reclined the seats before gently tucking the girls in, uttering soothing words to them as she did.

"Thank you," James said, as Scarlett began to walk back to the community centre.

"Walk quickly," she called over her shoulder. "If you walk too slow they won't fall asleep."

James nodded and began to push the buggy along the pavement. "She's a lot more competent than she looks."

"And a lot more competent than us," Tara said cheerfully. "The poor kids would have frozen to death while sitting bolt upright."

"I like to think we'd have figured it out."

"That's optimistic of you." Tara pulled her phone from her pocket as they walked briskly towards the village. "I might message Mum and see how's she's doing. Hopefully Nat isn't driving her crazy."

"I'm sure they're fine," James said, while Tara's fingers flew over the keypad.

They were walking along the road through the village when a reply came to say everything was going well at the shop.

"What on earth?" Tara said loudly as she read the rest of the message.

James gave her a nudge and looked pointedly at the buggy.

"Sorry," she whispered. "You won't believe this, though. Mum says some guy came into the shop and asked her out for dinner. Apparently he was there the last time she was looking after the shop and they'd had a long chat then."

James snorted a laugh. "I can't think of any of our regular customers who might ask your mum out."

Tara's eyes widened as another message came through. "She said she was going to turn him down but in the end she gave him her number. Apparently Nat encouraged her to go for it. What the hell is happening? We've only been gone for a few hours."

"Keep walking," James said. "If I slow down, I'll get in trouble with Scarlett. She's probably watching us from somewhere."

Tara hardly noticed she'd stopped and hurried to keep up. "I can't believe Mum agreed to go on a date with some random guy."

"I think I know who it might be," James said.

"Who?"

"Rupert."

Tara almost choked. "Rupert who never buys anything? And the one time he did he paid entirely in five-pence coins?"

"He often comes in the shop on Saturdays," James said.

"It better not be him. Not that it matters; she shouldn't be agreeing to go on dates with any man who she barely knows."

"Why not? It might be good for her."

"No. It won't."

"You know you treat your mum like a child a lot of the time?"

"Because she's the child in our relationship and I'm the adult. It's been that way for a long time."

"She's seemed much more stable recently. I don't think going on some dates would be bad for her. And what if she met someone she really liked?"

"It'd only end in tears," Tara said, staring at her phone screen, trying to decide how to reply.

James gave her an odd look. "We just got married a few weeks ago. We watched friends get married *today*. Our other friends had a baby today. Yet you can't bring yourself to be optimistic about relationships?"

She had to admit he made a good point. "I'm definitely feeling optimistic about relationships," she said, putting an arm around his waist and leaning her head briefly onto his shoulder. "Honestly, I just can't imagine Mum dating. She's never dated. Dad was the love of her life and he completely screwed her over."

James gave her a sidelong glance that was part amused, part exasperated. "I thought you'd decided to stop blaming your dad for everything."

"Yes. In theory, I decided that. In practice, it's a hard habit to break." Tara thought back to her sessions with the counsellor who had pointed out that Tara's thoughts about her parents were only thoughts and not necessarily facts or the truth. She was supposed to stop and look at situations with a more objective view. "Mum actually left Dad," she mused. "So I guess it was partly her decision. I still think it was rude of him to find another wife without fighting for Mum, but I suppose I don't fully know his side of it."

"Exactly. You made things very black and white, but they're not."

"Okay, so I'll keep an open mind about Mum dating. As

long as it's not Rupert." Finally, she channelled Nat and sent a couple of smiley faces in reply to her mum's message, then peeked around the buggy to check on the girls.

"They're both asleep!" she told James.

"Of course they are. I was pushing the buggy at the perfect speed."

"What are we supposed to do now?" Tara asked. "If we take them back to the wedding, they'll wake up with all the noise."

"Maybe we should walk around for a while," James said. "They'll stay asleep then."

After strolling a little further, they turned and headed back towards the village. "I'm freezing," Tara said, shivering as they passed the cafe. Unfortunately, Verity had closed up for the day so she could attend the wedding. "That would've been a good place to warm up. Do you think the pub does hot chocolate? We could sit at the picnic tables outside and have a warm drink at least."

"I'm fairly sure we can take them inside the pub. I think Max and Lizzie do it all the time."

"I know. They'll be too warm, though, won't they? They've got coats and blankets and hats on. I don't want to disturb them trying to undress them."

"They do look nice and snug," James agreed, parking the bulky buggy beside a weathered table at the front of the pub. "You wait here, I'll get drinks."

Tara was about to sit down when she realised her coat wasn't long enough to protect her dress from the bench, which looked slightly damp. After blowing into her hands she rubbed them together to warm them up and was grateful for the steaming mug of hot chocolate that James handed to her.

"The bench is damp," she said, bunching her shoulders up. "I don't want to mess up my dress."

James obviously wasn't as concerned about his trousers

and took a seat, then patted his right leg in an invitation for Tara to sit down.

"Are there many people in the pub?" she asked, perching on his lap and enjoying the warmth of the mug in her hands.

"No. A few old guys at the bar."

"I bet it's lovely and warm in there?"

"There's a fire roaring in the grate."

"Shall we just go inside?" Tara asked, looking at the peaceful toddlers all cosy under their blankets. Phoebe's eyes blinked open and stared up at her. "Don't wake up," Tara whispered, reaching out to rock the buggy. It didn't have the desired effect, and Phoebe squirmed to sit up, looking as though she might start screaming.

James nudged Tara off his lap and moved to undo the straps holding Phoebe in place. He pulled her from the buggy with the blanket still around her. While he rocked her on his lap, her eyelids got heavier until she fell back to sleep with her head on his chest.

"Well done," Tara said with a hint of sarcasm. "You're stuck like that now."

He scooped his arms under Phoebe and stood up. "I think going inside is a good idea."

It took a little while for them to manoeuvre the buggy and children inside, but soon they were parked in front of the fire and warming up rapidly. Tara had carefully removed Maya's hat and blanket and unzipped her coat without waking her. It left her with an odd sense of achievement. James still had Phoebe fast asleep on his lap. He could probably have transferred her back to the buggy, but he seemed to be enjoying the way she was cuddled into him.

"It suits you," Tara said as she watched James softly push a lock of hair from Phoebe's face. The words came without thought, and Tara regretted them as soon as she saw the flicker of sadness in James's features. She forced a smile, then turned her attention to the fire, hoping he wouldn't see the guilt in her features.

When they'd got together for the second time, James had insisted he'd be happy with it being the two of them. He'd promised he'd never push Tara on the topic of children, and in return he made her promise that she wouldn't spend her life assuming she was depriving him of something and feeling guilty for it.

She'd agreed.

Except it wasn't that simple. She *was* depriving him. Every week at story time she watched him interact with the kids and knew he'd make a wonderful father. And she loved him so much that it was impossible for her to not feel guilty for depriving him of a family that he would clearly love to have. Guilt and sadness hit her every time she saw him with other people's kids. She wasn't sure she was a good enough actress to hide it.

The fire crackled, dragging her from her trance. James was looking at her intently and reached his free hand out to her.

She was glad he didn't ask if she was okay. There wasn't much point.

Shuffling her chair closer to his, she entwined her fingers with his and watched little Phoebe sleeping peacefully in his arms.

CHAPTER 14

Lizzie wondered if Max bringing up the subject of having another baby right before Josie was due to give birth was a strategic move. Spending the afternoon at the hospital and having cuddles with a newborn definitely made her feel a little broody. She could barely remember the girls being that tiny. As she watched Max look lovingly down at their gorgeous niece, she could absolutely imagine them having another. It would cause a fresh round of chaos in their lives, but Max was right that they were better equipped for it now.

There was only really her work to consider, but she wouldn't seriously put her career before their family. She'd just make sure Max knew that he'd be the one to give up work this time. At least for a little while. And that shouldn't be a big problem since he was only working part-time.

She'd expected him to raise the subject the moment they left the hospital, but he managed not to bring it up at all on the drive. Once they re-joined the wedding, there was no chance to talk privately.

The twins barely seemed to have noticed their absence

and were having a whale of a time. As soon as the band started up in the evening, the two of them strayed to the edge of the dance floor, watching in fascination as people danced around them and joining in with their own moves, which mainly involved stamping their feet and bouncing up and down with bent knees.

"They're so cute," James said to Lizzie as they watched from the table near the dance floor.

"Are you sure they weren't any trouble?" she asked.

"They were really easy." Tara grinned as she took a sip of her wine. "I wasn't going to mention it, because I thought it might sound bad, but we took them to the pub."

"We take them in the pub all the time," Max said.

"We know." Tara had a mischievous glint in her eyes. "That became clear when they woke up there and seemed very at home. Everyone in there knew them. They're like tiny celebrities."

"We like to support local businesses." Max leaned back in his chair, turning his head in Lizzie's direction. "Scarlett's giving me one of her looks. I feel as though she's about to come and have a go at me."

"I think you might be right," Lizzie agreed as Scarlett strode across the room towards them.

In a bid to distract her, Lizzie reached for her phone. "Do you want to see photos of Josie's baby?" she asked. She'd been showing them off to everyone she saw.

Scarlett took the phone and scrolled through the photos. She handed it back without a word and glared at Max.

"Why did you ask James and Tara to look after the girls and not me?"

He rubbed at the back of his neck. "No reason. They were next to us and they offered."

"They have no clue what they're doing. Did you know that?"

He dipped his eyebrows. "I'll be honest, it's not a massive surprise."

"Hey!" Tara extended a leg to kick him but he moved out of her reach. "They were very well looked after."

"Only because I helped," Scarlett said.

"Thanks," Max said.

"You're welcome." Scarlett sat down beside Lizzie. "I need to have a meeting with you and Emily tomorrow."

"What kind of meeting?"

"A business meeting."

"If you want me to edit your next book, just send me the manuscript. We don't need a meeting about it."

"I haven't finished it yet." She pushed her tongue against the piercing below her lower lip.

"Did you publish the first book yet?" Tara asked.

"No. I want to get the whole series finished first. I don't have much time to work on the books at the moment because of uni assignments."

"If you need help with uni assignments that's fine too," Lizzie said. "Just come to our place tomorrow."

Scarlett rolled her eyes. "That's not what I'm talking about. I want to discuss business matters. We can meet at the cafe at ten o'clock tomorrow. I'll explain everything to you both then."

"Emily won't be able to."

"How do you know?"

"Well, she just got married. I'm guessing she has other things to do tomorrow morning."

"Like stay in bed?" Scarlett asked.

Lizzie avoided making eye contact with Max. "Yes. They're also going on their honeymoon tomorrow."

"That's why I thought the morning would be best. Before she leaves." Scarlett stood abruptly and waved at Emily, who was dancing with Jack.

"Leave her alone, Scarlett," Max muttered, then looked suitably sheepish when she glared at him in response.

Emily walked over when the song ended.

"Can you have a business meeting with me and Lizzie tomorrow?" Scarlett asked.

"No." Emily frowned. "Not really. I'm busy. What kind of business meeting?"

"I can't tell you now. But I came all the way back from Exeter this weekend so we could have a meeting and now you can't spare an hour?"

"I thought you came back for my wedding?" Emily said, amused.

"That as well." Scarlett sighed heavily. "So we can't have the meeting this weekend?"

"No. We can do it when I get back from my honeymoon."

"When's that?"

"We'll be back next Saturday night."

"We'll meet next Sunday then," Scarlett said.

"What exactly are we meeting for?" Lizzie asked.

"Top-secret book business." Scarlett looked down as Maya took her hand, pulling her towards the dance floor. "I can't have any of these commoners hearing about it." She waved a hand to gesture the rest of them at the table before going to dance.

"I don't know if it's the alcohol talking," Tara said, "but I really like her."

"She's pretty great actually," Max agreed before taking a swig of his pint. "Although I find it unnerving that I still have no idea when she's joking and when she's being serious."

"I love the way she can shut people up with a look." Tara mock scowled at Max, but he only laughed at her.

"I suppose we should take the girls home soon," Lizzie said. She was tired herself after all the excitement of the day and was happy to have the girls as an excuse to leave early.

Except the girls seemed to be full of energy still, and Lizzie couldn't bring herself to drag them away when they were having so much fun. She didn't object when Max pulled her onto the dance floor, and they boogied with the girls for an hour before finally coaxing them away from the party.

Assuming they'd fall asleep in the buggy on the way home, they'd put them into their pyjamas before leaving. At home, they only needed to lift them from the buggy to their beds. Creeping out of their bedroom, Lizzie noticed Max's trademark drunk smile.

"You look happy," she said in their own bedroom. She was desperate to get out of her dress and was certain she'd fall asleep as quickly as the girls had.

"It was a good day, wasn't it?" Max sat on the bed to pull his shoes off, then started undoing his shirt buttons. "Josie looked so happy with the baby."

"I knew you'd bring up the baby subject soon," Lizzie said, laying her dress neatly over the back of the chair at her dressing table.

"I was just saying they look happy."

"Maybe we should reassess how happy they look in a month when they can't remember what sleep is and they're tearing their hair out."

Having stripped down to his boxer shorts, Max walked over to her and slipped his arms around her waist. "So you don't want another baby?"

"I'm not completely against the idea." She looped her arms around his shoulders. "You did look very cute holding the baby today."

"Glad you noticed. I was aiming to look as cute as possible to persuade you."

"I definitely noticed." With a hand on his neck, she moved her face to his and kissed him. "Can we talk about babies tomorrow, when I'm not tipsy and half asleep?"

"I specifically chose this time," he said lazily. "I thought you'd be an easy target when you're tipsy and half asleep."

"Nice try," she whispered, then kissed him deeply.

~

In true Tara style, she danced the night away and made James stay at the wedding until the very end of the evening. She claimed she was having too much fun to leave, but there was another reason too. She wanted to go home as late as possible so Nat would already be asleep and she wouldn't have her evening ruined by having to make polite conversation with her. After a few drinks, Tara was much more brash and likely to offend. So far, she'd managed to be calm and patient around Nat, and she wanted to keep it that way.

"Did you have fun?" she asked James on the drive home. Sitting in the warm car, the buzz of alcohol soon left her and she felt increasingly tired.

"Yes." He kept his eyes on the road but put a hand on her leg.

Trailing her fingers over his knuckles, she was hit with an image of him cradling Phoebe while she slept. "You enjoyed looking after the twins, didn't you?"

"Yes. They're cute."

Tara nodded slowly. "Does it make you wish that we'd have kids?"

She felt him tense. He drew his hand away to change gear as he approached a junction.

"I'd rather not have this conversation," he said.

"Why?"

"Because it's pointless."

"I only want to know how you feel."

"I *feel* as though you've had too much to drink, and you're looking for an argument."

Tara had to admit she probably wouldn't have raised the subject if it weren't for the wine giving her courage, but she wasn't looking for an argument. She really did want to know how he felt. Except she already knew how he felt; he wanted kids, that was obvious. She just wanted to hear him say it. But what would that achieve? Maybe he was right and she was looking for an argument.

"Sorry," she whispered, then turned to look out of the window. As they neared Newton Abbot, the streetlights illuminated parked cars and cast shadows into people's front gardens.

Stopping at the traffic lights, James pulled the handbrake on and put the car into neutral. Confused, Tara turned back to him. He leaned across and put a hand on her cheek as he kissed her.

"I love you," he said with his face close to hers. "I'm happy. As long as I have you I'll always be happy. You're everything I need. You don't have to keep checking to see if I've changed my mind."

"I know." She ran a hand down his cheek and kissed him again. "I'm sorry for bringing it up."

He released her as the lights changed and put the car into gear. "Let's go home," he said with a smile.

CHAPTER 15

When Lizzie emerged downstairs late the following morning, she found Max lying on the couch with his eyes closed. Phoebe was nestled between his legs while Maya sat by his head, idly stroking his hair while she stared at the TV.

"Morning," Lizzie whispered.

The girls paid her no attention, but Max's eyes slowly opened and he stretched his neck. "Hi," he said, his voice croaky.

"Do you want a coffee?"

"Yes, please."

She'd just set the machine running when Max followed her into the kitchen.

"Did I ever tell you what a great husband you are?" she asked, creeping her arms around his waist as he yawned.

He rested his forehead against hers. "I think you've probably mentioned it. Usually when I let you sleep in."

"Thank you." She gave him a quick kiss. "You really are a great husband, and a brilliant dad. We're very lucky to have you."

His smile was fairly half-hearted, and Lizzie had a pang of guilt for not properly addressing his question about them having another baby. The more she considered the idea, the more she liked it. She should tell him she was onboard with the idea.

"I've been thinking a lot about having another baby," she said.

"You don't want to?" he asked, pulling back to look at her.

"I'm hesitant, but mostly because I feel so comfortable with our life now. A baby will throw everything off balance."

"Only for a little while. And things being off balance isn't really that bad."

"Yes. Sorry. I didn't mean to sound so negative. I intended to say that I don't hate the idea. I'm still trying to get my head around it, but I think having another baby would be okay."

"You should probably be a little more enthusiastic about it."

She rubbed at the side of her head. Agreeing to have another baby was more difficult than she'd expected. All she had to do was tell him she thought it was a good idea too. She was sure she'd be excited about it by the time she got pregnant. Until then, she might just freak out a little bit.

"You'd have to give up work," she said. "Or take paternity leave or whatever. It would be you who does the lion's share of childcare. You've got more patience than me, and you're better with the kids."

"I'm not sure that's true, but I'm happy to take paternity leave."

"Okay. Good." She turned to pour the coffee once the jug was full.

Max was staring at her when she handed him a mug. "So we're going to start trying?" he asked. "Straight away."

"Yeah. I guess so."

His smile softened his features and made her stomach flutter. If it weren't for the girls, she might suggest they go back to bed and start trying immediately.

"It might take a while," she told him, suddenly worried that he was going to get overexcited. "I need to finish my cycle with the contraceptive pill, and then it might take my body some time to get back to a normal rhythm. We got lucky with the girls and got pregnant straight away. It's unlikely to be like that again."

He nodded and his smile slipped. Maybe she shouldn't have dashed his enthusiasm, but she didn't want him to get his hopes up and then be disappointed if it took some time.

Tara's head felt as though it was gently pulsating when she woke. Coffee was needed, urgently. The sound of Nat chatting grated on her nerves the moment she opened the bedroom door, and she contemplated slipping back into the comfort of her bed. The pull of caffeine was too strong and she crept to the kitchen, hoping to get a few more minutes' peace before Nat redirected her incessant chatter away from James and onto her.

"Morning," Tara whispered when she forced herself to join them in the living room.

"Morning!" Nat said, too loudly. "I was just telling James that I finished the first Oxford Castle book so I borrowed the second one from your shelf. I hope that's okay?"

"It's fine." Tara sat beside James and wrapped her hands around the coffee mug. She should probably have asked if anyone else wanted one, but she wasn't capable of looking after anyone else yet.

James rubbed circles on her back. "How's your head?"

"I'm optimistic that it will be fine after about two cups of coffee."

"Did you get drunk?" Nat asked.

"A bit tipsy, maybe," Tara replied, wincing at the volume of Nat's voice. "How did it go with the shop?"

"It was great. Debbie's so lovely. We spent all day chatting and drinking cups of tea. I read a lot too."

"Any customers?" James asked.

"Oh! Yes." She laughed. "We sold some books. Everyone who came in seemed so friendly. I think there were a lot of regular customers because most people seemed surprised that you weren't there. There was this lovely lady who came in, I think her name was Bethany. She works in the chemist down the road and she said she was good friends with you."

"Belinda," Tara said on a sigh. The local gossip would have been thrilled to have new people to chat to.

"She's really funny," Nat said. "She stayed and had a cuppa with us."

"I bet she did," Tara said under her breath, then smiled when James gave her a playful nudge. "She's always very chatty."

"Working in a bookshop is so cool." Nat pulled her legs under her and leaned on the arm of the chair. "Oh, and this sweet old guy asked Debbie out on a date!"

Tara groaned as she remembered the messages from her mum. "Do you know his name?"

"Rupert."

"I knew it!" James said.

Tara curled her lip. "He's creepy. And he's old."

"I reckon he's probably about the same age as Debbie," James said. "It's his knitted waistcoat and cardigan that make him look old."

Tara shivered at the thought of her mum dating Rupert.

"Debbie went bright red when he asked her," Nat said

excitedly. "So I tried to help her out and suggested she could give him her number."

"Hopefully she was sensible enough to give him a fake number."

"I thought he seemed nice," Nat said. "And Debbie said she doesn't go out much socially, so a date might be fun for her."

"There's no way she'll go out with him." Tara inhaled the scent of coffee before taking a sip.

"I think she will," Nat said. "We talked about it afterwards and she agreed with me that it might be good for her."

Tara's fingers tightened around the mug until the heat got too much and she had to set it down on the coffee table. "It *wouldn't* be good for her," she said, trying not to lose her cool. Nat and hangovers clearly didn't mix well.

"Sometimes doing something different can be really refreshing," Nat insisted. "It gives you a boost to get out of your normal routines."

"And sometimes it's better to stay within your comfort zone."

Nat laughed as though Tara had told a joke. "Life would be so boring if people always stayed within their comfort zones."

"There's nothing wrong with boring," Tara mumbled as she stood. "I'm going to have a shower." If she stayed where she was, she'd end up in an argument, and her head hurt too much already.

Sundays were usually spent pottering around the flat. Sometimes she and James had a meal with Debbie or went for a drive along the coast. Every so often they had a day with James's sister, Kate, and her husband and kids. Since they only closed the shop for one day a week, it felt somewhat sacred, and Tara resented having Nat there. Thankfully, David messaged in the middle of the morning to say he was on his way.

"I don't know why he's coming to pick me up so early," Nat complained when the doorbell rang just after they'd eaten lunch. "I told him not to come until later."

Tara moved to the door and pressed the buzzer to let him into the shop. He arrived upstairs a minute later and gave Tara a hug.

"Nice to see you again," he said.

"You too. You're about ten minutes too late. You missed lunch. I can make you a sandwich if you want?"

"I stopped not long ago and ate. Thanks, though."

"I thought you were going to come this evening," Nat said as they walked into the living room. "I feel as though I only just got here. Tara was at the wedding all day yesterday so I've hardly seen her."

"Hi, Natalie," he said pointedly.

She slouched in the armchair. "Hi."

"You knew Tara was going to be at the wedding all day yesterday," David said, taking a seat on the couch. "You wanted to come anyway."

"I suppose I can come again soon."

Tara exchanged a look with her dad, wondering if she should be the one to oppose her on that one or if he would.

"It'll be Christmas before you know it," David said. "We'll definitely have to meet up with Tara and James over Christmas."

"That would be nice." Tara smiled widely. That was the sort of relationship she could deal with; they could get together on special occasions.

"Christmas?" Nat said, sitting up in her seat. "That's like two months away!"

"Well, you've got your studies. And I'm sure Tara and James are busy with the shop on the run up to Christmas."

"It's the busiest time," Tara said, backing him up.

"I thought I might come at half term," Nat said. "If the shop's busy I can help out."

"We're going away at half term," David said. "Your mum's already booked the cottage. You know that."

"I could come here instead. I'm bored of going to Norfolk."

David frowned. "We can talk to your mum about it, but I don't think it's a good idea."

"Is it okay with you, Tara?" Nat looked at her defiantly. "If Mum says it's okay."

"I'm not sure." Tara's brain worked overtime as she sought an excuse. "We usually do a stocktake around then so it might be difficult."

"I could help," Nat said quickly.

"It's really boring. I'd feel terrible keeping you cooped up here when you could be in Norfolk with your family."

"You're my family too," Nat said.

"Why don't you get your bag?" David said. "We should get going and let Tara and James enjoy the rest of their weekend."

Huffily, Nat pushed herself out of the chair and headed for the spare room.

"There's no way Gillian will agree to her coming here at half term," David said, when she was out of hearing range. "We always go to Norfolk at half term."

"That sounds lovely." At one time, Tara would have been jealous and resentful of their perfect little family holidays. Now she was quite happy with their plans.

"I imagine we won't get many more family holidays with them so we're trying to take advantage. Soon, they'll refuse outright." He tapped the arm of the couch. "How was the wedding yesterday?"

"Great fun," Tara said. "One of our friends went into labour during the service."

David's eyes sparkled as he smiled. "Really?"

"I have bruises to prove it." James rolled up his sleeve.

"Oh my goodness!" Tara grabbed his arm to look at the row of fingerprint-sized bruises. "I thought you were just being a wimp."

"No. It really hurt. She's stronger than she looks."

"Bless her. She must've been in agony, but she never made a sound. She gave birth in the ambulance on the way to the hospital," Tara told David.

"It sounds like an eventful day!" His gaze moved to Nat when she came back in. "And how was it at the bookshop?"

"Great," she replied without enthusiasm.

"How was the drive over?" James asked David, leading the conversation back to neutral ground. They spent a while chatting about the best route to take and the state of the roads. Eventually, David announced that they should get going.

Tara wrapped James in a hug as soon as she closed the door on them. "Thank you for your awesome small talk."

"Thank goodness for roadworks. If it weren't for half-finished roads I'd have had to resort to talking about the weather."

"I think you could even pull that off. You've got real talent."

"Thanks!" Chuckling, he went to the kitchen. "What do you want to do for the rest of the day?"

"I thought I might go and see Mum. Maybe bring her some flowers to say thanks for holding the fort yesterday."

"You mean you want to go and check she's not traumatised after her day with Nat?" He filled a glass with water and turned to her with a cheeky grin.

"I'd say there's a good possibility that she's traumatised."

"Nat's not so bad."

"Not to you. But you have the patience of a saint." She slumped into a chair at the kitchen table. "What was all that about half term? Did she want to come for a whole week or what?"

James raised an eyebrow. "That reminds me, what's all this about a stocktake?"

"I couldn't think of an excuse quickly." She was amused by the look of mock horror on James's face. "It was the first thing that came to mind. And compared to having Nat to stay for a week, stocktaking doesn't actually seem so bad."

"I hate it. Have we ever managed a stocktake without arguing?"

"No. But that's because you always make it more difficult than it needs to be."

"See, just talking about it causes bad vibes."

"I'm sure Dad and Gillian won't let Nat come again so soon anyway. Thank goodness. I can't believe she was encouraging Mum to go on dates."

"I have to say, I'm with Nat on this one; it really might be good for Debbie." His words were gentle and he gave her shoulder a reassuring squeeze.

Tara placed her hand over his. "I'm absolutely fine with you saying that. But when Nat says it I want to claw her eyes out."

"So it's safe to say she brings out the worst in you?" He smiled as he sat beside her.

"I hate how she comments on things that she has no idea about. She's so annoyingly naive. And I realise she can't help that she grew up in a perfect family and gets everything she wants, but it grates on my nerves."

"Well, you've been very patient with her."

"Not really. I leave the room when I can't cope with her any more."

"That's a good strategy," he said. "Shall we get going to your mum's?"

"Are you coming too? If you need a break from my family I completely understand."

"No, it's fine. I want to put that wardrobe together for her. Maybe she'll cook for us."

"It always seems as though you prefer Mum's cooking to mine," Tara said.

"That's because she's a really good cook, and you're terrible."

"Hey!" She took a swipe at his arm but he dodged out of the way. "At least say you were joking."

"Yeah, of course I was," he said with a grimace.

"You're mean." She picked up the car keys and grabbed her coat.

CHAPTER 16

Half an hour after they arrived at Debbie's house the spare room had pieces of wood laid out across the floor. James sat in the middle of it with an instruction manual in his hand and a look of intensity on his face.

Tara stood in the doorway. "If it's too much trouble you can leave it and I'll get Sam to come and do it sometime."

"I can do it," James said with a hint of a scowl. "You don't have to watch me. I'll shout for you if I need help."

"I'll bring you a coffee up," she said, leaving him to it.

In the kitchen, Debbie handed Tara a steaming mug and she savoured the taste as she took a sip of coffee.

"I still can't believe it about Josie," Debbie said. "Have you heard from her today?"

"She sent me and Amber a photo of the baby." Tara got her phone out and clicked into the group messages to find the picture. "They still haven't decided on a name."

"Oh, she's so precious," Debbie said as she peered at the photo. "Absolutely beautiful. Sam will be over the moon."

"I'd say so. We'll visit them next week sometime, when they're back home and settled."

"I'd like to go sometime too. I knitted a little blanket, so I'll take that around and see if I can have a cuddle with the baby."

Tara pulled out a chair at the kitchen table as she changed the subject. "Was it really okay at the shop yesterday?"

"Yes. We managed fine." She'd said as much already, but Tara thought she might get more out of her without James around.

"I hope Nat didn't drive you crazy. She talks a lot."

"Yes, she does." Debbie's brow creased.

"Was it weird spending a day with her?"

"It's a bit of a strange situation, but she is your sister and it seems as though she's going to be around so I'll have to get used to it."

"Oh no." Tara put her coffee down, hearing the hesitation in her mum's voice. "Was it that bad?"

"No." Debbie shook her head. "It wasn't bad at all. I just find her a little … I don't know how to explain it … she's sort of …"

"Annoying?"

Debbie laughed. "That's not what I was going to say. She asked me a lot of questions that's all. I wasn't expecting it."

"What kind of questions?"

"About how I met David, what our wedding was like, stuff like that. She's just curious, I suppose, and I didn't mind the questions. The problem is, I'm not sure how to talk to her. She's at that awkward age. I don't know whether to treat her as an adult or a child."

"I think I've opted to treat her like a child. It's easier to be patient with her that way. Plus, she's very immature for her age."

"She's a nice girl, though. And it's good that you're getting to know each other."

"I wanted to spend time with Dad. Now I feel as though that was a mistake."

"David's thrilled that you got back in touch with him."

"Have you spoken to him recently?"

"We email each other now and then. That's about it these days."

That had always been his preferred method of communication. When Tara had cut him out of her life, he'd sent her long emails at least once a week. She felt bad now that she'd mostly ignored them.

"He's really enjoyed getting to know you again," Debbie went on. "And meeting James. It means a lot to him that you want him in your life."

"I wish it was easier," Tara said wistfully. If it was just her dad it would be a lot more straightforward. Nat and Ben complicated things.

"It'll be all right. Nat will be off to uni next year so she won't be around so much."

"It'd be nice to spend time with Dad on his own sometimes. But I think he's worried about offending Nat."

"You need to stop thinking about it all so much." Debbie patted her arm. "I'll tell you something funny – that lovely man Rupert messaged me this morning. I must have made a good impression. I didn't know I still had it in me!"

"You can easily get a date if you want one. Don't go out with Rupert, though. If you want to date, find someone a bit more dynamic, please."

"I thought he seemed sweet."

"He's dull. And a bit creepy. Please don't go out with him."

"I probably won't. My dating days are long gone."

Tara stood and picked up James's coffee. "I better take this up and see how he's getting on."

. . .

It took a few minutes for James to notice Tara as he worked away, screwing the panels into place.

"Looks like it's all coming together nicely," Tara said,

"No need to look so surprised."

"I'll be honest, I thought I might have to call Sam to come and save the day."

"I can definitely manage to construct a wardrobe. Besides, Sam had a baby yesterday. I think he's got better things to do than help put a flat-pack together."

"You really don't know Sam very well at all. If I sent him a picture of a load of pieces of wood that needed assembling, he'd abandon his wife and newborn in an instant. He's like Batman of the DIY world."

"I've got it under control." He gave her a quick kiss and got back to work. "Stay here, though. I'll need some help soon."

She leaned against the doorframe, happy to watch him work. "I was thinking we could have dinner with Mum, then call in and see Annette later. I haven't seen her for a little while."

"Fine by me. Do you want to let her know we're coming? She'll probably bake something if she's expecting us."

"No. I don't want her going to any effort. And I'd like to test the theory that she always has something freshly baked regardless of whether she knows there's someone coming over or not."

~

In her childhood, Tara had spent a lot of time playing at Annette's house and she always had a rush of nostalgia whenever she visited. The dog kennels had been a wonderful place to spend time as a child. There were always some friendly pups to play with, and Annette and her partner, Wendy, always had homemade biscuits or cakes for them. Wendy had sadly passed away a few years earlier. Thankfully, Josie had come along and helped Annette with the kennels.

"I wonder why Josie's car's here," Tara said as they pulled up in front of the gorgeous brick house surrounded by rolling hills in all directions.

"She probably just left it here."

Tara walked to the kitchen door and let herself in. "It's just us," she shouted as she patted Charlie, the lovely old golden retriever.

"Come and look!" Annette said from the living room.

Puzzled, Tara walked through, then bit her lip at the sight of Sam perched on the arm of Annette's chair, gazing down at the tiny bundle that Annette rocked gently.

"I thought you were still in the hospital?" Tara said, clutching her chest as she looked at Josie on the couch.

"They discharged me this afternoon. We came straight here."

"Don't get up," Tara said, bending to give her a hug. "How are you?"

"Pretty sore. But otherwise really good."

"She's absolutely gorgeous," James said, crouching beside Annette's chair.

Annette wiped a tear from her cheek with a hanky. "I hate to break it to you, blondie, but I'm a lesbian."

"I meant the baby!" James said, shaking his head.

Tara crowded around too. "She really is beautiful."

"I'm an emotional wreck," Annette said, catching more tears on her cheeks. "Do you know what they've called her?"

"No." Tara looked to Josie. "I thought you hadn't decided on a name yet?"

"We wanted Annette to be the first to hear."

"Someone tell me then," Tara said, catching Sam's crooked smile.

Annette's chin twitched. "They're calling her Annette."

"I didn't realise it would make you cry so much," Sam said, rubbing her back.

"I'm just so touched."

"That's lovely," Tara said.

"We'll call her Annie so it doesn't get confusing," Josie said.

"Hello, Annie!" Tara beamed at the tiny baby. "Annie Blake. That's a gorgeous name."

"Do you want to hold her?" Sam asked.

"Yes, please." Tara went to sit beside Josie. "You'll have to pass her to me," she said to Sam. "I'm scared I'll drop her."

Carefully, he scooped her out of Annette's arms, pausing to drop a kiss on her head before passing her to Tara.

"She's so tiny." Tara's throat felt thick and she swallowed hard. Tears came out of nowhere, and she couldn't stop them. James gave her leg a squeeze as he sat beside her, leaning in to look at Annie.

"You're supposed to be the tough one," Annette said. "You're worse than me. Pass her the tissues." She nudged Sam to a box of tissues on a side table.

"Thanks." Tara wiped her eyes and looked at Josie, who gave her arm a gentle rub. "I'm a wreck," she said, sniffing and gazing down at the beautiful sleeping baby. "I can't believe I get to hold her when she's barely a day old. How was the birth, by the way?"

Josie's eyes widened dramatically. "Let's just say she's probably going to be an only child."

"Yep," Sam agreed. "I don't want to go through that again."

"Oh, it must have been awful for you," Josie said mockingly.

"It *was*!"

"I thought the wedding would be a bit much for me," Annette said. "But I wish I'd gone now. It sounds hysterical."

"It wasn't funny at all," Josie said. "I was in agony."

"Me too," James said, rolling up his sleeve to show off his bruises.

Immediately, Sam pushed his sleeve back. "Mine's the same. I'm black and blue."

"Oh, you pair of wimps," Annette said with a flick of the hand.

Josie laughed. "Do you really want to compare wounds? Because I promise you, I'm going to win."

Sam exchanged a look of mock horror with James and they hurriedly pulled their sleeves back down.

"Shouldn't you be in bed?" Tara asked Josie.

"Yes, she should," Sam answered for her.

"Just a minute," Josie said. "Give James a turn holding Annie before we go."

"Can I?" James asked eagerly.

Tara pouted. "I don't really want to let go of her, but okay." She shuffled to face James and carefully transferred little Annie into his arms.

"Hello," he whispered. "You're so cute."

"Honestly, James!" Annette tutted. "Stop flirting with me. You've got no chance!"

They all erupted with laughter. She'd always been a bit of a tease, but for some reason James got more than most. Tara took it as a sign of her approval.

"Isn't she adorable?" Tara said, touching the back of her finger to Annie's cheek. Her eyes filled up again and she hid her face in James's shoulder for a moment before discreetly reaching for another tissue. "No one's allowed to tease me for going soft," she said, as she felt everyone looking at her.

"We wouldn't dare," Sam said, then moved to take the baby. "I'm going to take my two beauties home now."

"Congratulations, again," Tara said to Josie. "I'm so happy for you."

"Thank you." Josie grimaced as she heaved herself off the couch. "Sorry about your arm," she said to James.

"I'll survive. Have a good rest."

Josie hobbled towards the door while Sam settled Annie into her car seat. He waved to them and followed Josie outside.

"That was lovely," Annette said. "I didn't know they were coming, so it was a wonderful surprise. I like that you all call in unexpectedly."

"We were at Mum's this afternoon," Tara said, "so we thought we'd pop in and say hello. We timed it perfectly."

Annette started to get up. "I'll put the kettle on."

"I can do it," James said, jumping up.

"Thanks." Annette settled herself back in her chair. "I made biscuits earlier too. They're on a cooling rack on the counter. Put them on a plate and we'll have a few of those."

James shot Tara a discreet wink before moving to the kitchen.

CHAPTER 17

Tara had only just opened the shop on Monday morning when Belinda waltzed in. Her voice calling out good morning was enough to make Tara's eyes roll.

"Hi," she said, her lips stretched to a tight smile.

"I've got a bone to pick with you." Belinda wagged a finger as she approached the counter. "I thought we were friends."

"Did you?" Tara asked dryly.

Belinda laughed. "Oh, you are funny! That's why I love coming in here. You always have me in stitches. Anyway, I can't believe you never mentioned you have a sister."

"Half-sister," Tara corrected her.

"A sister is a sister."

Tara stood up straighter. "And a half-sister is a half-sister. She mentioned that she'd met you."

"She's so sweet. We had a lovely chat. It's great that you've reached out to your father after all these years. I never realised you were estranged."

Tara rubbed at her temples. "Can I help you find a book?"

"Oh, there you go again with that dry humour. Of course I

don't want a book. I only came in to see you." Her eyes lit up. "What about your mum and Rupert?"

"What about them?"

"I think they'd make a lovely couple. And good on Rupert for having the courage to ask her out. I bet that wasn't easy."

"She's not going to go out with him."

"I told her she should. One date won't hurt. And you never know what might come of it." She turned, her eyes roaming the shop. "It's like there's something in the air here. First you and James, now Debbie and Rupert. So much romance. Maybe I should come and work here sometimes so I can find myself a man!" She let out a high-pitched laugh and slapped a hand on the counter.

"We've had some great books come in recently," Tara said. "I could show you some."

Belinda beamed. "Stop with your jokes!"

"There's a great non-fiction book called *Stop Gossiping and go Back to Work*. Shall I see if I can find it for you?"

"Oh, Tara! You're killing me!"

"Not yet, but I'm seriously thinking about it."

Belinda snorted with laughter. "This is why I love coming in here. Unfortunately, I really should get to work." She set off for the door, then turned back. "By the way, I've been thinking about organising some sort of Christmas event for the shops. I can't decide what … something to keep people shopping locally rather than going off to the big shopping centres or shopping online. I'll keep thinking and let you know what I come up with."

Tara clicked the computer mouse and navigated to the bookshop email account. "I'll be over here on the edge of my seat," she said in a dull monotone.

Belinda's shrill laugh reverberated around the shop before she finally left.

After checking through the emails for the bookshop, Tara

switched to her private account and found a message from her dad. She read through it quickly. He thanked her for having Nat to stay again and commented on how much he'd enjoyed seeing her at the weekend too. Then he told her that he'd spoken to Gillian about the upcoming school holidays and they were in agreement that Nat should join them on holiday as originally planned. He said she should also be concentrating more on her schoolwork, so they'd suggested waiting until Christmas before she met up with Tara again.

Smiling at the screen, Tara felt a rush of relief. Her eyes skimmed over the rest of the email where her dad wrote that she could call him any time if she needed anything or if she felt like a chat. It was the same way he always ended his emails, and Tara barely even registered it. She moved the message from the inbox to a separate folder which she'd imaginatively titled 'Dad'. Keeping them was a habit.

James was busy working on one of his web design projects but came down late in the morning kitted out in his running gear.

"I'm going for a jog," he said. "Then I'll make lunch. How are things down here?"

"All good." There'd been a few customers and an order had come in so she'd spent an hour cataloguing new books and finding shelf space for them. "Oh, except Belinda came in. Telling me all about her chat with Mum and Nat on Saturday."

"She'll have been in her element."

"Yep. I also got an email from Dad, which basically said they'd see us at Christmas sometime so that feels like a relief."

"It'll be Christmas before we know it."

"I can't wait," Tara said brightly.

"To see Nat again?"

"No!" She shook her head. "I can't wait to decorate the

shop. I love it." Her festive window display was always a big hit with children, and it had become something of a tradition.

"I'll see you in a bit," James said, as he left for his jog.

When he arrived back almost an hour later, Tara was scowling at her phone.

"What's wrong?" James asked.

"Nat messaged me to say that she's not allowed to come here in the school holidays but not to worry because she'll just keep nagging her parents about it until they give in."

"I wouldn't worry about it. David seemed pretty firm that she wasn't coming."

"Yeah, but she also seems used to getting her own way. I honestly couldn't cope with her for a week. Even a weekend is too much."

"Don't waste time worrying about something that isn't going to happen." He put his arms around her and attempted to kiss her as she wriggled away, complaining about how sweaty he was. "Come here," he said, holding a hand out to her as she backed away.

"I'm not touching you! You're disgusting." She couldn't help but laugh as he followed her around the shop with a flirty smile.

"I just want one kiss!"

"You're not having one," she said, darting around the beanbags to get away from him. "Go and have a shower."

"Fine." He stopped chasing her and walked towards the back door. "What do you want for lunch?"

"Whatever you want to make," she said.

"I might do jacket potatoes."

"Sounds good." She walked back to the counter, her mind on the tasks she needed to get done that afternoon. There were a few calls she needed to make, to the wholesaler and a couple of customers who were waiting on books that she'd ordered.

With her mind elsewhere, she didn't register James until he clamped his arms around her and pulled her close to him.

"James!" she shrieked. "You seriously stink. Leave me alone."

"One kiss," he said with a raised eyebrow.

She gave him a hasty peck. "There! Now go away."

"That wasn't a kiss." He moved his mouth back to hers, kissing her with such force that she had to take a step back. "Love you," he said when he released her.

"I love you too," she said, slightly dizzy from the kiss. She watched him leave with a huge smile on her face.

CHAPTER 18

Scarlett had sent Lizzie a message reminding her to be at the cafe on Sunday morning for their top-secret business meeting. She arrived exactly on time, but there was no sign of Scarlett or Emily so she took a seat at a table by the window.

"I'm sorry," Verity said as she came to take her order. "I had no idea what she was up to until yesterday. I've tried talking to her but I'm afraid you'll just have to let her down gently."

"You know why Scarlett wants to talk to us?" Lizzie asked.

"Yes. Another of her crazy ideas." She glanced around. "I'll let her give you her pitch. She's excited about talking to you. Try and be gentle with her. You know what she's like. Convinced she's had the best idea ever and then she gets tunnel vision."

"I'm intrigued," Lizzie said.

A cold draught wafted in when Emily opened the door.

"The newlywed returns." Verity said. "How was the honeymoon?"

"Really great. It just went too fast." She took her coat off and hung it on the hatstand by the door.

"And how's married life?" Lizzie asked.

"So far so good!" She sank into the chair opposite. "I'm dying for a coffee."

"Me too," Lizzie said, looking expectantly at Verity.

"Coming right up," Verity said.

"No!" Scarlett called, emerging through the door behind the counter. "No one's having coffee. Not yet. Business first, coffee later."

"Can't we drink coffee *and* talk business?" Lizzie asked.

"No. We need to go upstairs. You can have coffee later."

"Upstairs here?" Emily asked, pointing overhead.

"Yes." Scarlett hovered beside the counter. "Come on!"

"Is that okay?" Lizzie asked Verity as she and Emily stood up. She'd never been up to the flat above the cafe. Behind the counter was like a magical realm where she'd never ventured.

"Yes." She gave a small shake of the head. "Maybe you could at least pretend to mull over her proposition," she said quietly. "So she's not too disappointed."

"What's going on?" Emily asked Lizzie as they slipped behind the counter.

"I've no idea," Lizzie replied. It was interesting to see the back of the shop, though. She got a glimpse into the kitchen before Scarlett ushered them up the stairs.

"Look!" Scarlett said, sweeping a hand towards the door at the top of the stairs. On it hung a small frame with the words 'Scarlett Ink' written in thick red marker on a piece of paper. "We'll make a better sign. That's just to give you an idea."

"An idea of what?" Lizzie asked.

"Of how it will look when we have a sign on the door."

"I'm confused," Lizzie said as she followed Scarlett inside the flat.

"It's a play on words." Scarlett stared at her as though it was obvious. "Ink sounds like *incorporated.* So it sounds like it's a company name. Which it is, but it's actually ink like the kind used in printing. It's genius, isn't it?"

"I'm still a little confused," Emily said, looking around the short hallway.

"It's the name for the publishing company." Scarlett led them into the airy room, which had presumably been the living room when Verity was living there. All that was left was a couch in the middle of the room. "We can keep the couch if we want it or we can get rid of it. Verity doesn't want it at Bill's house. It's pretty old, but it might work depending on what style we go for. We need to look professional but also comfortable. If we have clients here we want them to feel at home, don't we?"

Lizzie raised a hand to stop her. "Slow down, please. What are you talking about?"

"Sorry! I got carried away. We're going to set up our own publishing company. The three of us can be equal partners. I don't have any money to invest to start with, but I think we can find a way to get around that. Like maybe you two put up some money initially and I don't." She beamed at them. "What do you think? It's a great space, isn't it? This window has a view over the beach, and one of the bedrooms does too. Come and see."

Silently, Lizzie and Emily followed Scarlett into the back bedroom, which still had a lot of Scarlett's things in it. "I'll clear everything out," she said. "I thought you two could each take a bedroom as an office. I guess that's only fair considering you're going to have to pay the rent to start with. I can have a desk in the living room. I'll also need to sleep here at the weekends, but the couch pulls out to a bed so that would be fine. I wouldn't mess the place up." She moved through to the front bedroom as she chatted.

"You're being very quiet," she finally said when Lizzie and Emily stood looking out of the bay window. The view was fantastic. You could watch people coming and going on the road below and also look out over the beach and the shimmering blue waters of the cove. "You like the idea, don't you?"

Lizzie tried to catch Emily's eye, but she was gazing blankly out to sea. "You want us to set up our own publishing company?" she asked, then remembered what Max had said about never knowing when Scarlett was joking. She felt the same.

"Yes."

"We can't set up a publishing company," Emily said. "That's crazy."

"It's not crazy." Scarlett's features scrunched up. "Between us we have all the know-how and most of the skills. Anything we can't do ourselves we can hire freelancers for, but we already have all the contacts so that's not a problem."

"Our own publishing company?" Lizzie said again.

Scarlett rolled her eyes and set off back to the living room. "Yes! You're a bit slow to catch on. How many more times do I need to say it?"

"I don't see how we could set up our own publishing company," Emily said, taking a seat on the couch. Lizzie sat at the other end of it and Scarlett looked down at them impatiently.

"Lizzie would be the in-house editor," she said. "Also the acquisitions editor."

Lizzie shifted in her seat. "What?"

"You'd look through the submissions and decide which authors we want to take on and which books we'll publish.

We'd all have to agree, of course, but you'd be the one to narrow down the choices."

"Sorry," Lizzie said. "I'm struggling to keep up."

"You understand how publishing companies work, don't you?" Scarlett asked huffily. "I thought you used to work for a magazine?"

"I did. But that's not the same as publishing novels."

"You have transferable skills," Scarlett said. "You know about budgets and business stuff as well as editing, right?"

"Yes," Lizzie admitted reluctantly.

"And Emily knows everything there is to know about the publishing process and marketing and advertising. I know a lot too. So between us we have all the skills we need. We'd need to hire a cover designer but that's not a problem."

"We can't start a publishing company," Emily said with a bemused smile.

"We can!" Scarlett beamed. "And you're the one who said we could."

"When did I say that?" Emily asked.

"When I showed you my first book and told you that my mum had said it was terrible and that I should give up." She smiled smugly. "You said I could do anything I set my mind to."

"I didn't mean start your own publishing company," Emily said.

Scarlett sighed loudly. "So you lied?"

"No. I just meant …" She looked to Lizzie for help.

"I think Emily was expecting you to start small and build up. Not jump straight into setting up a publishing company."

"I didn't just jump into it," Scarlett insisted. "First I wrote my own books and got them edited. And I learned a lot about marketing and advertising. Then I enrolled at uni. English with Creative Writing is the perfect course. I'll learn so much doing that, and it also gives me more credibility if I can tell clients I have a degree."

"Maybe you should get the degree first," Lizzie suggested. "And then think about setting up the publishing company."

"That was the original plan," Scarlett said. "But Verity's place is available now. If we wait, she'll rent it to someone else. This is a perfect place for our offices." She paused and glared at them. "I thought you'd be excited."

"I'm not sure you've really thought it through," Emily said. "You seem to be simplifying things."

"I never said it would be simple. All I said is that between us we have all the skills. It will be loads of work, but we're all used to working hard."

"You've got uni," Lizzie said. "How could you possibly juggle studying and setting up a business?"

"I can't," Scarlett said. "Not without you, anyway. But together we can do anything."

Lizzie rubbed her hands over her face and glanced at Emily, wondering which of them would be the one to let her down gently. Since it was Emily who'd given Scarlett the grand idea of being able to achieve anything, she thought it only fair it should fall to her.

"We can't," Emily said. "It's completely unrealistic. Have you actually thought about it in terms of business? You'd need to make a proper business plan to see if it could be a viable venture. And I just don't think it would be."

"I'm not good at business plans and stuff like that," Scarlett said. "But I know we could do it."

Lizzie sank back on the couch.

"Please say you'll do it with me," Scarlett said. "Otherwise I'll have to wait until I graduate and that's ages away. And one day when I go ahead and do it without you and end up being really successful, you're going to feel so stupid for turning me down."

"I suppose we can think about it," Lizzie said, hating the disappointment in Scarlett's features.

Scarlett beamed. "I'm sure you won't have to think about it for long before you realise it's a brilliant idea."

CHAPTER 19

Jack was getting out of the shower when Emily arrived home. He shouted a greeting to her and told her he'd be down in a minute. Their bags needed to be unpacked and there was a load of washing to do, but instead Emily plonked herself on the couch and contemplated what had just happened.

"You look miles away," Jack said, appearing in front of her. "How was your business meeting?"

Emily gave a slight shake of her head, still trying to digest Scarlett's proposition. "She wants us to set up a publishing company." It was hard not to laugh at the absurdity of the statement. As though setting up a publishing company was something you could breeze into and do on a whim.

"What?" Jack sat heavily beside her.

"The flat above the cafe is available to rent," she explained. "Scarlett wants the three of us to set up a publishing company and use the flat as our offices."

"Wow! That's …" Jack's eyes widened as he struggled for words. "Wow," he said again.

"I know. You can see why she's so good at writing fantasy books. She comes up with some far-fetched ideas."

"Genius ideas, more like." He sank back into the couch with a smile on his face. "How come you and Lizzie never thought of this?"

"Because it's ridiculous. We can't set up a publishing company."

"Why not? You know just about everything there is to know about publishing. Lizzie's an editor, and she has a great head for business. And Scarlett's brilliant when it comes to advertising and marketing. She's done a great job with your books."

"Yeah." Emily gave him a puzzled look, surprised by his reaction. "That's what Scarlett said."

"She's right. It's a fantastic idea. Aren't you tempted?"

"It's a nice idea in theory," Emily said slowly. "It's not realistic, though. You and Scarlett are both very good at simplifying things. You make it sound so easy, but it's not. And Scarlett really hasn't thought it out at all. She gets an idea and can't let it go, but she hasn't considered the business side of it or run any numbers."

Jack's eyes lit up. "We should make a business plan."

"We just got back from our honeymoon," she said, snuggling into him. "I thought we were going to have a lazy day together before we get back to work and real life."

He dropped a kiss at her hairline. "Okay."

With her head against his chest, she was lulled by the thudding of his heart. She smiled to herself yet again at the thought that they were married. Every time she thought of him as her husband it gave her a thrill.

"It would be pretty cool for you to have an office outside of the house," Jack said. "And you've always enjoyed working with Lizzie."

"That's true." An image of Verity's flat popped into her

head, except in her vision it was transformed into a workspace and there was a buzz in the air as she sat around with Lizzie and Scarlett discussing potential authors to work with. She pushed the thought aside.

"You could build up gradually over time," Jack mused. "So the initial costs would be low. There'd be some legal aspects I guess. You'd need to figure out what sort of contracts you'd have with authors."

"Max could probably help us with that. His background is law. He might have some contacts …" She sat up abruptly. "Why are we still talking about this?"

Jack shrugged and did his best to look innocent. "I think it's a pretty cool idea," he said eventually. "Don't you even want to consider it?"

"Maybe," she admitted. "But I keep telling you I'm going to work less, not more. Starting a publishing company would definitely be more work."

"I keep telling you I don't have a problem with you working long hours if it's what you want to do. It's not as though it's anything new. Besides, it's good for me. If you're really successful, it means that when we have kids I'll be able to stop working and be a househusband."

"You're quite excited about that prospect, aren't you?"

"Yes! I hang out with Max enough to see how easy he has it – he spends his days playing at the beach or the playground."

"You're such a big kid," she said.

He nodded his agreement. "Anyway, are you going to think about Scarlett's idea?"

With a sigh, she admitted defeat. "Let's start putting together a business plan." It couldn't hurt to do some research, and she was fairly sure the idea was going to niggle at her until she'd looked into it.

Three hours later, the dining table was covered in sheets

of paper, and Jack had several pages of scribbled notes on a notepad. Emily had first looked at the logistics and legalities of setting up a small press, printing out any useful information she found. Surprisingly, it didn't seem as complicated as she'd first imagined.

Since she'd been independently publishing her books, she had a fairly good idea of the sales and revenue figures they could expect. They scaled up from publishing her own titles to publishing titles from other authors, adding in all the costs they could think of. From there, they made projections for an initial five-year business plan.

"This was supposed to be a lazy day," Emily said, stretching her neck as Jack went over the figures again.

"I'm going to type all this up," he said, his eyes still on the papers. "Then you can give it to Lizzie to look over."

"Lizzie's going to think I'm mad."

Jack tapped his pen against the notepad, then looked at her seriously. "You're only mad if you don't put this plan into action."

Emily had intended to visit Josie on Monday and meet baby Annie, but after spending so long making a business plan for a hypothetical publishing company she felt like getting out of the house and thinking about something else for a while. Visiting on Sunday also meant that Jack could go with her. He was keen to meet Annie too.

They spent an hour drinking tea in Josie and Sam's living room, chatting about the wedding and honeymoon and the adorably sweet little Annie, who got passed between them.

Jack had her nestled in the crook of his arm when Sam went and touched her fingers and then her cheek.

"Do you think she's warm enough?" he asked, looking to Josie.

"I think she's fine." Josie discreetly rolled her eyes. "Stop fussing so much. In fact, why don't you take Jack up to the pub for a bit? Then I can get the juicy details of the honeymoon from Emily." She smiled mischievously and winked at Jack.

"That's disturbing." Jack shuffled along the couch and passed Annie to Emily. "But I suppose we can go up to the pub and leave you ladies to chat."

"Are you okay?" Sam asked Josie.

"Yes!" She laughed. "Go. Please." She waited until the door had closed behind them before speaking again. "He's very attentive, but I'm already looking forward to him going back to work and getting into some sort of normal routine."

"It's sweet how he looks after you," Emily said, gazing at Annie's dainty features as she slept.

"Yes, I know. I do appreciate it. I'm just slightly worried he might suffocate me. He barely gives me space to breath."

"Everything's okay, though?" Emily asked.

"Yes. I didn't mean to complain. Everything's great. How are things with you?"

"Really good. The week away was fantastic. I think I really needed the break from work, and it was lovely to spend so much time with Jack."

"I'm glad you had a good time." Josie moved from the chair to sit beside Emily on the couch. "Are you annoyed with me?"

Taken aback by the question, Emily's head shot up. Josie's features were serious.

"No," Emily said. "Why would I be annoyed with you?"

"Because I've been a rubbish friend." Josie's brow creased heavily. "I feel as though I wasn't supportive at all with the wedding. I was really happy for you, but I just had no energy for anything. I'm sorry."

"It's fine."

"You were annoyed with me, though, weren't you?"

Emily sighed. "I was a little bit disappointed. But I understand. You had your own stuff going on."

"I feel as though the past two years have been one big, awful blur." Josie pressed her lips together as though fighting off tears. "With the miscarriages and trying to get pregnant, everything was so stressful. And then I felt horrible the whole time I was pregnant."

"I know." Gently, Emily rocked Annie in her arms. "It's really fine."

"I sort of felt like you took it personally. But it was never that I didn't want to hang out with you, just that I felt ill all the time and I had no energy."

Emily focused on the baby to avoid looking at Josie. "You could have talked to me about the pregnancy. You just hid away. If you felt terrible, you could have spoken to me about it."

"I didn't want to talk to anyone about it. After the miscarriages, it felt wrong to complain about the pregnancy."

Finally, Emily looked up to find Josie's eyes shining with tears. Shifting Annie in her arms, she managed to put an arm around her for an awkward side hug.

"I'm sorry for being a rubbish friend," Josie said.

"You weren't. Stop worrying about it."

"I'll make it up to you." Josie wiped her hands over her cheeks. "I'll be able to come over and visit you all the time now. We can have lunches together and take Annie for walks on the beach."

"I'd like that," Emily said.

"What else is going on with you?" Josie asked. "Which book are you working on now? The smuggler one?"

“Yes. I’m still working on the first book in the series.”

“Did you really take a whole week off for your honeymoon?”

“Yes.” Emily laughed. “Why does everyone find that so surprising?”

“Because you’re a workaholic.”

“I’m trying to cut down my work hours,” Emily said.

“Sure you are,” Josie said, smiling.

Emily’s mind drifted to their dining room table, which was covered with plans for a publishing company. She opened her mouth to mention it to Josie, then stopped herself.

There was no point in talking about something that was never going to happen.

CHAPTER 20

The editing project Lizzie was working on was a struggle to get through and the week went incredibly slowly. Her mind wandered constantly, making it difficult to stick to the task. On Thursday morning, she set it aside after a couple of hours, deciding that fresh air and exercise would be good for her.

The wind whipped her hair into her face as she ambled along the path that led to the village. She was reminded of the first time she'd visited Hope Cove. It was like thinking about a different person. She'd been stuck in a relationship and a job that were both making her miserable, but she'd felt trapped and hadn't been able to see a way out of it.

In the end, it had been Josie who'd told her she could do whatever she set her mind to. With her sister's encouragement and support, Lizzie had walked away from her life and started from scratch. Tears stung her eyes as she imagined where she'd be if she hadn't been brave enough to take Josie's advice and make radical changes. With a deep breath, she relaxed her shoulders and began the steep descent on the path that brought her into the village.

"It's freezing," she announced, shivering as she walked into the cafe.

"What can I get you to warm you up?" Verity asked.

"A cup of tea and a scone please." Verity's scones had been her favourite when she'd first moved to Hope Cove, and she'd ordered one just about every time she was in the cafe. Eventually she'd decided they should probably be limited to a treat every now and again.

"Are you meeting Emily?" Verity asked when she brought her order over.

"No. Just me today." It had become unusual for her to visit the cafe alone. These days she either had Max and the girls with her, or she'd meet up with Emily. Chatting about work issues with Emily was always good. They just had to be careful to limit the time they spent together on workdays. The break from work was always welcome, but if they weren't careful they could lose a whole afternoon talking about all things writing and publishing.

"I hope Scarlett wasn't too pushy with you at the weekend," Verity said. "Once she sets her mind to something it's difficult to persuade her away from it."

"She seems determined."

"Yes. She says she'll have her own publishing company one day – with or without you and Emily. I'll be honest, I'm inclined to believe her. And God help anyone who stands in her way!"

Lizzie smiled lightly and switched her attention to her scone as Verity left her to eat. She'd drifted into a daydream when Verity returned to clear the table.

"Are you really going to rent the flat out?" Lizzie asked her.

"That's the plan. The extra income would be good. I'm just not sure what to do about Scarlett. She says it's the only place she's ever felt at home. At one time I would've been convinced she was using emotional blackmail, but sadly I think it might be the truth."

"Would you mind me asking what the rent would be?" Lizzie said.

Verity frowned. "You're not thinking of going along with this publishing company idea, are you?"

"No." Of course she wasn't. It was a crazy idea. "But I promised I'd consider it. No harm in looking at the numbers."

"I could give you a rough figure. If you rented it, I'd make it cheaper than if I rented it to strangers. I'd know the place was looked after, and it would be good for Scarlett. You are talking hypothetically, aren't you?"

"Yes." Lizzie scrunched her paper napkin on the plate as Verity cleared the things onto her tray. "Would you mind if I nipped upstairs and looked around again?"

"Help yourself. I'll write down a number for the rent to give you an idea."

"Thanks," Lizzie said as she walked behind the counter. There was an entrance at the back of the cafe, which would mean they wouldn't have to bring clients through the cafe if they had meetings. Not that they'd use the rooms for meetings much. Mostly it would be a haven for them to work alongside each other. Meetings with clients would take place over video calls or perhaps the occasional trip to London to meet with authors they were interested in working with.

Pausing at the top of the stairs, she pondered Scarlett's idea for the name of the business. Another possible name came to mind, and Lizzie wondered how hard it would be to negotiate with Scarlett on that. The back bedroom that had been Scarlett's should probably remain so, she thought, as she poked her head in there. She had the feeling that Scarlett had meant it when she'd told Verity that the flat was the only place she felt at home. Besides, Lizzie wanted a desk by one of the windows with a view. She'd happily take the living room if Emily wanted the more private space. Having Emily and Scarlett coming and going occasionally wouldn't disturb her much.

Standing at the window, she imagined having a desk there. Mixing up her usual editing work with phone calls and submissions might be interesting. Oh, goodness. She was actually considering it. Which meant she might be just as deluded as Scarlett.

Shaking her head, she hurried back out of the flat. Downstairs, she paid for her tea and scone and said goodbye to Verity. She was almost out of the door when Verity called her back, handing her a piece of paper with the rent on it.

"Are you okay?" she asked. "You seem a little distracted all of a sudden."

"I'm fine," Lizzie said.

She said the same thing to Max later when she kept drifting into a daydream while they were eating dinner with the girls. It was clear from the way he looked at her that he didn't believe her.

"What's going on?" he asked when she came down from putting the girls to bed. He'd just finished tidying up the kitchen and leaned against the sink.

"Nothing," she replied.

"Liar!" He smiled at her. "Tell me. Please."

"You'll think I'm crazy."

"I already think you're a bit crazy so that's no reason not to tell me what's wrong."

"Nothing's wrong. I just keep thinking about something …" She paused and bit her lip. "You're going to laugh at me, but I'd really appreciate it if you'd humour me for one evening and help me with something. Then I can stop thinking about it."

"I'm intrigued."

"It's Scarlett's idea of setting up a publishing company. I keep thinking maybe she's right and we could make it work."

"What do you want me to help you with?" Max asked, his features deadly serious.

"Can you help me do some research and draw up a business plan? Just something rough. I want to get an idea of whether it's possible. It's probably not, but at least that way I can tell Scarlett I've taken her seriously." She searched Max's features. "Do you think I'm being ridiculous?"

"No. There's no harm in looking into it."

~

Emily sat at the dining table on Thursday evening, staring at the papers in front of her.

"Do you remember when we were on our honeymoon," Jack said, breaking her thoughts. "And you said you were going to cut down on working in the evenings and spend more time with me instead…"

"Yeah. I know." Her eyes didn't leave the file until Jack closed it, making her look up at him in annoyance. "I was reading that."

"You've spent all week reading over it. What you should be doing is talking to Lizzie, not staring at numbers on paper."

Emily winced. "She's going to think I've lost the plot."

"Why? It's a solid business plan and the numbers speak for themselves. She'd be crazy not to go for it."

"Do you really think so?" She leaned her head back to look up at him.

Bending, he planted a quick kiss on her lips. "Yes. Remember the time I helped you make a business plan for your own books?"

"Yes."

"Did I get that wrong?"

"No." He'd been right in his projections back then, and she was certain the numbers added up this time too. Starting their own publishing company felt fairly daunting, but financially the idea seemed sound. As a small press, it would be relatively low risk.

"Just talk to Lizzie. What's the worst that can happen?"

"She might say no." She could also laugh at her for even considering the idea, but that didn't worry Emily as much as the idea of her just saying no. Over the week she'd tried to put the idea out of her mind, but the more she tried to forget it, the more she thought about it. And the more she thought about it, the more she wanted to do it.

Jack massaged her shoulders. "You really have your heart set on the idea, don't you?"

"Yes. But I also feel bad because I told you I was going to cut down on work and this is the opposite of that."

"I don't have a problem with you working long hours." He pulled out the chair beside her and took a seat. "I mean, I like to spend time with you now and again, but maybe just give me Sundays or something and I'll be happy."

"I can definitely give you Sundays," she said with a smile.

Jack tapped the folder in front of her. "I think this is a great idea. It's perfect for you and Lizzie and Scarlett. You're totally going to take over the publishing world."

"I'm not that ambitious. A small corner of the publishing world will be plenty for me. I just need to get Lizzie onboard."

"What if she doesn't go for it? You and Scarlett could do it alone."

She shook her head. "I want it to be the three of us. It wouldn't feel right otherwise." Although, if Lizzie turned her down she might re-think that. She really did have her heart set on the idea.

"Message Lizzie," Jack said. "You haven't seen her this week anyway."

It was fairly abnormal for them to go a week without meeting up for a coffee. Emily had even avoided knitting group while she plucked up the courage to speak to Lizzie. In the end, it was Lizzie who messaged her, asking if she wanted to meet up the following morning. Emily invited her around to their place and was determined to make her case for the business, which she was sure they could make a success of.

~

Lizzie arrived in the middle of the morning on Friday. She dropped her bag by the door, then followed Emily to the kitchen. Emily didn't even manage to switch the coffee machine on before she turned on her heel and walked out again.

"Scarlett's right," she said. "Business first and then coffee. I'm too nervous for coffee."

"What are you talking about?" Lizzie asked.

"I have to show you something. Come here." Standing beside the dining table, she beckoned Lizzie over. "Try to keep an open mind."

"What's that?" Lizzie stared at the folder in confusion.

"I kept thinking about Scarlett's idea," Emily said in a rush. "And I know it sounds completely unrealistic, but I made a few notes and I don't think it's as unrealistic as I originally thought." She flicked through the pages, which were considerably more than just a few notes. "Of course it's a lot of guesswork. But I did some projections and I think it's not a bad business idea." She took a deep breath. "If I'm honest, I think it's a brilliant idea."

She waited for Lizzie's reaction. A small smile played at her lips as she quietly pored over the numbers. Emily couldn't figure out if that was a good thing, or if Lizzie was amused that she was seriously considering Scarlett's idea.

"Say something," Emily said when she couldn't take the suspense any longer.

Lizzie moved to the door and retrieved her bag. Then she pulled out a blue folder. "Your figures are much more accurate than mine. I was going to ask if you'd share your book royalties to give me a better idea of what we'd be looking at, but you already did it."

"Some of my books sell better than others," Emily said, flicking through the file Lizzie had given to her. "So I took an average number to try and be realistic." She shook her head, not quite believing what she was looking at. "You made a business plan too?"

"Yes. I asked Verity about the rent on the flat so this number is accurate. And it's less than what you'd guessed so that's good."

Emily took a seat and stared up at Lizzie. "You think it's a good idea?"

"Yes." Lizzie chuckled as she pulled a chair out. "I was terrified that I wouldn't be able to convince you."

"I've been thinking the same all week." Emily felt the tension leave her, only to be replaced with a wave of fear a moment later. "Are we going to start our own publishing company?"

"I really want to give it a go," Lizzie said. "Max has gone through all this with me and he thinks it's a solid business plan."

"Jack thinks so too. And he's good at that sort of thing."

"And you want to do it?" Lizzie asked.

"Yes. The idea has been driving me crazy. I think it will always niggle at me if we don't at least try." Her gaze landed back on the file. "There are loads of things we'd need to discuss. Lots of details we'd need to figure out. But we've always worked well together so far." Emily had done a stint of working for Lizzie at the magazine, and more recently they'd worked together on Emily's books.

"I enjoy working with you," Lizzie said, "which is partly why this is so appealing."

"We'd have to talk about how involved Scarlett is," Emily said. "She's full of enthusiasm, but she's also young and inexperienced."

"She's going to be studying for the next three years," Lizzie added. "So I'm not sure how much she can realistically commit to running a business. Plus, I don't know if we'd take out a business loan to get started or invest in it ourselves, but Scarlett won't be able to contribute."

Emily nodded and they sat in silence for a moment. If they were going to go into business together, she'd have to get used to telling Lizzie how she felt. If she couldn't do that now, they were bound to hit problems down the road.

"I'd want her to be an equal partner regardless," she finally said. "I want it to be the three of us. Not just because it's her idea, but because she has a lot to offer. With guidance, she'll be an asset to the business."

"I think so too," Lizzie said without hesitation.

"Really?" Emily blew out a breath. "I thought we might have a difference of opinion there."

"No. I absolutely agree." A smile crept over her face. "I would like to suggest a different name for the business."

"Thank goodness. I'm not a fan of Scarlett Ink."

"That's going to be a fun conversation." Lizzie stood up. "Speaking of fun conversations, before we go any further with this I need to speak to Max."

"I thought he was onboard."

"He agreed it was a good business idea. But the conversation was hypothetical. I have to see what he thinks about it becoming a reality. We need to have a proper discussion about what it would mean for us as a family."

Emily knew Max well enough to know he'd be supportive of whatever Lizzie wanted, but she was right that it would mean big changes, which would impact them all.

"Give me a shout when you've talked it through with Max. I'm excited about telling Scarlett the good news."

Lizzie beamed. "I can't wait to see her face."

CHAPTER 21

Phoebe ran at Lizzie's legs as soon as she walked in the door. "Mummy home!" she shouted loudly as Lizzie crouched to give her a hug. She ran away again and Lizzie followed her into the kitchen where Max was unpacking shopping bags and Maya sat in her highchair munching on a piece of apple.

"I bought you a present," Max said without looking at her.

Phoebe stood beside him, looking eagerly up at him.

"Not for you," he said, running a hand over her hair. "For Mummy." He pulled a bottle from one of the bags and held it out to Lizzie. "I thought you might like to celebrate."

Smiling, she took the champagne from him. "I was expecting you to ask how it went with Emily, but it seems as though you already know."

"I spoke to Jack earlier. He said Emily had been trying to work up the nerve to talk to you about it all week."

"I think she's even more enthusiastic than I am, if that's possible."

"That's great. Do you want champagne with lunch or this evening?"

"I have to do some work this afternoon so I'd better wait." She checked her watch. "But we need to talk before we get carried away with celebrating. I told Emily I have to speak to you before I can discuss it seriously with her."

"Why?" He lifted Phoebe into her highchair and passed her a plate of fruit.

"Because it would mean a lot more work for me, and I need to make sure you're okay with that. I can't do it without your support. I wouldn't even want to try."

He slipped his hand into the waistband of her jeans and pulled her to him. "Do you really need to ask if I'll support you with this?"

"No." She looped her arms around his neck. "But I need to know it's really okay with you. It feels like bad timing. You want …" She lowered her voice. "*We* want another baby. I'm not sure the two are compatible."

"But you want to do this with Emily and Scarlett?"

She interlocked her fingers at the back of his neck. "I really want to do it. It's my dream job. I think that's why I didn't take Scarlett seriously at first. It sounds like a pipe dream. But I look at Scarlett and she takes a pipe dream and just refuses to stop until it's a reality. I want to be the same. And I want the girls to grow up believing that they can achieve anything they want if they set their minds to it."

"Then you should do it," Max said.

She looked at him sadly. "I don't know if I can do it *and* have another baby. At least not while we're starting out."

"I'm fairly sure you can achieve anything if you set your mind to it," he said with a hint of smugness to his voice.

Lizzie tried to smile, but she was hit by a wave of doubt. She liked to think she was the sort of woman who could juggle a career and a young family. With

Max being so supportive, she ought to be able to. But she also remembered how frazzled she'd been when the girls were tiny. She'd struggled to keep up with her sporadic editing jobs, never mind running a publishing company.

"Seriously," Max said. "You should move ahead with Emily and Scarlett. If a baby comes into the equation at some point we'll figure that out."

He was probably right. It might take her a while to get pregnant. And then they'd have nine months until the baby arrived. In that time, the business could be up and running and Lizzie having a few months off wouldn't be a big deal. With Max taking paternity leave, she wouldn't even necessarily need to take that much time away from it. And like Max said, one baby would probably seem like a doddle after having twins.

"Thank you," she said, resting her cheek against his. "I love you."

"Love you too." He planted a kiss on her forehead then moved away to continue unpacking the shopping. "I'm going to make sandwiches if you want one? Then we're going for a walk while you get on with your work. I think Jack will join us too."

"Jack!" Maya repeated, smiling. He was always a big hit with the girls. Probably because he had about as much energy as they had and would play with them for hours.

"I'll make the sandwiches," Lizzie said, pulling plates out of the cupboard. "Where were you thinking of going on this walk you've got planned?"

Max pretended to look thoughtful. "I guess we'll head towards the village. Probably have a run around on the beach."

"That sounds nice," Lizzie said. "I suppose you might be thirsty after that?"

"It's Friday afternoon," he said with a grin. "It'd be rude not to call into the pub for a pint."

"Just don't drink too much. You need to help me drink a bottle of champagne tonight!"

"How about I invite Jack and Emily over to help out with that? We could have a takeaway with them."

Lizzie nodded. "I'll message Scarlett and see if she's here this weekend or if she's staying in Exeter. It would be nice to tell her we're going into business together, and celebrate with her."

~

Lizzie forced herself to focus in order to get some work done that afternoon. When she felt as though she'd been productive enough, she set off for a walk to stretch her legs. On impulse, she called into the cafe and left a message for Scarlett. She'd already called her earlier so she knew she was driving back to Hope Cove that evening.

As she set off for home, she caught sight of Max and Jack walking up the road, each of them with one of the girls on their shoulders. They turned when she called out to them, and the girls shouted hello to her, both of them looking to be in high spirits.

"I hear we're going to your place to get drunk and celebrate the business venture," Jack said.

"It definitely calls for a celebration." She felt giddy every time she thought about the publishing company. An evening of drinking champagne and chatting it through was exactly what she needed.

Jack grinned at her, seeming oblivious to Phoebe patting him on the head repeatedly. "I've been saying to Max, this is going to work out really well for us. You and Em going off earning all the money while we take it easy and hang out with the kids."

"And I've been trying to tell him I've given him a distorted view of being a stay-at-home parent," Max said.

"It all seems like good fun to me."

"It's not," Max and Lizzie said at the same time, making them all laugh. Lizzie suspected Jack and Emily wouldn't wait long to have kids, and she could just imagine Jack and Max with a whole brood of kids around them. She smiled at the thought, grateful that they'd become such good friends and neighbours.

Emily arrived at the house at the same time as they did. "Is Scarlett coming?" she asked as they bustled into the hallway.

"Yes. I think she'll be here soon."

"Does she already know we want to go ahead with things?"

"I left her a clue," Lizzie said, stifling a laugh. "And she might be a bit unhappy with me."

"What did you do?" Max asked.

"You'll find out when she gets here. Let's order pizzas and open the champagne."

The pizzas were laid out on the coffee table and they were all crowded around helping themselves to slices when the front door opened. Scarlett stomped in, stopping in the living room doorway and holding up the frame which had been on the door to Verity's flat. When Lizzie had called into the cafe, she'd replaced Scarlett's business name with an idea of her own.

"What's this?" Scarlett demanded.

"Just an idea I had." Lizzie shuffled back on the couch

and helped Maya to balance her plate on her lap. "What do you think?"

"What do I think?" Scarlett repeated loudly. "So you're actually serious? In that case, I say we keep you away from any creative decisions we have to make. It's the most boring, unimaginative name possible."

Emily leaned forward in the armchair. "Hope Cove Press," she said, reading the sign in Scarlett's hand. "I like it."

"I hope you're joking." Scarlett knelt on the floor beside Jack and helped herself to a slice of pizza. "What do you prefer?" she asked him. "Scarlett Ink … Ink with a k. Or boring old Hope Cove Press?"

"Scarlett Ink sounds pretty cool."

"Thank you!" She looked questioningly at Max.

"I like Hope Cove Press."

"You would," she said, as Phoebe plonked herself on her lap.

"We're going to do it, though," Lizzie said. "We're actually going to go into business together. Whatever name we agree on doesn't really matter. The point is, we're going to have our own publishing company."

"I know," Scarlett said. "I told you this last week. It's not exactly hot news."

"Apparently some people are a bit slower than you," Max told her through a mouthful of pizza. "It's hot news for us. Do you want a glass of champagne so you can join our belated celebration?"

"Yes. Okay. I'll celebrate with you as long as we can agree that we're not going to call our business Hope Cove Press?" She used a dreary voice when she said it so it really did sound like an awful name.

"You've got to say it with more enthusiasm," Lizzie said. "Imagine answering the phone and saying 'Hope Cove Press! How can I help you?'"

"Is that your phone voice?" Scarlett asked. "It's awful. You've just made certain that you're not going to be the person to answer the phone. That job will have to go to Emily."

"What about you?" Emily asked, amused.

"Do you seriously want me answering the phone to potential clients? I'd tell them to send an email and hang up. Thanks," she said, taking the glass of champagne that Max handed to her.

"I was going to make a toast," Max said when Scarlett took a long sip.

"Please don't. You'll say something cheesy and make me uncomfortable. Let's skip it and talk business. My preference would be to publish mainly fantasy titles."

"I want us to take on a lot of romance," Emily said. "But not just commercial titles. I want us to sign diverse authors. Give people a voice who are struggling to be heard."

"I'd like to include thrillers and crime fiction," Lizzie said. "I've edited some great ones recently."

"As soon as we have a website we can put a call out for submissions," Emily said. "I know loads of social media groups where I can advertise that we're taking open submissions. We'll be inundated."

Lizzie happily sipped her champagne as they chatted away, bouncing ideas around between them.

When the girls were in bed and the remnants of the takeaway cleared away, they continued to sit around drinking and brainstorming for a couple more hours.

"That was such a great night," Lizzie said, when she and Max finally closed the door on their guests.

"It was fun," Max agreed, yawning. "And now I'm absolutely done in. Bedtime for me."

"I hope you're not *too* tired," she said in her most seductive voice. As she kissed him, she pressed her body against his. The gentle groan she got in response made every inch of her tingle with desire.

"You have a lot of energy these days," Max said, taking her hand and leading her up the stairs.

"I have," she agreed. The last couple of weeks had felt as though they'd jumped back to the beginning of their relationship, when they couldn't get enough of each other and struggled to keep their hands off each other.

At the top of the stairs Max took her in his arms and kissed her again. "I like it," he whispered against her lips.

CHAPTER 22

There was something very luxurious about spending an entire Sunday morning in bed. Tara was taking advantage of the fact that she and James had a day off without anyone else around. As an added bonus, she'd only had two messages from Nat in the two weeks since she'd seen her, so it felt as though normal life had resumed.

She ran a finger down James's chest until he twitched at the tickling and pushed her hand away. "We'll have to get up soon," he said with a lazy smile. "I'm hungry."

"Well, I would have made you breakfast in bed if we'd had any food in. Did the one slice of toast not sustain you?"

"A bit. But I'd say I've burned that energy off by now." He pulled her into his arms again.

She kissed his collar bone, tasting the salt from his sweat. "Okay. I'll shower first," she said, moving to get up. "Then we can go out for lunch."

"Where do you fancy?"

"Shall we eat at the Bluebell Inn? We can call in and see Mum after."

"Yeah. Hurry up then. I'm famished."

She had a quick shower, then finished getting ready while James showered. By the time they'd driven over to Averton, Tara was hungry too. They ordered drinks, then lingered by the bar while they looked over the menu.

Tara had just put an order in with Gemma, one of the regular waitresses, when Andy walked out from a back room. He greeted them cheerfully, leaning on the bar to chat, telling them how he'd seen Josie out for a walk with the baby the previous day.

"Is your mum all right now, by the way?" he asked, as they were about to move to a table. "She said she was fine, but I was a bit worried about her all the same."

"How do you mean?"

His features tensed. "Never mind."

"Andy! What were you going to say?"

"Nothing."

"Well, you clearly were. When did you see Mum? And what happened that made you worry about her?"

"I assumed she'd told you. She was a bit upset, but she promised she was going to call you …"

"Please, just tell me what happened," Tara said in a panic. "Is she okay?"

"Yes. But now I feel as though I'm gossiping."

"I swear if you don't tell me soon, I'm going to shake you," she snarled.

He held up his hands. "She was here yesterday having dinner with some guy."

"Oh, no," Tara groaned. "Rupert?"

Andy shrugged. "Glasses, bad dress sense."

"That's Rupert. What happened?"

"I wasn't really paying much attention. They had dinner together, then they asked to pay and things got awkward."

"Oh, he was a right weirdo," Gemma said, jumping into the conversation. "I felt a bit guilty because they seemed as though they were on a date so I gave them a joint bill. Actually, I gave it to him, which was a bit presumptuous of me."

"He's always funny about money," James said.

"Debbie offered to split the bill," Gemma went on. "Except when she gave him half, he started saying that her meal was more expensive than his ..." She rolled her eyes dramatically. "He was talking loudly so a few people were looking. And he was counting out exactly how much he owed in change. And no tip, of course!"

Tara sighed. "Poor Mum."

"She was okay," Andy said. "When he offered to drive her home, she was quite forceful in telling him she'd rather walk on her own. I think she just got a bit flustered about it all. I walked her home in the end. She said she was going to call you or I'd never have mentioned it. I don't want her to think I was gossiping."

"Thanks for keeping an eye on her," Tara said.

"I was surprised to see her. It's not often she comes in the pub, and I know she doesn't always get out much, so I felt bad that it didn't go well."

"I'm sure she's fine," James said. "We're going to see her after we've eaten anyway."

"I hope she wasn't too upset," Andy said. "Don't say we were talking about it. Just say I mentioned I'd seen her or something."

Tara's whole body was tense when they sat at the table near the window. "I told her not to go out with Rupert. What was she thinking? Why didn't she listen to me?"

"Maybe because she's a grown woman and can make her own decisions."

"And look where it gets her."

"Don't be like that," James said. "It could just as easily have worked out well."

"But it didn't. As I predicted. Now she's probably sitting

at home, crying on her own. I can't eat. We'll cancel the food and go straight over to check on her."

"I'm sure she's fine. We can eat lunch and then go over there. Give her a quick call if you're worried."

Tara pulled her phone out. "I can't eat while I'm worrying what state she's in." They fell silent while she listened to the phone ringing. It seemed to take ages before Debbie answered. Tara was about to give up and go around there instead.

"Are you okay?" Tara asked at the sound of her mum's voice.

"I'm fine. Are you coming over today?"

"Yes. We just called into the Bluebell for lunch. We were planning on coming over afterwards."

"Oh. That's why you're calling to check on me. The gossip mill reached you?"

"Andy mentioned he'd seen you yesterday. When I badgered him, he said you were with a man. I presume you went on a date with Rupert?"

"Yes." She laughed. "And I presume that's not all Andy told you. It didn't go brilliantly, but it's not a big deal."

"Are you sure you're okay?"

"I'm fine. Enjoy your lunch and I'll see you later."

James's smile was fairly smug when Tara ended the call. "So she's okay? Not completely traumatised by her evening with Rupert?"

"It doesn't seem like it, no."

"Should I say I told you so?" James asked.

"Not if you want me to continue speaking to you for the rest of the day."

"Now I'm torn. A quiet day might be nice."

"You're really annoying sometimes," Tara said, grinning.

"I'm your husband, I thought it was part of the job description."

"I hope the food doesn't take long," she said. "I want to go and see Mum."

"She just told you she's fine."

"I know, but I want to hear about her date. I can't imagine what Rupert would talk about."

Thankfully, the food came quickly. They ate in silence, both of them ravenous. When they arrived at Debbie's house, she had a pot of coffee ready and waiting.

"Give us the gossip then," Tara said, settling on the couch with James. "How was your date?"

"A bit of a disaster," Debbie replied cheerfully.

"You don't seem to have let it get you down," James said, flashing Tara a knowing look.

"Well, that wouldn't make it any better, would it? It was just embarrassing really. But Andy reckoned it was Rupert who should've been embarrassed, not me. He was very sweet and insisted on walking me home. We even had a bit of a laugh about it, so that made me feel better."

"That was good of him," Tara said. "I suppose Rupert's put you off dating."

"I think I'm too old to be dating anyway. Although Andy told me off for saying that. He said if I am, then so is he, and he doesn't like to think of himself as past it yet."

"There's no way Andy's as old as you."

James gave Tara a friendly slap on the leg.

"Sorry," she said. "I didn't mean that you're old."

Debbie laughed. "I suppose I probably am a bit older than him. I've no idea how old he is."

"I'd say around fifty," James said.

"Do you reckon?" Tara frowned. "I've actually no idea how old he is. Now that I think about it, he doesn't seem to have aged in all the years I've known him."

"You just don't notice it," James said. "It's always the

way. If you see someone every day, you don't notice the subtle changes."

"I do not see Andy every day!" She couldn't help but laugh at James's cheeky grin. "I'm hardly ever in the pub any more."

"Yeah, right!"

"I'm not."

"When was the last time you were there?" James looked at his watch. "How many minutes has it been exactly?"

"You're really enjoying teasing me today, aren't you?"

"I've got to keep myself entertained somehow."

"Well I'm glad you amuse yourself at least."

She was also glad that her mum hadn't let her bad date affect her too much. In fact, she was in an extremely good mood. It had been like that for a while. The longer it went on, the more Tara hoped that it might be her new normal. But she was fairly sure that kind of thinking would only invite heartache.

CHAPTER 23

Tara was pottering around the shop on Friday afternoon, straightening out books, when her phone rang. It was on the counter and she hurried back there to grab it as it vibrated across the polished wood surface.

"Hi," she said, answering the call from Nat. After not hearing much from her over the last few weeks, the call was a bit of a surprise.

"What are you doing this weekend?" Nat asked, her voice upbeat.

"Same as always," Tara said. "Working and chilling out."

"Great! I have some good news."

"What is it?"

"I'm on my way to see you."

Tara kept quiet for a moment. She felt as though she'd been tricked. If she'd realised Nat was still set on coming to stay, she'd have made an excuse for why it wasn't convenient.

"You're coming today?" Tara said when she found her voice.

"Yes. Just for the weekend. That's okay, isn't it?"

"Erm … I thought you were going to Norfolk?"

"We leave on Monday, so Mum and Dad agreed that I could come to you for the weekend. Then I can still go away with them next week like they want."

"Right." Tara was seriously annoyed. She thought she'd made it clear to David that she didn't want Nat's weekend visits to become a regular thing, and now he'd agreed to it without even checking it was okay with her. Which it wasn't. Why on earth couldn't they just say no to their spoilt little princess?

"What time were you thinking of setting off?" Tara asked. "Because we have a few things we need to do this weekend, so it might not be the best weekend to come."

"Don't say that." Nat went a little shrill. "I'm already on the way."

"But you didn't think to ask me first? Can you put Dad on the phone?"

"I'm not with him. He's got loads of work to do before we go on holiday so he agreed I could get the train."

"You're on the train now?"

"Yes. I arrive at Newton Abbot at 16:23. Can you meet me at the station?"

"I suppose so. It really would have been better if you'd checked it was okay beforehand."

"I wanted to surprise you. And I knew you wouldn't say no."

"It means I have to rearrange my weekend."

"I can fit in with whatever you're doing. You don't need to change any plans. We'll have a great time whatever we do."

"I'll see you in a little while then." Tara ended the call and slumped against the counter as she typed out a message to James, telling him she needed him to come down and look after the shop for a while.

A customer walked in as she hit send. Tara switched into professional mode and smiled brightly as she greeted her. The old lady was just browsing and Tara left her to it. Two teenage girls came in next, at the same time that James appeared from upstairs.

"Nat's on her way," Tara said, then paused and called hello to the woman who came in with a baby in a buggy. "Why does the shop always get busy when I want to talk to you?"

"Remember we like customers? We need them."

"I know." Tara watched the woman with the buggy head straight to the children's corner. "Do you need any help?" she asked her. When she said she was fine, Tara turned back to James. "Nat decided to surprise us with a visit, so she's on her way now. I said I'd go and pick her up from the station."

"David isn't driving her this time?"

"No, he's working."

"I thought they were going on their family holiday?"

"On Monday. So I guess she'll stay until Sunday."

James gave her shoulder a squeeze. "She really loves her big sister. You should see it as a compliment."

"I see it as an inconvenience." She kissed his cheek. "I won't be long."

He snatched at her hand and drew her back to him. "Don't let her put you in a bad mood. Maybe you can take her out somewhere tomorrow. If you spend some quality time together, it might make things easier."

"Or it might mean that I finally snap and tell her how I feel about her visits."

"That would be one way of putting a stop to them."

"Except the guilt would eat me up. I'll go and get her. Hopefully the weekend won't be as bad as I imagine."

After pulling into the small car park at the train station, Tara stayed in the car, watching for the train. She blew into her hands in an effort to warm them up and was playing with the heat settings when her phone rang. It was tempting to ignore the call from her dad. She was pretty ticked off that he'd told Nat she could visit without running it by her first. Surely he knew Tara wouldn't be happy about it.

"Hi," she said when she answered.

"I don't suppose you've heard from Natalie recently?" he asked.

"I'm fine!" she said mockingly. "Thanks for asking. How are you?"

"Sorry. I'm worried about Nat …"

"Of course you are. The precious little princess is all alone on a train. You realise she's seventeen and not seven?"

"She's on a train? So she's on her way to you?" His tone was part surprise, part anger.

"She didn't tell you?"

"No! We told her she couldn't and she was in a bad mood about it all week. Today, she didn't come home from school as usual, so Gillian called around her friends and found out she didn't even go to school."

"Oh."

"Oh? You don't sound particularly concerned."

"She's not *my* kid. And she's barely even a kid anyway."

"Thanks a lot for the support," he said angrily. "Do you know which train she's on?"

Tara checked her watch. "The one that's arriving here in two minutes."

"Do me a favour and put her on the next train back here."

"No," Tara said with amusement.

"Can you please not make things more difficult?"

"This is not my problem. Or it shouldn't be. It's quite annoying for me that she turns up here after only giving me half an hour's warning. I had plans for the weekend." At least, if you counted lazing around with James, she had plans. Lots of them.

"Sorry," he said begrudgingly. "So she didn't cook this up with you?"

"Definitely not. I didn't know anything about it until today. But I refuse to stand on the train platform arguing with a stroppy teenager. If you want her to go straight back again, you need to be the one to talk her into that. Or come and pick her up."

"I can't leave work for a while." He sighed. "Do you mind if she stays with you tonight and I'll collect her in the morning?"

"Fine by me. The train's here now. I better go." She hung up and opened the car door to wave at Nat as she stepped off the train.

"It's so great to see you," Nat said as she enveloped Tara in a hug by the car. "The train was pretty fun too. It felt like an adventure being on my own."

"It might have been a good idea for you to tell your parents you were going on an adventure."

She looked suitably sheepish. "Did Dad call you?"

"Yeah." She got back in the car, and Nat moved around to the passenger side.

"How angry was he?" Nat asked, not seeming too bothered by the fact that she'd probably landed herself in a load of trouble.

"Pretty angry. But surely you knew they'd notice you were missing? What exactly was your plan?"

"I thought if I was here by the time they noticed I'd gone, it would be too late for them to stop me."

"That's a terrible plan," Tara said as she put the car in reverse. "If you want to disappear for a weekend, tell them you're staying at a friend's place or something. That way they won't look for you."

Nat clicked her seatbelt into place and looked at Tara with wide eyes. "Did you used to do that?"

"Erm …" Perhaps this wasn't the best advice to be giving. "No comment!"

"So what did Dad say?"

"That he'll pick you up tomorrow morning."

"He's so annoying. Can you talk to him again and tell him to pick me up on Sunday night? Or better still, tell him I'll get the train on Sunday night."

"I don't want to get involved." She rolled her eyes. "Any more than I already am. If you want to negotiate with him, you need to do it yourself."

"There's no way he'll listen to me. I'm probably grounded for the foreseeable future. Which will suit Dad perfectly. He prefers it when I have no social life."

"What do you usually do when you're not grounded?"

"Mostly hang out with Winnie. I told you about her. She's my best friend. Her mum and my mum are good friends. We hang out at each other's house, or sometimes we go shopping or to the cinema. Normal stuff."

"Do you go to the pub? Or parties?"

"We can't go to the pub because we're underage."

"That would never have stopped me at your age."

"Yeah. But you didn't have Dad breathing down your neck. He'd kill me if he found out I'd been drinking."

"I don't get it. That's normal teenage behaviour. Why's he so dramatic about it?"

"Because he's annoying. You're lucky. Your mum's so nice. I bet she was never strict like my parents."

Tara smiled sadly. Her mum definitely hadn't been strict. A lot of the time, Tara had the feeling that she didn't have the energy to enforce rules. Which probably worked out for the best. If she'd tried to dictate what Tara could or couldn't do, she might have been even more wild in her teenage years.

"They just care about you," Tara said. "They're strict because they want the best for you."

"As soon as I turn eighteen they won't have a say any more, so they'll have to get used to me doing what I want then."

Tara stifled a grin. "Unless you find yourself financially independent at eighteen I guess they're still going to have a lot of say."

She flopped her head to one side. "Can I just come and live with you?"

"No." Tara laughed. "I'm afraid not."

Nat went straight upstairs when they got home, and Tara hung around in the shop and explained the situation to James.

"That's not good," he said when Tara relayed how angry David was on the phone.

"No." Tara's lips twitched to a smile as she looped her arms around James's waist.

"This is the first time I've seen you look happy about having Nat here. What's going on?"

"It'll sound bad." Tara screwed her face up. "But I think I quite like rebel Nat! She's much more fun. I can relate to a rule-breaker."

"Have you led her astray?" James said. "I feel as though she was completely naive until she met you."

"Yes," Tara said with a shrug. "It's probably my fault. But I don't really care!"

"I can see that." He pulled her hips against his and gave a quick glance at the shop door before kissing her slowly.

"What happened to the rule about not being affectionate in the shop?" Tara asked.

"I think we scrapped that a long time ago."

"I'm glad. It was a stupid rule."

"You would say that. You're a rebel."

"True. I'm going upstairs. I need to think of more ways to

lead Nat astray this evening. Shall we take her to the pub? I could introduce her to my friend, Tequila."

"No." James chuckled. "Absolutely not."

"I was kidding," she said, blowing him a kiss as she left him alone in the shop.

CHAPTER 24

The evening with Nat was completely painless. After dinner, she got a message from her best friend, then disappeared to the spare room to have a video chat for an hour. Tara and James could hear her laughing away while they sat in front of the TV. When she finally joined them, she regaled them with the story of how her friend had got into trouble for knowing Nat's plans but not saying anything. Apparently Nat was quickly forgiven and had told her all about her little adventure of skipping school and getting the train to Newton Abbot.

Nat was in the shower the following morning when Tara went downstairs to do a few things in the shop before she opened up. She was surprised when her dad knocked on the door shortly before they were due to open. He must have set off early.

"Morning," Tara said, letting him in and locking the door behind him.

"Hi." Tension radiated from him as he followed Tara to the back of the shop. "Sorry your weekend was disrupted."

"It's fine. I hope Nat isn't in too much trouble."

"She skipped school and got on a train without telling us what she was doing. I'd say she's in a fair bit of trouble."

"No harm done, though," Tara said.

He gave a small shake of the head. "When you have kids of your own, you'll understand better."

Tara tensed at his condescending tone. She refrained from mentioning that she didn't ever intend to have kids.

"She's a teenager," she said, trying to stay calm. "And she seems like a good kid, so I think you're being too hard on her."

"She is a good kid." He ran a hand across his forehead. "It's only recently she's gone off the rails."

"I hope you're not going to blame me for being a bad influence," Tara said, trying to keep her tone light. "I definitely didn't encourage her to come and visit."

"Except you let her drink and take her to parties. There's no wonder she'd rather come here than go on holiday with her family."

Tara refrained from mentioning that she was her family too. "I don't let her drink," she said instead. "And I don't take her to parties."

"She told us you gave her alcohol."

"One glass!" Tara wanted to laugh. If she'd wanted to lead her sister astray, she'd have done a much better job than one glass of Prosecco at the world's tamest hen party.

"She wasn't like this before," David said, pacing beside the counter. "She would never have missed school or lied to us."

"Before what?" Tara asked, her stomach twisting uncomfortably.

He shook his head but refused to meet her gaze.

"Before I came on the scene?" she demanded.

"I didn't say that." He pushed his hands through his hair. "Gillian and I think it would be best if Nat didn't see you for a while. She should be focussing on her studies."

Tara glared at him as her heart rate sped up. "I agree. And for the record, I never intended to mess up your perfect little family."

"You didn't mess anything up," David said on a sigh. "I didn't mean that."

"Don't worry about it," Tara said. "I get it. My life was much easier before I got in touch with you again too."

"Don't be like that. Please."

"But it's true. This doesn't work. I don't want Nat in my life. Or you."

"Tara, I want you in my life."

"But you don't want me being a bad influence on your favourite daughter?" She could hear how bitter she sounded, but she couldn't help it. She *was* bitter.

"I didn't say you were a bad influence, just that Nat has other things to focus on at the moment."

"You don't need to justify it to me. I'm sure you know what's best for her."

"I didn't mean to upset you."

"You haven't." Swallowing her emotions, she forced herself to smile. "I already wanted to go back to how things were before. I hate Nat messing up my weekends, so you telling her she can't see me any more is doing me a favour." She turned to walk away. "You can wait in the car, I'll send her out to you."

"Can you stop and talk to me properly? We need to figure out where we go from here."

"I'd say you should go home, back to your family. And you should stay away from me. I don't want to see you again. I don't want you here ever again."

He called after her, but she didn't stop. She just wanted him to leave and not come back. Upstairs, she found Nat in the kitchen chatting away to James.

"Your dad's downstairs," Tara said. "Grab your things and go down."

"Why didn't he come up?"

"He's waiting in the car. Go and get your things."

While Nat disappeared to the spare room, Tara tried hard to keep her composure and ignore the questioning look James was giving her.

"Are you okay?" he asked.

"Fine," she replied with false cheer.

"I take it Dad's really angry?" Nat asked when she reappeared with her backpack on her shoulder.

"He'll calm down. Don't worry about it."

"Did I get you into trouble?"

"No. Come here." Tara took a couple of steps and wrapped Nat in a tight embrace. "I might not see you for a while."

"Why not?" Nat asked.

"It's just probably not a good idea at the moment."

"If they say I can't visit again, I'll come anyway."

"Don't," Tara said as she released her. "It'll only make things worse. You can always message me, though. Even if they tell you not to. Message me anyway, okay?"

"Of course. But I'll see you soon."

Tara smiled tightly. Considering she was now getting exactly what she'd wanted, it didn't feel very good. "Bye," she whispered.

Nat turned in the doorway. "Bye."

Silence fell for a moment before James spoke.

"What happened?"

"David doesn't think it's a good idea for Nat to spend

time here." She forced a smile. "So that's solved that problem."

"What did he say?"

"That she has other things to concentrate on at the moment and they don't want her to be distracted."

"And you're okay with that?"

"I'm very happy about it," she replied, ignoring the tightness in her chest. "I only ever wanted to patch things up with Dad. I didn't really want him to suddenly be a big part of my life. And I definitely didn't want his family hanging around."

"They're your family too."

"Yeah, but distant, extended family. The kind you see on special occasions, not the kind that you visit for no reason."

"Did you tell David you'd like to meet up with him without Nat around?"

"Not exactly, no." She managed to keep smiling as she walked to the door. "I better go and open the shop."

"How did you leave things with him?"

She shook her head, wanting to drop the subject. "We're going to take a step back and see how things go."

"That doesn't sound good."

"I think it's for the best. It was all getting a bit stressful." She continued to walk away, even as James followed her.

"You don't want to talk about it?" he asked.

She bit her bottom lip as she descended the stairs without looking back at him. If she talked about it, she'd fall apart. "There's not much to say. I'll see you later."

The next few days went in a similar way. Tara insisted she was quite happy with the way she'd left things with her dad. She told herself that as well as James. By the middle of the week, she almost had herself convinced. Except she'd turned into one of those people who checked their phone obsessively. She'd had two calls from her dad, which she ignored, and an email from him that she'd moved to the 'Dad' folder without even opening. There'd been no contact from Nat.

On Thursday morning, she and James always opened the shop together. Story time always made it a busy morning and they really needed to both be there. Tara was picking out stories to read when she was distracted by someone knocking on the glass of the front door.

"It's Josie," James said, walking out from behind the counter.

"What are you doing here?" Tara asked, when Josie walked in with Annie in her car seat.

"I've missed coming for coffee. When I was pregnant I didn't feel like doing anything. Now I feel human again, so I'm desperate to get out and about."

Tara peered at the sleeping baby. "She might be a bit little for story time."

"I know. We're not staying for long. It'll be a big germ fest with all those snotty toddlers so we'll disappear before they arrive, but I had this great idea …"

"What?" Tara asked, amused by Josie's energy. She'd thought new mothers were supposed to look constantly frazzled, but Josie looked better than she'd seen her in a long time.

"I thought Annie could be your youngest customer! You can get a photo with her and put it up on the wall with all the other pictures. You can post about it on social media too."

Tara looked to the wall that was adorned with framed photos of her and James with the authors who'd been to visit the shop. "It's just authors on the wall," Tara mused.

"I realise that," Josie said, sounding slightly irritated. "There's a photo of you with Emily. But considering I'm never going to write a novel, I'll never make it onto the wall. I thought this might get me up there!"

"You really want to get your picture on the wall that badly?" James asked.

"Yes! It's like a dream of mine."

Tara raised her eyebrows. "Really?"

"Not really, no. But I feel left out. Emily's up there, and all these authors. I used to be an actress, you know. I'm practically famous. I should definitely be on the wall."

James crouched beside the car seat. "Annie can definitely have her photo on the wall for being our youngest customer."

"Great." Josie unclipped the straps of the car seat and lifted Annie out.

"I can hold her for the photo," James said, his hands outstretched. Cradling Annie in the crook of his arm, he walked to the children's corner, flashing Tara a mischievous smile as he went. "We could stand here with the kids' books in the background. That should be a good one." He beckoned to Tara with a flick of his chin, then looked back at Josie. "Try to get it quite close up, but make sure you can see Annie." He tilted her slightly.

"I need to be in it!" Josie said.

Tara pointed at the other photos on the wall. "I think you'll notice none of our other celebrities had their assistants in the photo."

"I'm not her assistant, I'm her mother!"

"None of them have their mothers in the photo either," James said, grinning.

"Oh, you're a pair of jokers today!" Josie stood beside James to get a picture of the four of them.

"We'll cut Josie out," James mock-whispered in Tara's ear.

"You will not cut me out." Josie took another couple of photos as they all laughed. "I'm going to print it out and frame it myself so you don't mess with it. I'll post it to my social media accounts and tag you. It's so nice to have something to post about again."

"You've had plenty to post about for the last nine months," Tara said.

"About how fat I was and how terrible I felt? No one wants to hear that."

Tara looked at James, who was beaming down at Annie.

"She's got her eyes open," he said.

Tara moved to look. "I think she looks like Sam."

"Me too," Josie agreed. "Speaking of which, we better get going. See if we can get home before Sam gets back from shopping and realises we've done a runner."

"Are you supposed to be housebound?" Tara asked, amused.

"He's a bit overprotective. Thinks I should be taking it easy and we should just be relaxing at home. But that's all I've done for nine months. I want to get back out and do things."

"It was nice to see you," James said as he passed Annie back.

"Oh, I meant to ask how it went with your dad when he picked Nat up?" Josie bent to secure Annie back into her seat. "It cracked me up when you said she'd just turned up. She didn't seem the rebellious type."

Tara had sent a message to the group chat with Josie and Amber on Friday evening, telling them about Nat's unexpected visit. She felt a pang of regret and sadness as she was reminded of the heated conversation with David. "I don't think she'll be allowed to visit again for a while," Tara said lightly.

"Really?" Josie straightened up. "That's a shame."

"Not really. She was driving me crazy."

"That's little sisters for you," Josie said. "Just ask Lizzie!"

"You two get on really well," Tara pointed out.

"Yeah. But if you asked her to describe me, I'm fairly sure *annoying* and *irritating* would be the first words you'd get."

"Maybe, but she'd say it in an affectionate way."

"Now she would. Five years ago would have been a different story. She couldn't stand me. We came very close to disowning each other."

"Are you serious?" James asked.

"Yes. We could barely be in a room together without snapping at each other. And the only time we saw each other was when Mum insisted on it."

"I never knew that," Tara said. "You always seemed close."

"I think it was the age difference for a while. It makes it harder. Nat seemed sweet, though."

"She's okay, I guess," Tara agreed reluctantly.

Josie walked towards the door. "I'll come back soon with the photo for the wall."

They called goodbye and James turned the sign on the door to *open* when she left. Tara got back to preparing for the story time.

The hectic morning went quickly as always. In the afternoon, James went upstairs to get on with some work, leaving Tara alone in the shop. The conversation with Josie played on her mind, and in a quiet moment she typed out a quick message to Nat, asking how she was. No reply came, and when she realised the message hadn't even gone through, she felt a flutter of nerves deep in her stomach. Maybe David and Gillian had blocked Tara's number from her phone. Or made her change her number.

A customer came in, and she forced the thoughts aside to make small talk before leaving the middle-aged woman to browse. When she finally closed the shop at the end of the day, she checked her phone again, but the message still hadn't gone through.

Trudging upstairs, she found James working on his laptop at the kitchen table. She said hello but couldn't bring herself to return his smile.

"What's wrong?" he asked.

"Nothing." She took her own laptop and opened it on the kitchen counter. There was a new email from her dad. The subject line read 'Sorry'. She was startled when James's hands landed at her hips, then slipped around her waist.

"Tell me what's going on." He dropped his chin to her shoulder as she clicked the mouse to move the email to the folder with the rest of them. "Did you even read that?"

"No. I don't want to read his emails."

"Why not?"

Her features crumpled as she turned in his arms. Tears filled her eyes and she sobbed as she buried her face in James's neck. He kissed the side of her head and held her while she cried, then quietly wiped his thumbs over her cheeks when she finally pulled away.

"He said everything was better before I came along and messed up their perfect lives." She sniffed and ran her fingers under her eyes.

"He really said that?"

She shrugged. "I'm not sure if he said it or stopped himself from saying it or just implied it, but it was quite clear. He said Nat never got into any trouble before I showed up in her life and that I've been corrupting her. Which is also what you said."

"I was joking when I said it."

"Dad wasn't."

"What did you say to him?"

"That I don't want Nat in my life anyway, so he's doing

me a favour. And I said I don't want to see him any more either."

"Did you mean it?"

"Yes." She took a deep breath. "Life was much easier when he wasn't a part of it."

"Why are you so upset then?"

"I don't know. But I haven't heard from Nat since she left, and she didn't reply when I messaged her earlier. I don't think she even got the message, so I guess she's not allowed to be in contact with me."

"That seems extreme. Maybe David explained in his email."

With a sigh, Tara turned back to the laptop and opened up the folder.

"Are they all from David?" James asked.

"Yes."

"There are loads of them. And a lot of them are marked as unread."

"It's about fifteen years' worth of emails. And they're marked as unread because I don't always feel like reading them."

"But you keep them?"

"Yes." She opened the latest email. "He doesn't say anything about Nat, just that he's sorry that I was upset on Saturday and would like to talk."

"Has he called you?"

"Twice. I didn't answer."

"Maybe you should call him."

"I don't think I can face it. I'm not that keen on listening to him explain why I'm like poison to his precious little family."

"I think you might be being unfair."

"Maybe. But he'll always put them first. I'll always be the one on the side-lines." She rested her forehead against

James's. "I'm a grown woman with a husband and a business and a really great life. I don't need him making me feel like crap."

"Okay." He pushed her hair behind her shoulders and kissed her nose. "Whatever you want."

She smiled sadly. "When it comes to my dad, it's never been about what I want."

CHAPTER 25

Saturday afternoon was unusually quiet in the bookshop. Tara told James she was going upstairs and he should give her a shout if he needed her.

"Why don't you call David?" James said as she was leaving.

"Because I don't want to speak to him."

"At least find out what the situation is with Nat. It's going to eat away at you otherwise."

Tara flashed him a smile and left him alone. He had a point; she wasn't going to stop thinking about Nat until she found out what was going on. And the only way to do that was to speak to David.

As soon as she walked into the flat, she took her phone out, knowing that if she hesitated she'd think of reasons not to call him.

There was a note of relief in his voice when he answered the phone and told her he was happy to hear from her.

"I messaged Nat," she said frostily. "But she didn't reply. Isn't she allowed to speak to me?"

"Of course she's allowed to speak to you. Didn't you get my emails?"

"I got them," Tara said. "I just haven't had a chance to read all of them"

"Right," he said on a sigh. "Well, if you'd have read them, you'd know that Nat had her phone confiscated for a week."

Tara opened her mouth to tell him what she thought of that, then decided it was best not to comment. If they wanted to be controlling and over-bearing it was nothing to do with her.

"I told you in the email that she'll be in touch when she gets it back. We'd never tell her she can't have any contact with you. I think it's a good thing if you two have a relationship."

"You didn't sound so keen the last time we spoke."

"Because I was tired and stressed and I'd had a huge argument with Gillian. I wasn't thinking straight and I'm sorry I upset you. That was never my intention."

"Okay. Good. That's all then. I just wanted to know what was going on with Nat."

"Did you mean what you said to me?" he asked. "About not wanting to see me?"

She pulled out a chair at the kitchen table and took a seat, trying to figure out how to answer him. "I don't really know what I want. But I feel as though I'll always end up getting hurt. The more I see you, the clearer it is that even though I'm your first child, I'll always come last."

"That's not true," he whispered.

"It's how it feels. But it also doesn't really matter. I'm all grown up and I don't need you in my life. I thought it might be nice for us to have some sort of relationship, but maybe we both need to accept that it's not going to happen."

"I want you to be a part of my life," he said firmly.

Tara took a deep breath. "I appreciate the sentiment, but in reality you don't have space for me in your life."

"Don't cut me out again, please. It will take time to figure things out but we'll get there."

Staring at the grooves in the wooden table, Tara couldn't think of anything to say. Now that he was back in her life, even in a small way, it would be hard to cut him out again completely. Especially if she wanted to have a relationship with Nat.

"I have to go and help James with the shop," she finally said, needing to get off the phone and get her thoughts in order.

"Tara?" he said as she was about to hang up. "Do you ever read my emails?"

She squeezed her eyes tight shut, but couldn't bring herself to reply.

"Do you want me to stop sending them?" he asked.

She inhaled deeply. "I honestly don't care."

After ending the call, she sat staring at the phone for a long time. It had been a stupid thing to say. Sometimes, she just wanted to hurt him, as though that would lessen her pain. How on earth could she ever have a relationship with him when she couldn't get past her anger at him? When their family had fallen apart, he'd left to get himself a new family, and she wasn't sure she could ever forgive him for that. Getting back in touch with him only meant that she was regularly reminded of how much he'd hurt her when he'd abandoned her.

Eventually, she moved to the comfort of her bed, lying in silence until darkness fell around her. She felt utterly pathetic when James switched on the light in the hallway and peered into the bedroom at her.

She reached to turn the lamp on and squinted in the

sudden brightness. "Winter's depressing. I hate that it's dark already."

"Are you okay?" he asked, concern causing the skin around his eyes to crinkle.

"Just feeling sorry for myself," she said with a small smile. "Sorry I left you alone all afternoon."

"It wasn't busy." He sat on the edge of the bed. "I take it you spoke to your dad?"

"Yeah."

"And?"

"They confiscated Nat's phone. She's allowed to message me as soon as she gets it back."

"That's good."

"I have mixed feelings. I only wanted to be in touch with her when I thought the option had been taken away. Now, I keep thinking how annoying it was to have her interfering in my life."

James smiled lightly. "She's your sister. You're allowed to find her irritating and still care about her."

"It feels strange."

"You'll get used to it."

"I'm not sure what to do about Dad. I honestly don't know how to have a relationship with him. Is it normal to hate someone and still care about them?"

James shook his head. "You don't hate him. You're just angry with him."

"But what happens if I can't figure out a way not to be angry at him?"

He patted her thigh. "I've no idea."

"You're supposed to have all the answers," she said, rolling her head to the side.

"You could try asking me something easier."

She gave a knowing smile. "Are you hungry?"

"Yes!"

"What do you want to eat?"

"I thought we could go to the Rose and Crown for dinner and drinks."

"The food's not great there," she pointed out.

"I know. I just like it because it reminds me of the night we met."

"That was a surprisingly good night." She hadn't expected anything good to happen that day – it had been the funeral of Annette's partner, Wendy. Tara had ended up drinking alone in the Rose and Crown at the end of the day. Until James had walked in and struck up a conversation.

"Let's go then," James said, taking her hand to pull her up.

"How about we eat at the Jolly Farmer, then go for a drink in the Rose and Crown?"

"A pub crawl?" He nodded approvingly. "I like your thinking!"

Tara had just stood up when her phone lit up on the bedside table.

"Looks like your annoying little sister got her phone back," James said, glancing at the screen.

Tara scrolled over the long rambling message and smiled when she reached the row of smiley faces and hearts at the end of it.

CHAPTER 26

Emily seemed to be spending most of her time with Lizzie. In the few weeks since they'd decided to go ahead with the publishing company, they'd drawn up a more professional-looking business plan and had been approved for a small business loan from the bank.

They'd signed a contract with Verity for renting out the flat that morning and were excited about kitting it out with furniture and having their very own workspace. As much as Emily enjoyed working from home, she loved the idea of having an office.

The only trouble was, her mind seemed to be constantly on the publishing company so she wasn't getting much writing done. She assumed that would change when the novelty wore off so, she was trying to enjoy the journey rather than panic about her productivity.

After the quick meeting at the cafe to sign the contract, she walked with Lizzie as far as her place, then continued on alone. She let out a sigh of frustration when she saw Josie's car outside the house. It had only been the previous evening that Josie had messaged, but it had completely slipped her mind that she was coming over.

When there was no sign of her in the car or on the doorstep, Emily unlocked the front door, then called out to Josie as she stepped inside.

"We're in the kitchen," she called in reply.

Emily hurried through. "I'm sorry. Lizzie called me this morning and asked if I could meet her to sign a contract with Verity. I completely forgot you were coming over." She patted her pockets. "My phone's probably on silent too. Is Jack here? How did you get in?"

Josie finished filling the kettle and switched it on. "When you didn't answer, I called Jack. He told me to try the back door. He said you usually forget to lock it."

"He's always going on at me about that. It feels very safe living in a village." She peered at Annie, who was asleep in her car seat on the kitchen table. "I'm sorry I forgot. My head is all over the place at the moment."

"That's okay. It seems as though there's a lot to do when you're setting up a publishing company. It's all Lizzie can talk about too."

Emily wasn't sure if that was meant as a dig at the fact that Emily had talked constantly about the new business venture when she'd met up with Josie the previous week.

"We've been pretty busy," Emily said. "It's amazing how quickly it's all coming together. I posted in a couple of my online writing groups to gauge if there'd be much interest, and now my inbox is full of writers wanting to send their manuscripts for consideration.

"I thought self-publishing was the way to go these days," Josie said, dropping tea bags into two mugs.

"It's not for everyone." Emily moved to get the milk out of the fridge. "A lot of writers just want to write and aren't interested in the publishing side. Marketing and advertising can be daunting too. I knew we'd get a lot of interest, but I was slightly overwhelmed by the response. And that's without having a website or anything set up. Once we have more of an online presence and a professional website we'll no doubt be inundated with submissions."

"It's exciting." Josie stirred the tea and handed Emily a mug. "No wonder you forgot about me."

Even though Josie's tone was light, she was clearly annoyed. "I'm sorry," Emily said, feeling a little irritated by the guilt trip. "I'm here now."

Josie leaned against the sideboard, cradling her steaming mug. "It just feels as though you don't have a lot of time for me these days."

Emily spluttered a humourless laugh. "Well now you know how I feel most of the time with you."

For a moment, they stared at each other in a deadlock.

"Sorry," Emily said. "That was uncalled for."

Josie shook her head and moved to sit at the table. "You don't need to apologise. You're right. I haven't had time for you, and now I'm jealous that you and Lizzie hang out all the time. I'm also very jealous that you're going into business together. It must be so exciting."

"It is." Emily sank into the chair opposite her. "But things are pretty exciting for you at the moment too." She tipped her head towards Annie.

"Yeah." Josie smiled at her daughter. "I'm very lucky. She's perfect and obviously I adore her but …" She looked slightly sheepish. "She doesn't *do* a lot."

Emily chuckled. "She's a tiny baby!"

"I know, but people make out that kids are a lot of work and you never have time for anything else, but she's actually really easy. We feed her now and again, change her nappy, smile at her, cuddle her. With Sam and I both at home, we seem to spend most of our time twiddling our thumbs."

"I thought you were supposed to be exhausted from night feeds and drowning in washing."

"She only wakes a couple of times a night for a quick feed. It's really not so bad. And it's not as though she's crawling around in mud … she doesn't really get her clothes dirty. Besides, her clothes are so tiny that you could get her entire wardrobe in one wash."

There was a knock at the front door, and Emily had just stood up when Lizzie's voice drifted in.

"I didn't know you were coming over today," she said to Josie as she wandered through to the kitchen.

"It was a surprise," Josie said, shooting Emily a playful look.

"Sorry to barge in." Lizzie switched her attention to Emily. "I know I just left you and you wanted to get on with writing, but I was looking over the website again, trying to figure out what we should do about it. I'd like to finalise it as soon as possible. Maybe we could get together this evening or tomorrow morning and try and hammer it out."

"What's the problem with the website?" Josie asked.

"I've designed it," Emily said. "But it's not the right vibe somehow."

"Get your laptop and show me," Josie said.

Emily moved to do as she was told. When she came back, Lizzie had lifted Annie out of her seat for a cuddle.

"Look," Emily said, opening up her laptop and showing Josie what she'd got so far.

Josie screwed her nose up as she browsed through the website. "Yeah, it's not great," she mumbled.

"Thanks!"

"Sorry. It's not bad. It's too clinical, though. If you're calling the business Hope Cove Press, you should incorporate the setting into the website. Add some photos of the area. If I understand your vision correctly, you want to appear professional, but also friendly and approachable. Authors should feel connected to you and feel as though they're part of a team. The website should reflect that."

"Photos of the area might be a good idea," Lizzie said. "Maybe as a banner across the top of the page. I like that."

"I've got some great sunset photos from the summer," Josie said. "Make me an admin of the site and I'll play around with it for you."

"You'll set up the website?" Emily asked.

"Yes. You know I'm good at this sort of thing. Why didn't you ask me earlier?"

"Sort of thought you had enough on your plate at the moment," Lizzie said, looking pointedly at the baby in her arms.

Josie waved a hand in front of her face. "She's a piece of cake. Setting up the website will be great. It gives me something to do."

"We really couldn't be more different, could we?" Lizzie said. "You hated every moment of being pregnant, while I breezed through it. Then you think having a newborn is a doddle whereas I spent most of my time wondering how Max would cope if I packed my bags and left."

"To be fair, you had two," Josie said.

"I think I'd have still been tearing my hair out with one of them." Lizzie gently rocked Annie. "Although I've yet to hear this child cry. I think you just got an easy baby."

"She can definitely cry," Josie said. "Stops pretty quick when she gets fed though."

"It would actually be great if you could have a play around with the website," Emily said. It had been annoying not being able to get it right, and she suspected it was partly because she was too close to the project.

"I'll do it this evening," Josie said. "But that means you have to involve me in things more."

"Like what?" Lizzie asked.

"Like when you decided to start your own publishing company and spent an evening drinking champagne to celebrate but forgot to invite me!"

Emily grimaced as she looked at Lizzie. "It was an impromptu thing. And I suppose we thought that you wouldn't be able to …"

"Why? Because I've got a baby? Am I supposed to sit at home all the time now?"

"Most people keep a fairly low profile in the first weeks after they've had a baby," Lizzie said.

"I've kept a low profile for the past nine months. I'm ready to get back out into the world. In fact, I might open the kennels again."

Lizzie shook her head. "I thought you were taking six months off."

"That was the plan, but it seems a bit daft now. If you two can set up your own publishing company, I can walk a few dogs while looking after a baby. I can take Annie in the sling."

Emily exchanged an amused look with Lizzie. "You don't just walk dogs, you run a business."

"Yes, but I can still do it and look after Annie. Or I could leave her with Annette sometimes. Annette would love that."

"She's only a few weeks old," Lizzie said. "Relax and enjoy the time."

"I wouldn't start up again immediately," Josie said. "It would take a while to get the word out that we were open and get bookings. I'm going to talk to Sam about it."

"I'd like to be a fly on the wall for that conversation," Lizzie said.

Josie laughed. “He’s not going to be happy, is he? He’s such a worrier.”

“You can usually get him to come around to your way of thinking,” Emily said. “And if you want to open the kennels again, I say go for it.”

“I think I will,” Josie said firmly.

CHAPTER 27

Tara had taken to checking her emails as soon as she woke up in the morning, but there was never anything from her dad. He hadn't called her either. She'd received one text message from him asking how she was, which had felt overly polite and formal. Tara answered it in much the same tone.

Oddly, she now enjoyed her messages and calls with Nat. Her enthusiastic nature felt much more of a positive trait as Tara got used to her. Nat was getting excited about Christmas in a fairly childish way considering she was seventeen, but Tara could relate to that. She enjoyed the festive season too.

It was the run-up to Christmas she enjoyed rather than the day itself. December was her favourite month. Everyone was cheerful and there was a buzz in the air.

As usual, she started to feel twitchy as November dragged on. It was the same every year while she impatiently waited to decorate the shop for Christmas. She had a rule that the decorations went up on the first of December at the earliest. Some of the shops started putting up Christmas displays straight after Halloween and it drove Tara crazy.

"Maybe I'll break my rule this year," she said to James when he came down to the shop that Friday morning to see how she was getting on. "I don't think I can wait any longer."

"What are you talking about?"

"The Christmas decorations. I think I'll put them up already."

He leaned against the counter. "You say this every year and then you force yourself to wait. There's only another week until December anyway."

"Yes. I probably should wait. It's just annoying. I've got no patience."

"You might want to disappear for a while then," James said, as the door opened, bringing a blast of cold air through the shop.

Tara groaned at the sight of Belinda, who was rubbing her gloved hands together.

"It's lovely and toasty in here," she said. "And it's good to see you both. It feels like it's been ages since I've seen you. The last couple of weeks have been busy, as I'm sure you can imagine. I never knew organising a little Christmas raffle would be such hard work." She beamed at Tara. "I'm sure you've been busy too."

Tara glanced around the shop. "Not particularly."

"Oh, you're going to be coy with me, aren't you?" She tilted her head. "I'm expecting something spectacular from your window display this year. I always love the Polar Express theme, but I'm sure it will be even bigger and better this year."

"I'm doing the Polar Express again," Tara said. The window display with the train track was a source of pride year-round, but the way she transformed it into a winter scene with a Santa figure, reindeer and fake snow was even more special.

"Really?" Belinda looked puzzled. "I assumed you were

working on something different for this year. You don't have to, of course. Anyway, I've come for your raffle prize."

"What prize?"

"The Christmas prize," she said, in a tone of voice that made Tara feel like a child.

"I have no idea what you're talking about."

Belinda stared at Tara for a moment, then switched her gaze to James, who shrugged.

"You must have got my emails?" she said, looking slightly horrified.

"No," Tara said.

"Oh my goodness. This is a disaster."

"What was in the emails?" James asked.

"All the information about the Newton Abbot Christmas shopfront competition."

"That's a bit of a mouthful," Tara said. "And I still don't know what you're talking about."

Belinda pulled her woolly hat off and put a hand across her forehead. "We're having a competition. All the local shopkeepers have agreed to it. We're dressing up our windows for the festive season. I can't believe you haven't heard about it from anyone else. We haven't done the official social media posts yet, but a lot of the shopkeepers have been talking about it."

"Edith from the flower shop was saying something to me about the window," Tara said thoughtfully. "But everyone decorates every year. What's so different about that?"

"Most of them just put up a bit of tinsel. This year it's a competition. Shoppers will vote for the shop with the best decorations. When they vote, they'll be entered into a prize draw. Every shop is donating a prize. I can't believe you didn't receive my emails. Maybe they got lost in cyberspace."

Tara felt herself getting increasingly annoyed. "Which email did you send it to, the bookshop or my private one?"

"The bookshop, I think." She looked thoughtful.

"Didn't it occur to you to wonder why we hadn't replied?"

Belinda shifted her weight. "It's not entirely unusual for you not to reply to my emails. And I know you can get a bit competitive, so I sort of assumed you'd got straight to work planning your display and putting a prize together."

"How long have you been planning this for?"

"A couple of weeks. I feel terrible now. I should have come and spoken to you when you didn't reply."

"It is slightly suspicious considering you're usually in here every few days. And that suddenly stopped."

"What do you mean suspicious?"

"Oh, come on. Everyone knows I'm the queen of the window display. I think you've purposely not let me in on it until the last minute so I don't have as much time to prepare. You're trying to cut down the competition."

Belinda stared at her in shock. "I would never do that."

"Yeah, right. When do we unveil the window displays?"

"They should be ready a week on Monday," Belinda said.

"Good. No problem. I'll still win."

"I hope you don't really think I'd try and sabotage you like that." Belinda's cheeks were flushed as she looked at Tara. "We're friends. I wouldn't even do something like that to an enemy. And it was you who inspired the event. I wanted to involve you as much as possible."

"That might be more believable if you'd actually sent me the email or come to speak to me," Tara snapped.

Belinda looked to James. She was quite an actress and had the distressed routine perfected.

"Don't look at him like that," Tara said wearily.

"Like what?" she asked, her voice high-pitched.

"As though you're expecting him to back you up. Here's a bit of news for you – he's *my* husband, so he's not going to take your side." She stood up straighter as her anger intensified. "And since we're on the subject, I've never liked the way you look at James. The flirting has never been subtle. He's married now, so I think it's time it stopped."

Belinda's jaw hung open for a moment, then her gaze shot to James.

"Are you deaf?" Tara snapped. "Get your roaming eyes away from my husband." She sounded a bit dramatic, but the issue had been building for years.

James dropped his chin to his chest, then covered his face with his hands. "How about I bring the prize over to you later?" he said from behind his hands.

"I'd appreciate that," Belinda said. "Thank you."

The bell tinkled as she left.

"Can you believe her?" Tara fumed.

James peeked between his fingers, before removing his hands from his face.

"Can I believe *her*?"

"Yes! Claiming the emails got lost in cyberspace. Does she really think I'm that gullible?"

James puffed his cheeks out, a small smile playing at his lips.

"What are you looking at me like that for?"

"Did you really just tell her to *get her roaming eyes off your husband*?"

Tara stifled a laugh. "Yes! But she's had that coming for a long time."

"You made me feel like a piece of meat!"

"Sorry."

"And I don't think she does flirt with me, but let's ignore that issue for now. I'm sure she didn't maliciously leave you out of the planning for her little Christmas event. She can be a bit much to take sometimes, but I think she genuinely considers you a friend."

"So you *are* taking her side?"

"Yes!" He laughed. "I love you, but I can't believe you freaked out like that."

"She's trying to make me look bad. You know how I love my window display."

"Yes." He wrapped his arms around her when she walked over to him. "But you understand it's just a window, not life or death stuff. You should be flattered that your creativity inspired the event."

"Inspired her to try and out-do me, more like. Well, she's going to be disappointed. I may not have as long to prepare, but I'm still going to win. She's going to find out she's messed with the wrong shop owner."

"I'm fairly sure she's already figured that out," he said with a raised eyebrow. "*If* she was trying to mess with you."

"Don't be so naive. It's absolutely the sort of thing Belinda would do." She put her hands on her hips. "I need to decide what to do with the windows."

"I can watch the shop if you want to go and start planning."

"Great. Can you organise the prize? Grab a few books, I suppose."

He nodded and she hurried away. The lack of planning time didn't worry her. She still had more than a week to come up with something brilliant. And she had every intention of winning and putting Belinda firmly in her place.

By the time James came up after he'd closed the shop, Tara had a load of notes and sketches, but still hadn't made any final decisions.

"I took a selection of books to Belinda for the prize," he said, hovering beside the coffee table in the living room. "She arranged them neatly and tied them with ribbon. She's taking photographs of all the prizes so she can start posting about it on social media. We're supposed to post about it on our page too."

"Right," Tara said, tapping her pen on her notepad. "I need you to help me choose a design." He stayed where he was until she finally looked up at him.

"I need to tell you something," he said, rubbing at his temples. "But you're not going to like it, so you need to remember it's all your fault. Don't take it out on the messenger. Okay?"

"What's all my fault?"

"Remember a while back when Belinda sent one of her group emails about wanting the local shop workers to get together for a monthly social event?"

"How could I forget? The worst idea ever. I got really annoyed at our email filters—" She stopped abruptly and slapped a hand over her mouth. "Oh no," she mumbled. "No, no, no! I complained that the email filter wasn't intelligent enough to realise her emails should go straight to the junk folder …"

James nodded. "And then you changed the settings …"

"You've got to be kidding me? Please, don't tell me she really did email me?"

"I'll keep quiet then."

A feeling of dread swept through her as she lifted the computer onto her lap and opened the email account for the bookshop. She saw the emails as soon as she went to the junk folder. With a hand over her mouth, she stared at the screen, unable to bring herself to read the messages.

"There are a couple of group emails that went out to all the shop owners," James said in a gentle tone. "And a private one to you about how much she loves your energy around the Christmas season and how great it is that you always get into the spirit of things."

Tara flopped back onto the couch. “I’m a horrible person,” she said sadly.

“The current evidence might suggest so,” James said.

“Stop it. I can’t joke about it. I am a horrible person. What is wrong with me? I had such a go at her, and she hadn’t even done anything wrong.”

“She’ll get over it.”

“I need to apologise.”

“You might need to grovel and offer to be her best friend or something.”

“I can’t believe I had such a go at her.” She covered her face with her hands as she remembered everything she’d said. “And why did I snap at her for looking at you? I swear I’ve lost my mind.”

“Just call her and tell her you’re sorry. It’ll be fine.”

“I should’ve realised as soon as she mentioned the emails that they’d be in the junk folder.” Her eyes widened as a thought occurred to her. “What if his emails went to my junk mail too?” she said in a panic. “Maybe the settings just got messed up …”

“What are you talking about?” James asked as Tara clicked away on her laptop.

“He stopped emailing me. Or I thought he had but perhaps …” She opened up her personal email account and went into the junk folder. After scrolling for a moment, she closed the laptop and set it aside. “Never mind.”

James looked at her questioningly. “Who stopped emailing you?”

“Dad,” she said, sinking back into the couch. “He always used to email me once a week or so. But he’s stopped.”

“That’s strange. When did you last hear from him?”

She swallowed hard. “He messaged me once, but apart from that I haven’t heard from him since the day I called him to find out why Nat had stopped messaging me. And I sort of told him that I didn't read his emails a lot of the time, and that I didn't care whether he sent them or not."

"That's clearly not true," James said, taking her hand.

Forcing a smile, she stood up. "Do you want a drink? I think I'm going to have a glass of wine."

He declined but followed her to the kitchen where she pulled an open bottle of white from the fridge.

James watched her intently as she filled her glass. "Do you think maybe you should start seeing the therapist again?"

Tears pricked her eyes. "Great! Now you think I'm a head-case."

"I don't think that. But I think you're dealing with a lot at the moment and it's causing you a lot of stress. I know Belinda has a tendency to wind you up, but you wouldn't normally snap at her like that. Maybe it's all this stuff with your dad and Nat getting to you."

Tara took a swig of her wine, then shook her head. "You don't need to make excuses for me. I was completely out of line."

"I'm not making excuses. But I think that bottling up how you're feeling about your dad isn't good for you."

"I'll be fine," she said, taking her wine to their bedroom.

"What are you doing?" James asked.

"Calling Belinda. I'd rather do it in private. I'm mortified enough without you listening to me grovel." She closed the bedroom door and took a deep breath as she scrolled to Belinda's number.

"How did it go?" James asked, muting the TV when she joined him ten minutes later.

"She was really lovely." Tara sat beside James and snuggled up to him.

"That's good."

"I still feel terrible. In fact, I think I feel worse. When everyone around me is so nice it makes me feel even more of a horrible person."

"Don't be daft." He hugged her tightly. "You're not a horrible person. You're just stressed."

"Getting in touch with Dad was supposed to help me sort out my issues, but my life feels more of a mess now than it did when I was ignoring him. It's worse – he's ignoring me now."

"I'm sure he's not. What's he supposed to do if you tell him you don't read his emails?"

"I seem to have a habit of snapping at people and saying things I don't mean." Shuffling along the couch, she lay down and rested her head in James's lap.

"Well, you sorted things out with Belinda." James ran his fingers through her hair. "I'm sure you can sort things out with your dad too."

"I just feel like giving up on him."

He looked at her kindly and shook his head.

"Thanks for marrying me," she said.

"That's a strange thing to say."

"Sometimes I think you must be a bit crazy to marry me. But I'm glad you did. You are the best thing in my life."

He interlocked his fingers with hers. "And you're the best thing in mine."

CHAPTER 28

After the incident with Belinda, Tara lost some of her enthusiasm for the Christmas decorations. Now, the window display would be a reminder of her outburst. Belinda really had been very understanding on the phone. When Tara told her that she was stressed and dealing with some stuff, she'd forgiven her immediately. She'd also offered a sympathetic ear if Tara ever needed someone to talk to. At one time, Tara would have sworn she just wanted to get some juicy gossip, but she'd sounded genuine.

On Sunday, she spent most of the day wallowing in self-pity until she was forced to admit that James was right about the tension with her dad getting to her. His lack of emails bothered her a lot more than she'd care to admit. Even when she was angry with him, the emails had been her connection to him, and now it felt as though that had been cut. Except it hadn't, really. All she had to do was get in touch and apologise. That had been difficult enough with Belinda, but with her dad it felt monumental.

"I should probably arrange to see Dad and Nat over Christmas sometime," she said to James over dinner.

"Before or after Christmas?"

"I'm not sure." They'd spend Christmas Day at her mum's house and Boxing Day at James's sister's house. There would also be the usual Christmas Eve celebration in the Bluebell Inn, which she was looking forward to. "Maybe the week before. I'll find out what their plans are and see when they have time."

James swallowed his mouthful. "Will you message Nat or your dad?"

"I should probably arrange it with Dad. It'd be good if Ben would come too. We could meet for dinner somewhere." She put a forkful of pasta in her mouth and fell silent while she chewed. "I messaged Sam earlier too. Told him I have a woodwork project I need help with and asked him to come over sometime. I'm surprised he's not turned up yet."

"I could help with the window display."

"Josie was complaining they're driving each other crazy around the house all the time anyway. A little project will be good for him."

"And you think I can't manage it?"

She stifled a smile as she nodded.

~

When the bell tinkled at lunchtime on Monday, Tara smiled at Sam walking into the shop.

"How's Annie?" she asked.

He smiled widely. "No one asks how I am any more."

"Why would they? You're completely unimportant!"

He gave her a quick hug. "Annie's great. I could sit staring at her all day. She's so cute."

"Cute enough to make it onto our wall of fame," Tara said, gesturing to the picture.

"Josie told me about that." He moved for a closer look. "That's a good photo."

"How long are you off work for?" Tara asked.

"Until January. Which was probably a mistake. Annie's such an easy baby that having both of us at home feels a little redundant. Josie's even talking about opening the kennels again."

"She mentioned that in a message."

He continued to hover by the back wall, poring over the framed photos. "It's great to see her enthusiastic about things again. Pregnancy really didn't agree with her."

"Reopening the kennels will be good for her. And for Annette. I bet she's been bored without Josie and the bustle of dogs around the place."

"I think so." He turned back to her. "How's everything with you guys?"

"Everything's fine."

"And what's the woodworking emergency?" he asked, quirking an eyebrow.

Moving to the counter, Tara took her notepad from the shelf underneath and pulled out a sheet of paper. "This is my plan for the window display. All the local shops are doing elaborate displays this year, so I need something different." They had two large bay windows and she'd decided to stick with her Polar Express scene on one of them. The kids always loved it.

"An elf village," Sam said, looking at her sketch.

"I thought I'd have little elf houses around the edge, and a miniature Christmas tree and a Santa in the middle."

"What do you want from me?"

"The wood for the houses. I found these templates online. I thought maybe you had some wood that you could cut for me. Then I can put them together."

"When do you need it for?"

"I need to set it up on Sunday. I'd need the wood before then so I can put it all together."

"How are you going to construct it? With nails or wood glue?"

"I'm not sure. What do you think?"

"Either would be fine. You could paint them too. Brightly coloured elf houses would be cute. With snow on the top."

"Yes! I'll hang paper snowflakes too."

"Do you have a Santa sleigh?"

"No, I was going to order one online."

"I can make one." He looked thoughtful. "I'll get back to you by the end of the week." He folded her piece of paper and put it in his coat pocket.

"You're the best."

"I know! I'll see you soon."

She shouted thanks as he left, then wandered to the back of the shop, her eyes drawn to the photo wall. There were so many memories in the photos, but her eyes were drawn to the one with little Annie in it. James seemed so at ease with her in his arms; the laughter in his eyes lit his face up, and he looked as happy as she'd ever seen him.

~

James was in the shop with Tara on Friday morning when Sam arrived with a large cardboard box in his arms.

"Is that the wood?" she asked excitedly.

"Kind of," Sam said, setting the box on the floor beside the counter.

James peered over the counter as Tara eagerly pulled back the flaps.

"I know you only wanted me to cut the wood," Sam said as Tara lifted a little wooden house from the box. "But I got carried away and put them together. Then I painted them."

Passing the bright red house to James, Tara took out an orange one, then peered into the box.

"Here's the sleigh," Sam said, lifting it out. "And I also managed to make reindeer. I cut them out of the wood and then smoothed them down and painted them. They're not perfect, and if you don't want to use them it's fine."

"I love them," Tara said, feeling a little choked up.

"I hope you don't mind that I took over."

Tara shook her head. "I knew you would. As if you'd trust me to construct the houses! It's way more than I expected, though."

"These are really good," James said, turning one of the reindeer over in his hand. "You could sell these."

"No!" Tara said protectively. "I need them."

"I meant generally. They're good enough to sell."

"I don't think so," Sam said. "But Josie was impressed too. So now I have to make another set for Annie and one for the twins. I'll probably do one for Kieron too."

"That'll make a really beautiful gift," Tara said, taking out all the pieces and looking at them in awe. "You're very talented."

"Keeps me out of trouble," Sam said.

Tara's lips twitched as she was struck by an idea. "I might move the elves around so the scene is slightly different every day. Kids would love that, wouldn't they?"

"We'll probably end up with a crowd at the window every day," James said.

"It might be *too* good." Tara sighed. "We'll probably win the competition."

Sam raised an eyebrow. "Isn't that the aim?"

"Not really. I was hoping the chemist shop would win."

"I thought Belinda would be the one you definitely want to beat."

"I had an argument with her," Tara explained. "It was my fault, so now I feel awful. I'm in no mood to be competitive."

"Well, one of Belinda's redeeming traits is that she's quick to forgive. I've snapped at her several times over the years and it's always soon forgotten. I wouldn't worry about it." He flashed Tara a reassuring smile. "I ought to get back. I've got more elf villages to get on with."

"Thanks so much for this," she said.

"I'll come back for a look when it's all set up."

After he left, Tara spent a while looking over his creations with James and admiring his handiwork. The window really would look fantastic. She'd just set everything back in the box when her phone beeped.

"It's Dad," she said to James as her eyes scanned the message. She'd messaged him earlier in the week about Christmas and he'd told her he'd speak to Ben and Nat and get back to her. "He's suggesting dinner on the 23rd. They'll come over here."

"That's fine, isn't it?" James said. "It's a long way to come for dinner, though."

Tara's phone vibrated in her hand, startling her. "It's Nat," she said as she answered the call.

"Is the 23rd okay with you?" Nat asked excitedly.

"Yes. But you don't need to come here. We can meet you somewhere halfway."

"I want to see how you decorate the shop," Nat said. She knew about the competition from Tara's messages. "It's a Saturday so we thought we could come in the afternoon and have a look around Newton Abbot at all the shop windows. Then we can go for dinner somewhere. Dad says he'll book a hotel for him and Ben, but can I stay at your place?"

"Yes," Tara said, smiling at Nat's enthusiasm. There was some bustle in the background and she could hear her dad's voice.

"Dad says if that's not okay with you we can meet somewhere halfway. It's okay with you, though, isn't it?"

"Yes. Absolutely." She liked the idea of showing them around Newton Abbot. With the windows all dressed up, it would be wonderfully festive.

CHAPTER 29

By the middle of December, the offices of Hope Cove Press were starting to take shape. The homemade sign on the door had been replaced by an engraved silver plaque, which made Lizzie smile every time she arrived. Inside, the furniture and decor were still minimal, but Lizzie and Emily both had desks and had taken to working there rather than from home. Mostly, they worked on their own editing and writing projects but had also been looking over submissions they'd received from authors keen to work with them.

Scarlett was back from university for the Christmas break and Lizzie enjoyed the extra bustle around the place. That Friday afternoon, the three of them sat down together to discuss the submissions so far. As per their guidelines, they'd received the first three chapters from authors. Now they needed to decide on their favourites and request the full manuscripts.

It didn't take long for the discussion to become heated. Lizzie had a few clear favourites. Predictably, Scarlett had completely different ideas, and Lizzie was surprised by Emily's preferences too.

The confident knock at the door broke through their lively conversation, silencing them in unison.

"Do you think we have a walk-in?" Lizzie said. "Some author has heard about us and is dying to work with us?"

Scarlett looked suspiciously in the direction of the hallway. "I'd say it's more likely to be Aunty Verity with a tray of tea and scones."

"That would be good too," Lizzie said as she set off towards the door. When she opened it, she found herself looking into incredibly sparkly blue eyes. "Hello," she said when she finally found her voice.

"Hi." His smile was warm as he raised a hand to the sign on the door. "I think I have the right place."

"You were looking for Hope Cove Press?" Lizzie asked in confusion. He was only young but had a confident stance. His perfectly fitting crisp blue shirt was clearly expensive, with a designer logo embroidered on the breast pocket.

He pushed his silky blonde hair to one side. "Yeah. I wasn't sure it actually existed. That's cool, though."

"What can I help you with?" Lizzie asked.

He shook his head as though clearing his thoughts. "I'm looking for Scarlett. She works here, right?"

"Yes. She's a co-owner."

His features morphed to something Lizzie would have sworn was pride. "I didn't know if she was having me on about that. Sometimes it's hard to tell with Scarlett."

"That's true," Lizzie agreed. "Sorry, who are you?"

He dragged his teeth along his bottom lip and seemed to be searching for an appropriate answer. "Fraser," he said, extending his hand.

"Lizzie," she replied. "How do you know Scarlett?"

He looked thoughtful again. "We both go to uni in Exeter," he said after a pause. "I'd like to say we're friends, but she'd probably say acquaintances. If she was feeling generous."

"It sounds as though you know her well."

"I'm not sure about that." He glanced over Lizzie's shoulder. "Is she here?"

"Yes. Sorry." She stood aside and motioned for him to come in. "Just down the hall."

Scarlett groaned when she set eyes on him. "Are you kidding me? You've decided you don't annoy me enough in term time so you thought you'd stalk me over the holidays too?"

His laugh was gentle and melodic. "I'm not stalking you. I came to visit. There's a big difference."

"I didn't invite you, and I'm sure I've never given you the address. You've tracked me down and turned up unannounced. It definitely feels like stalking."

The look he gave her was so intense that it seemed to change the atmosphere in the room. "I wanted to see you," he said eventually, a flash of teasing in his eyes. "After all you are my—"

"Study partner," Scarlett said frantically, while Fraser looked highly amused, as though he knew there was no way she'd let him get to the end of the sentence.

Lizzie glanced at Emily, then perched on the arm of the couch wondering what on earth was going on.

"He's my study partner," Scarlett said, her cheeks flushing to a shade of red that made her name very apt. "We study together sometimes." She took his arm to propel him back towards the door, but he didn't seem keen to leave and held his ground. "We agreed to have a break from studying over Christmas," Scarlett said, more flustered than Lizzie had ever known her. "So you should leave now. We were in the middle of a very important business meeting and you've barged in and interrupted us."

"Sorry," Fraser said, looking to Emily and Lizzie.

They both told him it was fine and not to worry. He was definitely a welcome interruption, and Lizzie was mesmerised by the interaction between him and Scarlett.

"This place is really great," he said, glancing around with the same look of pride that Lizzie had witnessed at the door. "I thought you might be messing with me about setting up a publishing company."

"Why would I say it if it wasn't true?" Scarlett asked. "And why exactly was it so unbelievable?"

"It wasn't." His eyes were full of kindness as he looked at her. "I believed it when you said you were going to do it after uni. It's pretty amazing that you're already going ahead with it."

"Whatever," she said, shaking her head. "Can you please just leave?"

He took a step towards the door, then hesitated. "I wanted to apologise for the other day and check you were okay after the party. I'm sorry you were upset."

"I wasn't upset. I was annoyed. Like I'm annoyed now. Please go away."

He took a step away from her before pausing again. "If you're in Exeter at all over the holidays maybe we could get together for some extra *studying*." He winked at her, then headed quickly for the door.

"You're so annoying," she growled, following him and slamming the door behind him. "There's nothing going on between us," she said when she re-joined Lizzie and Emily. "He did that wink thing to make you think there's something going on with us, but there definitely isn't."

"So you and he just study together?" Emily asked, stifling a giggle.

"Yes."

"And by *studying*," Lizzie said. "You really mean …?"

"I mean studying! I realise he made it sound as though we're sleeping together but we're not. He's gross."

"He's gorgeous," Emily said.

"And he seems very sweet," Lizzie added.

"He's not." Scarlett's features were set in a frown, but she crept towards the window, trying to surreptitiously look out while staying far enough back that he wouldn't be able to catch her looking.

Emily grinned at Lizzie before turning to Scarlett. "If you hurry you might be able to catch up to him. Run into his arms and snog him on the street."

Scarlett moved quickly back from the window and glared at Emily. "Haven't you got a romance novel you need to write?"

"Do you really not like him?" Lizzie asked.

"No. He's awful."

Emily walked to the window and peered out. "He obviously likes you. He came all this way to check you were okay."

"He doesn't like me."

"If you don't like each other, why do you study together?" Lizzie asked.

"We just ended up together and now we're stuck with the situation. I can't do anything about it."

"Surely you can't be forced to work with someone you don't want to," Emily said. "And what did he do to upset you?"

"Nothing! Can we stop talking about it?" Scarlett indicated the papers spread out on the coffee table. "We've got work to get on with."

"I think we need a break from it actually," Lizzie said. "We all know each other's opinions. Let's take some time to mull things over and then regroup."

Emily picked up her notepad from the table. "I'm going to

head home. Let's meet on Monday and see if we can make some firm decisions then."

"I'll walk with you," Lizzie said. "I promised Max I wouldn't be late."

"This is how it's going to be then, is it?" Scarlett said. "You two slacking off and me always being the last one in the office?"

"You live here!" Lizzie reminded her as she put her coat on. "By the way, have you decided what you're doing for Christmas?"

"I won't be doing much, just lunch with Verity and Bill on Christmas Day. I can babysit on Christmas Eve if that's what you're getting at. I already told you that."

"Are you sure?"

"Yes. And I was thinking I can sleep in your spare room so you can stay out as late as you want."

"You don't need to do that," Lizzie said. "We won't be late."

"I'll stay. You can have a wild night in the Bluebell Inn." She rolled her eyes.

"Thanks!" Lizzie chuckled and called goodbye as she walked out with Emily.

"Who the hell was that guy?" Emily said as soon as they were outside the cafe.

"I've no idea. But he's really cute."

Emily zipped her coat up. "Should I point out that you're old enough to be his—"

"No! You definitely shouldn't. You're kind of mean sometimes, you know."

"Sorry. But he's about twenty years younger than you."

"Okay, stop now! What do you think's going on between him and Scarlett?"

"It's hard to say with Scarlett. There's probably some

obscure reason why she's hanging out with him. She certainly doesn't seem to like him."

"Do you think she's somehow using him for money?" Lizzie asked. "He seemed to be head to toe in designer gear, and there was a hint of posh to his accent."

"I hope you're not suggesting she's sleeping with him for money?"

"No!" Lizzie laughed. "I'm intrigued, though. It was sweet of him to come and check on her. It's made me feel all Christmassy and romantic."

Emily gave her a sidelong glance as they ambled up the road. "You've been very cheerful recently."

"Yes." Lizzie let out a sigh. "I should probably have mentioned it to you before, but Max and I are trying for another baby."

"Really?" Emily's eyes widened. "That's great. I'm happy for you."

"Thanks. At first I was quite hesitant about it, but now I love the idea of having another baby. I feel a bit bad, though."

"What about?" Emily asked.

"Because we're just setting up a business. A baby will mean me taking a backseat for a while which will leave you taking up the slack."

"It'll be fine," Emily said. "You didn't need to let me in on your plans. Although, I appreciate the heads up. Hopefully I'll be asking you to return the favour sometime in the not-too distant future."

"Are you and Jack talking about kids?"

"Jack's been talking about it for ages. He's keen to get started on a family straightaway. I've convinced him to wait a couple of years. I want to enjoy it being the two of us for a while."

"That's a good plan. Max and I rushed things. Not that I regret it, but it put a lot of stress on our relationship."

"You'd never know it. You two always seem so together."

"There was definitely a rocky patch, but now …" She trailed off, feeling like a giggly schoolgirl with a crush.

"What?" Emily asked.

Her shoulders slouched as she sighed. "I apologise if this is too much information, but the last couple of months while we've been trying to get pregnant …" She paused, choosing her words carefully. "It's reignited our physical relationship …"

"You're having lots of sex?" Emily asked bluntly.

"Loads!" she admitted. "Everything feels so great between us. It's like I've fallen in love with him all over again."

"I'm very happy for you. You really do seem to be glowing recently. Are you sure you're not already pregnant?"

"Not yet," Lizzie said. "Which means we get to keep trying!"

They laughed together then came to a stop outside the cottage.

"There's something I've been wanting to run by you," Emily said, her features turning serious. "How would you feel about us publishing Scarlett's books?"

"That's not a bad idea. Since this whole thing was her idea, it would be fitting for her books to be the first ones that we publish."

"That's what I thought."

"It might also give her the motivation to get on and finish the third book in the series."

"I'm fairly sure it's finished," Emily said. "I suspect she's holding off on giving it to you to edit because then she has to publish them. I think she's nervous."

"Are you serious? She's been adamant about publishing her books for ages."

"Talking about it and doing it are two very different

things," Emily said. "And putting your book into the world for anyone to read and comment on is daunting. That's why I think we should give her a nudge. If she thinks we're confident enough to publish them, it might be the ego boost she needs."

"It's a good idea," Lizzie said. "Let's talk to her about it on Monday."

"Have a good weekend," Emily called as she continued up the road.

When Lizzie walked inside, Max was plating up chicken, rice and veg while the girls waited patiently at the table.

"Perfect timing," he said.

She kissed his cheek. "I don't know how you manage to cook with the girls under your feet."

He raised an eyebrow, then turned away from her to put plates in front of the girls. As they ate, Lizzie asked about their day, then told Max about Scarlett's mystery visitor and the idea to publish Scarlett's books through Hope Cove Press.

The girls got down from the table as soon as they'd finished eating. A few minutes later, Phoebe started crying in the living room, followed closely by Maya.

"They're tired," Max said. "I'm going to put them in the bath, then get them into bed early."

"I can do it," Lizzie said.

"I'll clean up in here then."

She put a hand on the back of his neck as she kissed him. "Why don't you grab a beer and chill out on the couch? I'll clean up later."

His features tensed and she caught his subtle eye roll but decided not to comment on it. He was quieter than usual, but he was probably worn out after chasing the girls around all afternoon. She gave him another quick peck before going to see what the girls were fussing about.

When Emily walked into the house, she checked her watch. "I didn't think you'd be home yet," she said to Jack as she joined him on the couch.

"It was all quiet in the office so I left early."

"I had great plans to have dinner on the table when you got home. You've ruined it now."

He put an arm around her and pulled her close. "What were you going to cook?"

"Whatever I could find in the fridge."

"I'm surprised you're home so early too," he said. "I thought you'd be a while yet. Have you got more work to do this evening?"

She frowned and looked around. "I actually forgot to bring my laptop home."

"Do you want me to go back for it?"

"No. I think I can probably survive without it for the evening."

Jack sat up straighter, a look of mock surprise on his face. "What's going on? You haven't worked any evenings this week."

"I'm more productive when I don't work at home," she told him happily. "I don't get distracted as easily. Plus, seeing Lizzie hard at work motivates me to get on with my work too."

"So this new business venture might mean that I see more of you?"

"It's probably not always going to be like this." She shuffled to get comfortable against his chest. "But for now it feels like a nice routine."

"Why are you getting comfy?" he asked. "I thought you were cooking dinner."

"I'm losing motivation fast." She smiled up at him. "How about dinner at the pub?"

He feigned a look of deep contemplation before nodding eagerly.

CHAPTER 30

December saw a marked increase in customers at the bookshop. Tara was astounded by the amount of extra business Belinda's raffle brought in. Word quickly got out about the window displays – not only attracting locals but people from the surrounding towns and villages. She could see why too. A stroll around Newton Abbot, checking out the Christmas displays, was wonderfully festive. The atmosphere around the town made it all the more special. Tara took Belinda a big bunch of flowers a few days before Christmas as a thank-you for organising it.

When her dad arrived to visit with Ben and Nat, Tara felt a rush of pride at their reactions to her window displays. She told them how she rearranged the elves every day and how the local kids would come on a daily basis to see what the elves were up to. She'd arranged them in a snowball fight and building snowmen. One day she'd even got James to help her tie the reindeer from strings with the elves attached to their backs so it looked like they were joyriding on flying reindeer. Thinking up ideas had been great fun, and she loved showing it off to her dad and Nat and Ben.

After they'd spent enough time looking at her window display, Tara left James to man the shop while she took them on a tour of the town. When they'd seen all the other shop windows, they declared that the bookshop was the best and were certain it would be voted the winner.

Tara didn't care at all about winning. She was just happy to be a part of such a lovely event. Besides, the extra business it had attracted was a win for all the local businesses. A bit of fuss on social media for the winning shop wouldn't make much difference.

After a relaxed afternoon wandering around the town, they went back to the shop to pick James up before heading out for dinner at a local Italian restaurant.

As usual, Nat kept the conversation moving smoothly, and Ben even put his phone away and made an effort to chat. Tara's worries that things might feel tense between her and her dad were unfounded, and the evening was surprisingly easy.

After saying goodnight to David and Ben outside the restaurant, Tara and James set off for home with Nat. The blast of freezing air and exercise on the short walk was welcome, and Tara linked her arm through James's as Nat chatted away beside them.

"Now I feel like dessert," Tara said as they unwrapped their outer layers in the warmth of the flat. She'd had no room for dessert after the meal, but following the walk she could definitely eat something sweet.

"I don't think we have much," James said, pausing in taking his coat off.

"There must be ice cream," Tara said. "Let's pig out on ice cream."

"Hmm." James looked sheepish. "I think someone might have finished it and forgotten to buy more."

Tara went to the freezer, sure he must be wrong; there was

always ice cream. "That's disappointing," she said as she shuffled things around.

"Shall I go and see if I can find some?"

"I don't know which shops will still be open," Tara said. "Don't worry about it."

Nat rubbed her hands together to warm them. "I don't know how you can eat ice cream in the middle of winter."

"We can always eat ice cream," James told her, zipping his coat up again. "I'll find some."

"Thank you," Tara called as he left.

Nat made herself at home, curling up in the armchair and pulling a blanket around her.

"James is so sweet," she said. "You want ice cream so he just goes out to get you some."

Tara smiled. "It's not completely selfless. Just knowing there isn't ice cream in the flat will make James nervous. He has a bit of an addiction."

"He's lovely, isn't he?"

"Yes." Tara smiled as she sank back into the couch, enjoying the glow of the room with the Christmas lights twinkling on the tree by the window. "He's very lovely."

"Do you think you'll have kids soon? I can't wait to be an auntie."

Surprised by the question, it took Tara a moment to formulate a response. She decided she may as well be honest. Otherwise Nat would probably continue to pester her about it.

"We're not going to have children," she said, proud of her ability to keep her voice level. It wasn't a subject people generally broached, so Tara wasn't used to talking about it.

Nat didn't manage to hide her shock. "Oh my God. You can't have children?"

"It's not that we *can't*. We just decided it's not for us." With anyone else, she was sure that would be the end of the conversation, but she had the feeling it wouldn't be enough for Nat.

"Don't you like kids?"

"I like them," Tara said slowly. "But we decided not to have them."

"I don't understand." Nat pulled the blanket up to her chin. "You'd be great parents."

Tara swallowed the lump in her throat. "Thanks. It's not going to happen, though."

"That's such a shame. I'm really surprised. I could totally imagine you having a big family."

"It's not something I've ever imagined," Tara said. "When I was growing up it was only me and Mum, so having a big family is completely foreign to me."

"You remember when Dad lived with you, don't you? And when you had Reuben and it was the four of you?"

"Yes. But that's sort of the problem. I know what can happen."

"What do you mean?"

"I mean Reuben dying put me off ever having kids of my own." As soon as she said it, she wished she could take the words back. It wasn't a conversation she wanted to have with Nat.

"But his death was one of those freak things that happens sometimes. It's not normal for babies to die."

"I know that," Tara said wearily. It had been a big topic of discussion with the therapist. But knowing it wasn't the norm didn't change the fact that she knew first-hand that freak things *did* happen. Babies got sick, families fell apart. These things happened.

"Doesn't James want children?" Nat asked.

"We agreed that we aren't going to have them," Tara said, dodging the question.

"So you talked about it before you got married?"

"Of course." Tara was beginning to lose her patience.

Nat screwed her features up. "And he was really fine with that?"

"Yes." Tara stood, deciding she needed to put an end to the conversation. "You look cold. Do you want a warm drink? I can make hot chocolate."

"Okay."

In the kitchen, Tara took a deep breath and tried to put the conversation out of her mind. She'd just pulled the milk from the fridge when Nat wandered in.

"It seems unfair that James doesn't get to have kids because you don't want them."

Tara set the milk on the counter, keeping her back to Nat as she inhaled deeply.

"It's kind of selfish," Nat went on, her voice annoyingly soft, as though she wasn't saying something offensive. "And I can't understand why Reuben's death—"

"Of course you don't understand!" Tara swung around to face Nat. "You don't understand because to you he's an anecdote. You talk about him as though he's an interesting story. But he's not. He was a baby. My baby brother. He wasn't your family and you don't get to claim him as some interesting part of your life.

"Your life is living in a nice house with your perfect family and going on holidays together and getting everything you want. So, no, you don't understand me, and you never will. Don't come into my home and tell me I'm selfish. You have no right to comment on my choices."

Finally, she took a breath. Her hands were balled so tightly that her nails dug into her palms. As her blood pumped furiously, she felt a pang of regret deep in her stomach. Why couldn't she ever keep her cool?

She watched Nat's eyes fill with tears before she hurried

to the spare room. The door slammed so hard that it felt as though the whole building shook.

Tara slumped into a chair at the kitchen table. She probably sat staring at the wall for ten minutes before her phone pulled her from her trance.

"Hi," she said to her dad when she answered his call.

"Natalie called and asked me to come and pick her up."

"I upset her," Tara said without emotion. "Sorry. I didn't mean to."

"What happened?"

Tara drummed her fingers on the table. "She was talking about Reuben. Sometimes I can't stand the way she talks about him so casually."

"Are you okay?" David asked.

"Me?"

"Yes, you."

"Yeah. I feel bad that I upset Nat."

"I'm sure it wasn't entirely your fault. She has a tendency to say whatever springs to mind without a lot of thought."

"I've noticed that."

"Do you want me to come over?"

"I'll talk to her. It's probably better if I deal with it."

"I think so too. But call me if you want me to come and talk to her or if she still insists she doesn't want to stay there."

"Okay. Thanks."

Tara had just ended the call when the front door opened.

"They only had small tubs of ice cream at the petrol station," James said. "But they did have mint choc chip so it's not all bad. Where's Nat?" he asked as he began to unpack the shopping bag.

"Crying in the spare room, I think."

James stopped what he was doing. "What happened?"

"I snapped at her, like I snap at anyone who says something I don't like."

"What did she say?"

"It doesn't really matter. I shouldn't have had a go at her." The chair scraped as she stood. "I need to talk to her."

"Can I do anything?"

She gave him a quick kiss on the cheek. "Save me some ice cream."

Tara knocked quietly before opening the door to the spare room. Nat lay on her side on the single bed with tears running silently down her face.

"Can I come in?" Tara asked. There was a small twitch of Nat's shoulder, which Tara took as a shrug. She sat on the edge of the bed beside Nat's legs. "I'm sorry. I shouldn't have shouted at you like that."

"It's okay," Nat said quietly.

"It's not really." Tara's gaze dropped to the cream carpet as she pondered what to say. She decided honesty might be the best strategy. "I find all of this difficult."

"What?" Nat shifted to look up at Tara.

"Having you here. Having a sister." She paused. "I spent so much time hating you. You had the childhood I should have had and the family I wanted. You got my dad."

Nat sat up and wiped at her eyes. "I hated you too."

"Really?" Tara asked, surprised but not at all offended. "Why?"

"Because Dad always wanted you and not us."

"Don't be daft," she said, slightly bemused by the idea.

"He'd get in these moods and it was like he wasn't there any more. He'd stare into space when we talked to him, then he'd nod and smile and pretend he'd been listening when he hadn't. He'd shut himself away in his study with his photo albums of you and Reuben." Her chin quivered. "When he got really bad, he'd go to see you and he'd come back okay again. And I hated that it was always you who could cheer him up."

Tara frowned. It didn't make any sense. "Until earlier this year, I hadn't seen him for a long time."

"I know that now. He had to tell me the truth before I found out from you."

"I'm confused," Tara said hesitantly.

"Mum knew for years. That's what all the arguments were about, I suppose."

"Knew what?"

"That when Dad said he was going to visit you, he was actually meeting up with your mum."

Tara had always known that they met up sometimes. She'd gone too – until she'd been old enough to refuse. She was surprised that he'd kept it a secret. "Mum never coped very well after Reuben died," she explained. "Sometimes she'd call Dad and want to see him. And she had to tell him how I was getting on at school and stuff …" Tara trailed off when she caught the look of sympathy on Nat's face.

"It was *him* who wanted to meet up," Nat said. "He's still in love with her."

"No," Tara said with a hint of a laugh. Nat had absolutely no idea what she was talking about. "That's ridiculous."

"He always wanted to be with you and Debbie, not us." She sniffed. "So you might want my family, but I always wanted yours."

"Wait." Tara struggled to get her thoughts in order. "Are you saying Dad was having an affair with my mum?"

Nat shrugged. "Mum thought so. That's why they argued so much. I only figured that out recently. Ben overheard them talking. Mum thinks Dad's only sticking around until Ben and I move out, then he'll leave her."

"No," Tara insisted. "None of this makes any sense. There's no way they were having an affair. Dad was always happy with you. He left us and started a new family." At least that was what Tara had always told herself. That was the story as she knew it.

"When I asked Dad, he said he wasn't having an affair, but I didn't know whether to believe him. Then I volunteered to come and help Debbie in the shop that day—"

"That's why you were asking her all those questions about her and Dad?"

"She told you?"

"Yes. I don't think she thought too much of it – possibly just that you're a bit odd!"

Nat's features were serious. "I don't think Debbie loves him. Not any more. And I don't believe she'd have an affair with him."

"I don't think she would either."

"I think my parents are going to get divorced anyway. And sometimes I think it might be for the best. They seem to make each other miserable."

"I had no idea," Tara said. "I'm sorry." When she was younger she used to daydream about her dad divorcing Gillian and coming back to be a family with them. Now the thought of them divorcing just made her sad.

"When I realised that you hadn't seen Dad for all those years, I felt guilty that I'd spent so long being angry with you. And I sort of thought that if my family was falling apart, maybe having a big sister would be a good thing." She paused and chewed her bottom lip. "But sometimes I feel as though you don't like me."

Tara felt a pang of regret and wished she was better at hiding her feelings. "I'm a really bad big sister," she said. "You should have a great sister – someone like Amber who's patient and kind. She'd be a brilliant big sister. I'm sorry you got stuck with me. I do like you, but I found this whole situation hard."

"I'm still glad I got you as a sister."

"Well that's because you have a very generous spirit," Tara said, giving her leg a gentle pat.

"Do you wish I didn't exist?" Nat asked as more tears filled her eyes.

"Of course not. Why would you ask that?"

"Because if Reuben hadn't died, Ben and I wouldn't exist. I think about it a lot."

A lump formed in Tara's throat and tears stung her eyes. "You can't think like that," she said, shaking her head and reaching out to pull Nat into a hug. "I'm really glad you and Ben exist."

"But—"

"There are no buts." Tara pulled back and looked at Nat sternly. "Okay?"

She pushed tears from her cheeks and nodded.

"Can I tempt you to ice cream?" Tara asked in a bid to lighten the atmosphere.

"I think I might go to sleep, if you don't mind."

"Of course. But give Dad a call and let him know you're okay."

"I will." She reached for her phone as Tara headed for the door. "I'm sorry I called you selfish."

Tara smiled at her. "Don't worry about it."

Feeling emotionally drained, Tara grabbed a tub of ice cream and joined James on the couch. She pulled the blanket up to her neck, with an arm sticking out the side so she could eat.

"Is it strange to wrap up in a blanket and eat ice cream?" she asked.

"It makes perfect sense to me." Moving closer, he intercepted the spoon and stole the ice cream.

Tara tipped her head in the direction of the discarded tub on the coffee table. "You already ate a whole tub."

"There are about five mouthfuls in a tub! Don't make me sound greedy."

"If the portions are small, don't steal mine."

He sat back and put an arm around her. "How are things with Nat?"

"She's a really messed-up kid and she reminds me a lot of myself sometimes. But I think things are okay." She took another mouthful of ice cream. "You know, I think it was rude of you not to warn me that siblings are a complete nightmare before I invited them into my life. Why are you looking at me like that?" she asked, noticing the twinkle of amusement in his eyes.

"Because you said that in an affectionate way. Like when I complain about Kate."

"So I'm making progress?"

"Seems like it."

She paused with the spoon halfway to her mouth. "I always thought they were a perfect, happy family. But I suspect I got that very wrong."

"Really?"

"Yes. And it doesn't make me feel better."

James looked at her intently. "What did she say to make you snap at her?"

For a moment, Tara concentrated on her ice cream, trying to decide whether to make something up or tell him the truth. "She asked if we planned to have kids. When I explained the situation she said it was selfish of me. And that it was unfair to you."

"I can see why you snapped at her. I would have done too."

"She was only saying what she thinks. What everyone thinks."

"No one thinks that," James said. "And it was inappropriate of her to comment on it. It's none of her business."

"Maybe."

"Definitely. I love you. We're happy."

"I hate thinking that I'm depriving you of a family that you want."

He gave her a crooked smile. "You're not depriving me of a family. You *are* my family."

Abandoning her empty ice cream tub to the table, she snuggled into James. "You're right," she said.

"I'm always right," he replied cheekily.

CHAPTER 31

Tara was already showered and dressed when her phone buzzed on the kitchen table the next morning. She was the only one up and the flat was completely quiet.

"I didn't wake you, did I?" her dad asked when she answered the call.

"No. I'm up. Nat's still fast asleep. Do you want me to wake her? What time are you leaving?"

"No rush. I doubt Ben will be awake for a while. I was hoping I might be able to get a coffee with you before they get up?"

"Sounds good." She managed to hide her surprise. "Where are you?"

"Outside your place. I thought we could go somewhere for a chat. It's never just the two of us."

"No, it's not." It had annoyed Tara at first, but sometimes it also felt like a good thing. After Tara's conversation with Nat the previous evening, she wasn't sure she wanted the chance to speak to him alone. There were so many questions she wanted to ask him, but she wasn't sure she wanted to hear the answers. "Hang on," she said. "I'll come down."

As she ended the call, she knew she'd take the opportunity to ask her questions. The answers might be unsettling, but so would not knowing. Her mind whirred, trying to decide where they could go so they could talk. She wasn't sure she wanted to have a private conversation in a cafe. Especially since she was sure to see someone she knew.

"I don't think I've ever shown you our second kitchen," she said when she opened the door of the shop to let him in.

"That sounds quite fancy," David said, stepping inside. "Having two kitchens."

"It's not at all." Tara locked the door behind him. "But it's a bit more private than going out somewhere." She led him through the shop to the little kitchen at the back. "One of the neighbouring properties just put an extension on the back. I said to James we could do the same and knock the wall through at the back of the shop to add a cafe." She wittered away, filling the silence while she got the coffee machine up and running. "We probably won't do it, but I like the idea of having a cafe."

David took a seat at the small table in the centre of the room. "You're very ambitious, aren't you?"

"Not really. Well, maybe when it comes to the shop. I like to find ways to improve things." The coffee machine hummed, slowly filling the cup while Tara busied herself getting milk and sugar. "I had a good chat with Nat last night," she said, thinking she may as well get straight to the point.

"Me too," David said. "She called me after she spoke to you."

Tara passed him a mug of coffee and indicated that he should help himself to milk and sugar. "Did she tell you what we'd spoken about?"

"Yes. I hope you don't mind."

"Why would I mind?" Tara's brow creased as she got her own mug of coffee and joined him at the table.

"I wasn't sure if you'd spoken to her in confidence …"

Tara stared at him for a moment before she figured out that they were talking about completely different things. "She told you I don't want to have children?"

"Yes." He looked slightly puzzled, so she presumed he had no idea what else they'd been talking about.

"I wish I hadn't told her. But she asked when we were going to have kids. I didn't realise that if I said never, she'd think it was okay to have an opinion on that." Her fingers gripped the mug so tightly that the heat made her hands tingle. "Is that why you wanted to talk to me? So you can give me your opinion too? Because it's not up for discussion. It's none of Nat's business, and it's none of yours either."

"I know. I'm sorry. I only wanted to make sure you're okay."

"I was going to ask you the same thing," she said tersely.

"What do you mean?"

Tara took a sip of her coffee as her confidence wavered. Maybe his personal life was none of her business and she should keep quiet. But she knew she couldn't do that.

"Nat has it in her head that you and Gillian are going to get divorced."

"She said that?" he asked in surprise.

Tara nodded and stared into her coffee. "Is it true?"

He hesitated. "I don't know. Not now, but I suspect she'll leave me eventually."

"Why?"

"Because I'm a pretty bad husband," he said lightly.

"Are you in love with Mum?" Tara asked, forcing the words out.

The pain was evident in his features. "Yes."

"Did you have an affair with her?"

"No." He took a deep breath. "Not in the way you're suggesting. But it was inappropriate for me to meet up with her, even just to talk."

"That's what caused the problems with Gillian?"

He closed his eyes briefly. "The problem was that half of my heart always belonged to you and Debbie. I missed the two of you, and Reuben. All the time. My mind was always on what I'd lost instead of what I had."

That was pretty much what Nat had said, but Tara struggled to process it. She'd spent most of her life hating him for leaving them without thought or remorse. But apparently that wasn't the case.

"It doesn't make sense," Tara said. "If you cared so much about us, why did you leave in the first place?"

"It was a difficult time." His voice turned wooden, as though he was retelling a story he'd told a thousand times. "Debbie wanted space, and I wanted to help her however I could. That meant giving her space."

"Surely that didn't mean going off and marrying someone else?"

"I thought I'd lost Debbie forever. She couldn't stand to look at me. I worked with Gillian and she was caring and supportive."

"Did you even love Gillian?"

"Yes. I did, and I still do."

That was something at least. "I still don't understand why you let Mum take me. Why didn't you want joint custody?"

There was a flicker of something in his eyes; a hint of a thought that he kept to himself.

"What aren't you telling me?" Tara asked.

"Nothing. I didn't want you to be pulled between us. It was never that I didn't want you." His eyes shone with tears before he stood and walked to the sink.

"I hope you can work things out with Gillian," Tara said,

through the lump in her throat. "Nat seemed really upset about it."

"I'm glad she feels she can confide in you," he said, keeping his back to Tara. "I worry about her."

"I've noticed that," Tara said dryly.

His eyes were damp when he turned around. "What's that supposed to mean?"

"Sorry." Tara shook her head, wishing she wasn't so careless with her words. "I didn't mean anything. It's just been hard to see how close you and she are. You constantly worry about her. She's seventeen and you practically have her wrapped in cotton wool. Sorry," she said again. "How you choose to parent your children is none of my business." She put her hand over her mouth as she realised the irony of that statement. David flashed her a sad smile.

"I do wrap her in cotton wool," he said, his tone serious. "Ben too. It's another source of tension between me and Gillian. I can't seem to help it."

"They're teenagers," Tara said. "You have to let them live their own lives at some point."

"The thought terrifies me." He leaned heavily against the sink. "I've spent their entire lives being terrified."

"Because of Reuben?" Tara asked, her eyes filling with tears. It was the same reason she'd decided never to have children. She knew she'd spend her whole life worrying about losing them.

"And you," David said.

"Why me?"

His eyes narrowed, as though the answer should be obvious. "I lost you too."

"No." Tara's lips stretched to a bemused smile. "You didn't lose me."

"I didn't see you for more than ten years." He swiped at

the tears that rolled down his cheeks before turning quickly away from her.

Tara stared at his back, wishing she hadn't caught the pain in his features. She'd cut him out of her life to protect herself from the hurt of seeing him with his new family. Her mum had often told her how upset he was and how badly he'd wanted to see her, but Tara had never really believed it. She'd always believed he didn't really care about her.

"I'm sorry," she whispered. "I always thought you were happy without us."

"No," he sniffed. "I wasn't."

The silence was uncomfortable. All Tara was aware of was the dull thudding of her heart and the sound of her breathing, which made her suddenly self-conscious.

"Nat's probably up by now," she said. "And James. I should go up so they don't wonder where I am."

"I'll wash the mugs and be up in a minute."

Tara opened her mouth to tell him to leave the mugs, then realised he was looking for an excuse to be alone.

Pausing for a moment at the top of the stairs, she took a few deep breaths, then forced herself to smile as she walked inside. James and Nat were sitting at the kitchen table.

"Good morning," Tara said brightly.

"We were just wondering where you'd got to," James said, then craned his neck as she bent to kiss him.

"Dad arrived early. We had a coffee downstairs so we wouldn't wake you."

"Where is he?" Nat asked.

"I made him do the washing up," Tara said with a grin. "He'll be up in a minute."

When he appeared a few minutes later, it was only to say he was going to head back to the hotel and make sure Ben was up in time for them to check out. The two of them returned an hour later and Tara made pancakes for them all for breakfast.

"You can stay for longer if you want," she said when David mentioned leaving. "We don't have anything planned apart from drinks with friends this evening."

"Thanks. But we should probably get back. Gillian might be missing us."

"I bet she's enjoying the peace," Ben quipped.

"That's probably true," David said. "But we ought to get back anyway."

"Oh, I have Christmas presents for you." Tara went to the Christmas tree to retrieve them, handing her dad a gift bag with wine and chocolates for him and Gillian. Then she handed Ben a card. "We were going to get you a video game, but we didn't know which ones you had so there's money for you to choose your own."

"Thanks," he said, smiling enthusiastically.

"Can I open it now?" Nat asked, when Tara gave her a dainty gift bag.

"It's not Christmas until tomorrow," Tara said, with mock consternation.

"I don't care. I'm opening it, and I want you to open the one from us too." She nodded to the square box that she'd put under the tree when she'd arrived.

"You're such a rebel," Tara teased. "I can't believe you're trying to lead me astray." She watched as Nat excitedly opened the necklace and earring set, exclaiming over how much she loved it.

"Go on, open yours!" She reached for the box and thrust it at Tara, then turned to James. "You didn't say anything, did you?"

"My lips were sealed," he replied.

"Do you know what it is?" Tara asked in confusion.

Nat beamed. "James had to help me with it a little bit."

"Now I'm intrigued." Tara pulled the ribbon away and opened the box. "You made us a wedding album?"

"I love doing stuff like that," Nat said, while Tara sat down and lifted the album from the box. "And I know you said you'd probably never get around to it. Do you like it?"

"I love it," Tara said as she turned the pages to look at the photos from their wedding day. "Thank you so much. Have you seen it?" she asked James when he perched beside her to look over her shoulder.

"No. I just emailed Nat the photos."

"It's so lovely," she whispered, choked up by the thoughtful gift and by the reminder of their wedding day. When she came to the last page, she passed it to James and stood to hug Nat. "It's the best gift ever."

"I'm so happy you like it," Nat replied, squeezing her hard.

"Come on then," David said. "We really should hit the road."

Tara and James walked outside with them, and they stood chatting by the car for a few minutes before they all began to shiver against the freezing wind.

"Thanks for coming," Tara said, as she hugged Nat again. "Hey!" she called to Ben as he opened the car door. "Where's my hug?"

"Dunno." He flashed a mischievous grin. "Where did you leave it?"

"You've got no chance," David said as he put his arms around her. She relaxed in his embrace and felt tearful when he pulled away.

"We'll have to get together again soon," she said.

"I'd like that." He shook James's hand before getting into the car.

James draped an arm around Tara as they watched them

drive away. "It's good that you managed to grab some time alone with your dad."

"Yeah," she agreed vaguely. If only it hadn't left her feeling so awful. Discovering how much she'd hurt him when she'd cut him out of her life left her wracked with guilt.

It niggled at her for the rest of the morning. After lunch, she waved away James's suggestion to go out for a walk and instead curled up with a book that she was halfway through. She must have been staring at the same page for almost half an hour when James gently pried it from her hand and asked her what was wrong.

She sat up straighter on the couch. "I keep playing everything over in my head – the conversations I had with Nat and my dad. Everything is such a jumble."

"Do you want to talk about it?"

"Not really. I feel as though you spend enough time dealing with my family drama. It must be pretty boring for you."

"Do you really think I mind?"

"No." She curled her lip and scowled at him dramatically. "Because you have the patience of a saint."

"I love how you make that sound like a bad thing."

"It's kind of annoying to live with," she said lightly. "You set the bar too high. It makes me look bad."

"I have yet to see you look bad," he said with a flirty smile

"You're such a charmer." She kissed his cheek. "I might nip over and visit Mum."

"Shall I come with you?"

She shook her head. "No, I won't be long."

CHAPTER 32

The Christmas wreath shuddered on the door when Tara let herself into her mum's house. Debbie checked her watch as she stepped into the hall.

"I wasn't expecting you," she said. "I'm going out soon."

"Where are you going?" Tara asked, shrugging her coat off on the way to the living room.

"I'm meeting some friends."

"Since when do you have friends?" Tara grimaced as she flopped onto the couch. "Sorry. That sounded mean. But you don't usually go out with friends."

"It's a new thing. And it actually started with that date I went on. Turns out it wasn't such a bad thing after all."

"Oh, no." Tara sighed. "Please tell me you're not still seeing Rupert?"

"No chance. But a few days after I went out with him, Andy turned up at the door. He was worried that I'd think he'd been gossiping when he told you about Rupert, so he came around to apologise."

"Oh my goodness! You're dating Andy? How old is Andy anyway?"

"Slow down! Let me finish the story." She glared at Tara with mock annoyance. "Andy invited me for a drink in the pub as way of an apology. I refused because I hate going in the pub on my own, but he said loads of people go in the pub on their own, and any time I felt like going down I could sit at the bar and chat to him so I wouldn't be alone. And I wasn't going to, but one evening I thought what the hell and I walked down to the pub, sat at the bar and had a drink and chatted to Andy. It was really nice."

"So you *are* seeing Andy?" Tara struggled to get her head around the idea.

Debbie rolled her eyes and looked impatiently at Tara.

"That's not the end of the story, is it?" Tara said.

"No. While I was in the pub, Sheila came in, Amber's mum. She was meeting a couple of friends and invited me to join them. I had a great evening. They invited me to go out for a meal with them the following week. Then they added me to their messaging group and invite me along whenever they're doing anything. This afternoon we're having mulled wine and mince pies at Sheila's house as a Christmas Eve treat."

"That's nice," Tara said, slightly shocked at the idea of her mum socialising. "Do you still talk to your online friends?" Debbie's online support group had been her lifeline over the years.

"Of course I do. But I can have other friends too."

"That's good. I'm glad."

"I need to get ready soon," Debbie said, glancing at her watch again.

"Oh, okay. I'll talk to you another time."

"Sorry." She patted Tara's arm when she went to stand up. "I didn't mean to shoo you away. I've got a bit of time. And it won't matter if I'm late. Tell me how it went with David and the kids."

"They're not really kids," Tara said. "But it went okay. It always feels emotionally draining, but I think things are slowly getting better."

"I'm happy to hear it."

"Dad explained a lot of stuff to me. About how he always missed us. I had it in my head that he didn't really care about us."

"I always told you he loved you and he wanted to see you."

"I know, but I didn't believe it."

"I'm glad you're sorting things out now." Debbie seemed as though she was trying to wrap the conversation up.

"I just have one question," Tara said, drumming her fingers on her thigh. She swallowed the lump in her throat and looked her mum directly in the eyes. "Why didn't Dad want joint custody of me? I don't understand why he let you take me away from him. If he cared about me so much, why would he do that?"

Debbie had the same fleeting look that David had.

Tara's eyes brimmed with tears. "He wanted custody, didn't he?"

"Yes," Debbie whispered.

"What happened?"

"It doesn't matter what happened. It's in the past. You need to move on. We all do."

"How can I move on when I don't understand what happened? Just tell me, please. Then I'll drop the subject and never ask about it again."

Debbie paused, and when she eventually spoke, her words were calm and controlled. "I blamed David for Reuben's death. That's why I left him. When he threatened to try and get custody of you, I told him he'd never be able to." She wrung her hands in her lap. "Who'd give custody to a man who'd already caused the death of one of his children?" Tears sprang to her eyes and overflowed down her cheeks. "That's what I said to him. He backed off then, left us alone, more or less."

Tara's chest felt tight. "But Reuben died of a virus. How can that have been Dad's fault?"

"It wasn't," Debbie said, taking a steady breath. "When Reuben got ill he went downhill quickly. I panicked and wanted to take him straight to the hospital. David suggested we wait a while."

"Oh my God." Tara dropped her face to her hands.

"We didn't wait long. And the doctors said an hour probably wouldn't have made any difference. But when I needed someone to blame, David was an easy target."

"It wasn't his fault," Tara said quietly.

"No. Of course it wasn't. But he blamed himself too, so I used that to get him to stay away from us. He still came to see you, of course, but it was all on my terms. By the time I stopped blaming him, he was with Gillian."

"He still loves you," Tara stated, the pain of all that her parents had been through feeling as though it might suffocate her.

A smile played on Debbie's lips. "And I still love him. He'll always be the love of my life. But grief pushed us apart instead of pulling us together. We've both accepted that."

"You must really hate Gillian," Tara said, wiping furiously at her cheeks.

"No." Debbie laid her hand over Tara's. "I will be eternally grateful to her for being there for him when I couldn't. I had you, but he had no one. She saved him."

"Do you know they're not happy?"

"I know they've had their ups and downs. They'll be okay."

"I'm not so sure."

"Stay out of it," Debbie said firmly, then stood up. "I should get changed."

"Are you still going out?"

"Yes." She sounded slightly defensive. "I've spent enough time hiding away, feeling terrible. I have to get on with my life."

"I'm glad you're doing well," Tara said, giving her a kiss on the cheek before heading for the door. "Have a nice time," she called behind her.

Almost on autopilot, Tara drove into the village instead of heading home. Passing the pub, she kept going until she reached the sign for the kennels. The car tyres crunched on the gravel driveway as she crawled towards the house. Smoke billowed from the chimney and a smile hit Tara's face as she stepped out of the car.

"It always smells delicious in here," she said, walking into the kitchen.

"I've just baked a cake," Annette said, turning to Tara. "It was for tomorrow really but we can have a slice now with a cup of tea."

"That sounds perfect." Tara draped her coat over a chair and bent to stroke Charlie, who sniffed around her legs. "How are you?" she asked Annette.

"I'm fine. I'm cooking Christmas dinner for Josie and Sam tomorrow so I'm looking forward to that. Max and Lizzie will call over in the afternoon too. It's good to be busy. You and James are with your mum tomorrow, aren't you?"

"Yes, then we'll visit James's family on Boxing Day."

"Will you come over here on New Year's Day? I'm having an open house. Call in whenever you want."

"Yes. We'll be here." She'd already heard about it from Josie.

"Good. I'm lucky that all you kids still come around and look after me."

Tara couldn't help but chuckle as Annette set a slice of Victoria sponge in front of her. "I think it's you who looks after us." It had always been the way. Annette and Wendy's house had felt like a second home to Tara for as long as she could remember. Glancing at the door to the living room, she was hit by a vision of Wendy. She could just imagine her wandering in and beaming at Tara. She'd been the one who Tara had confided in when things hadn't been good at home.

"You look miles away," Annette remarked, putting two cups of tea on the table and taking a seat.

"I was thinking about Wendy," Tara said, a slight quiver to her voice.

"Oh dear," Annette said. "That's a bad sign."

Tara warmed her hands on her drink. "How do you mean?"

"You used to tell Wendy all your problems. But I thought you were doing well? You seem happier."

"I am," Tara mused. "Mum's doing really well, and everything is great with James and the bookshop."

Annette sipped her tea. "And you're seeing your dad and siblings?"

"Yes." She paused. "It's hard but it's getting easier. I think it's a good thing."

"I'm glad. Wendy would be happy that you're doing well. You were her favourite," she said conspiratorially.

"No!" Tara said, amused.

"You were. Wendy didn't have an easy childhood, and I think you reminded her of herself sometimes."

"So that's how she always seemed to know the right thing to say," Tara mused.

"Probably."

"I always felt as though she understood me."

Annette nodded. "She'd be so proud of all you've achieved. Amber tells me that the bookshop is the heart of the community in Newton Abbot. She says how welcoming it is and how everyone loves to call in."

Without warning, tears filled Tara's eyes. It was true that the bookshop was doing well, but she struggled to focus on her achievements. Instead, her mind raced to how impatient she'd been with Nat when they were first getting to know each other, and to how snappy she'd been with Belinda. And then there was James …

"Did you ever regret not having kids?" Tara blurted out as tears spilled down her cheeks.

"So that's what's really on your mind?" Annette looked at her sadly, then fetched a box of tissues. "Took you a while to get to the point."

Tara sighed. "Josie wanted to have a photo of Annie in the shop, as our youngest customer. So now there's this picture on the wall of James holding her and it feels as though it's taunting me. James would be such a great dad, and I can't help thinking he's missing out because of me."

"What does James say?"

"That he has everything he wants and he doesn't need anything else."

"There you go then."

"I'm worried it's something I'll regret later." She took a deep breath as she tried to get her emotions under control. "You and Wendy never regretted not having kids, did you?"

"No. We didn't." She pushed Tara's cake towards her. "But it doesn't matter about me and Wendy. You need to figure out what's right for you and James."

CHAPTER 33

Lizzie wanted to put the girls to bed herself on Christmas Eve, so she was slightly irked when Scarlett arrived two hours earlier than expected. She ate dinner with them, then took the girls into the living room while Max and Lizzie tidied up the kitchen.

"Do you think she arrived early so she can charge us more for babysitting?" Lizzie asked quietly. "That's probably why she offered to stay over too. She's going to hit us with a massive bill tomorrow."

"I don't think so," Max said, collecting up the plates from the table.

"It's a bit odd that she came over two hours earlier than I asked her to. You're the one who says she's cunning and always has something up her sleeve. There'll be an ulterior motive rather than just wanting to see the girls before they go to bed."

Max put the dishes on the counter and looked at her seriously. "I think that's exactly why she came over early."

"Really?"

He glanced at the door before lowering his voice.

"Clearly she's not on good terms with her parents, and I get the impression she's uncomfortable around Verity and Bill. Where else would she go? I think she just doesn't want to be in the flat on her own at Christmas."

Lizzie let out a sigh. Why hadn't she thought of that instead of assuming Scarlett had some devious motives?

"I'm surprised she didn't stay in Exeter with her boyfriend," Max said, his eyes flashing with mischief.

"She swears he's not her boyfriend," Lizzie hissed. "And I've told you you're not allowed to mention it to her."

"I'm going to ask her about it later. I'm intrigued."

"So am I. But she's not going to tell us so it's better not to bring it up." She stroked Tilly's head when the loving dog nuzzled her knee. "I always think of Scarlett as being tough. But maybe underneath she's actually insecure. I'm still surprised she wasn't more excited when Emily and I talked to her about publishing her books." When they'd mentioned it, they'd got a decidedly lukewarm response and Scarlett said she'd think about it.

"Emily's probably right that she's nervous about putting them out in the world. I'm sure she appreciates the offer."

"I hope she comes around to it. It'd be fitting for her books to be the first ones that we publish."

"I'm sure she will." Max opened up the dishwasher, then gave a small growl at finding it needed unloading. He began pulling out clean plates. "What time are we picking Jack and Emily up?"

"We're not any more. Emily messaged to say they were going over to Josie and Sam's for dinner so they'd just see us in the pub." She checked the time. "I'm going to get ready, then I can help Scarlett put the girls down before we leave."

She was almost at the door when she turned back. "I'm happy to drive tonight if you want to drink?"

“I don’t mind driving,” he said, putting glasses away in the cupboard and not looking at her.

Lizzie had expected him to jump at her offer to drive. Actually, she’d been counting on it. Her period was a few days late and she strongly suspected she was pregnant. Her excitement had been building for a few days, but she didn’t want to get Max’s hopes up until she was sure. She’d bought a test but had chickened out of taking it, worrying that her disappointment would cast a shadow over Christmas if it was negative. She decided to wait until Boxing Day. The result should be accurate by then too.

Having to drive home was a convenient excuse not to drink on Christmas Eve without raising any suspicions.

“You should have a few beers,” she said, trying to sound casual. “You deserve it after all you do for me and the girls.”

Still he didn’t look at her but gave a small shake of the head. “Whatever. I thought you were going to get changed?”

“I am,” she said, leaving him to finish tidying up.

She didn’t need to make too much effort for an evening in the Bluebell Inn, but it was nice to get a little bit dressed up. By the time she was ready, the girls were in their pyjamas and Scarlett was in their bedroom with them.

Lingering in the doorway, Lizzie watched the girls snuggling affectionately into Scarlett as she read them one of their favourite stories. None of them noticed her until the story was over, then she gave Phoebe and Maya cuddles before settling them in their beds.

“I think they’ll fall asleep quickly,” Lizzie whispered to Scarlett as they crept down the stairs. “Neither of them napped today.”

In the living room, Max was waiting, wearing jeans and a crisp white shirt.

“I thought you were going soon?” Scarlett said, looking him up and down. “Don’t you need to get ready?”

As Max rolled his eyes at her, Lizzie slipped an arm around his waist. "I think you look very handsome."

"Thanks," Max said.

Scarlett dropped onto the couch. "Off you go then. Leave me in peace."

"Speaking of being left in peace," Max said, "what's your boyfriend doing over Christmas? Will you be seeing him at all?"

"You told Max about Fraser?" Scarlett glared at Lizzie, then shook her head. "He's not my boyfriend."

"He's not really just a study partner, though, is he?" Max asked with eyes full of mischief.

Lizzie shot him a look. "Leave her alone."

"You wouldn't understand," Scarlett said wearily. She looked forlorn as she stroked Tilly, who leaned against her legs. Lizzie had expected her to put an immediate end to the conversation, but she got the distinct impression that Scarlett wanted to talk about it.

"We're not *that* old," Max said. "If you're seeing someone, it's a good thing, isn't it? There's no need to hide it."

"I'm not seeing him. He's my housemate."

Lizzie failed to hide her surprise. "I thought you were living with a girl. Verity thinks so too."

"I let her think that. If she knew the truth she'd freak out."

"I'm sure she'd be okay with you living with a guy," Lizzie said. "She's pretty open-minded."

"It's a weird situation." Scarlett's gaze was trained on the Christmas tree by the window. "He helped me with money. If Verity or my parents knew, they'd have a problem with it. But it's none of their business so I don't need to tell them."

"He lent you money?" Max asked, moving to perch on the arm of the chair.

"He didn't *lend* me money," Scarlett said.

The conversation was making Lizzie uncomfortable. She

had the feeling she wouldn't like whatever Scarlett said, and she didn't like the thought of keeping secrets from Verity.

"He *gave* you money?" Max ventured.

Scarlett shifted her gaze to Tilly as she stroked her head. "I couldn't get a student loan. It's a stupid system. I couldn't get a loan because my parents have enough to pay the fees, but they didn't think I should go to uni so they wouldn't pay for it. Fraser helped me get around the system."

"He helped you with the paperwork?" Max asked.

"No. Well, yes. Kind of."

"I'm confused," Lizzie said.

"Don't be weird about it if I tell you. It's not a big deal. Okay?"

Not at all sure she wanted to continue the conversation, Lizzie nodded despite herself.

"If you're married, the loan company assesses your eligibility based on the income of you and your spouse," Scarlett said flatly. "Not your parents' income."

Lizzie and Max remained silent for a moment.

"But you're not married," Lizzie said. "So that wouldn't help you."

"I *wasn't* married. But I thought that if it was a way for me to get my degree, then it would be much easier than working at some stupid job while I saved up."

"So you're saying you married this guy so you could get a loan?" Max asked.

"Yes. Fraser is my husband. Legally. We agreed we'll get divorced as soon as we finish uni."

Lizzie put a hand over her mouth, trying desperately to hide her shock but sure she was failing.

"It's not a big deal," Scarlett repeated. "But you can't tell Verity. She'd freak out."

Horrified, Lizzie turned to Max, but he only looked amused.

"So you're married?" he asked, with a crooked smile. "You have a husband?"

"That's what I just told you."

"It's the most absurd story I've ever heard." Max stood up, rolling his eyes. "You can tease me for being old all you want, but I'm not gullible. Nice try, though."

"Please say you're joking," Lizzie said, staring at Scarlett.

"Of course she's joking." Max held his hand out to Lizzie. "Come on, let's get going. Call if there are any problems, Scarlett."

"Have a nice evening," she muttered in reply.

Lizzie followed Max out of the room, pausing in the doorway to look back at Scarlett, who finally met her eye. Her stomach lurched as she continued after Max.

"She wasn't joking," she whispered when they'd closed the front door behind them.

"She was definitely joking," Max said firmly. "Ignore her."

"I think she actually did it," Lizzie said in a daze as she got into the car.

"You think Scarlett's married? Seriously? I know I sometimes struggle to tell if she's joking, but that was pretty obvious to me."

"Once Scarlett gets an idea in her head, she won't let it go. She wanted to go to uni. I know her parents refused to pay. Verity told me that."

"But if your parents refuse to pay, there's definitely another way to get the student loan." Max turned the engine on and put the car in gear. "The system can't really be that rigid."

"I honestly think she was serious," Lizzie said, trying to process the information. "And it's the sort of crazy thing Scarlett would do. Remember how she pierced her own lip for book research?"

"Yeah, but getting married to cheat the student loan system is extreme even for Scarlett."

"I think it's exactly the sort of thing Scarlett would do."

Max gave a small shake of the head and the subject was dropped. They drove the rest of the way to Averton in silence, which made the pub seem incredibly loud when they walked in. Their group of friends were sitting at the usual table at the side of the pub and they waved at them as they walked to the bar.

"Do you want wine?" Max asked as he waited to be served.

"No," Lizzie said. "I told you I'm happy to drive. You can drink."

He shrugged. "I don't mind either."

"Tonic water for me," Lizzie said when Andy approached them.

Max ordered a beer, and they set off across the room to join their friends. Emily and Jack were there with Tara and James and Amber and Paul.

"Are Josie and Sam coming?" Lizzie asked.

"No," Emily said. "They're staying at home with Annie."

"I thought Sam might at least come for one celebratory drink," Tara said, then beamed at Lizzie. "The bookshop won the prize for the best window display."

Lizzie smiled back at her. "Congratulations!" She and Max had taken the girls over to Newton Abbot the previous week to look at the window displays, and she'd had no doubt that Tara would win.

"Thanks. I have to give Sam most of the credit, though."

"He did a great job but I think it was moving the elves around every day that made it such a hit." Lizzie glanced at Max, who was keeping very quiet and didn't seem to be listening to the conversation.

He took a long swig of his beer, then looked up at the

table at large. "You won't believe what Scarlett just said to us."

"What now?" Jack asked.

"I don't know if you should be telling people," Lizzie said, frowning at Max. "I honestly don't think she was joking."

"She was joking. She must have been."

James chuckled. "What on earth did she say?"

"She claims she's married," Max said.

Emily's brow creased. "Of course she's not married. She's eighteen. And surely we'd know if she was married."

"According to Scarlett, the guy who came to the office the other day is her husband." Lizzie felt guilty for discussing it. If it was true, which her gut told her it was, she didn't think Scarlett would want them to share it with anyone.

Max took a sip of his pint, then wiped his thumb across his top lip. "She told us she couldn't get a loan because her parents earn enough to pay for her to go to uni. But they refused to fund her, so she got married in order to get the loan."

"Wow," Tara said. "I'm glad I never thought of that trick."

"What do you mean?" Max asked.

"Remember I was thinking of going to uni? But I realised I couldn't get a loan because they'd look at my dad's income as well as my mum's."

"That rings a bell," Max said.

"I don't understand," James said. "If your dad could have afforded it, he'd have paid for you, wouldn't he?"

"Yes. That was the problem. I hated him and refused to give him any opportunity to do anything for me. I couldn't stand the thought of being indebted to him. So I scrapped the idea of getting a degree."

Emily looked at her sympathetically. "That's sad."

"Don't feel sorry for me." Tara's eyes sparkled as she pushed her hair over her shoulder. "Everything worked out well. I learned to lie to get jobs. Did I tell you I own a bookshop now?"

"I think you've mentioned it," Jack said, amused.

Max's features tensed as he leaned with his forearms on the table. "So you're saying Scarlett was right that the only way to get the student loan was to get married? Couldn't she just tell the loan company that her parents refused to pay?"

"Not unless they've changed the system," Tara said. "I looked into it quite a bit at the time. You have to be estranged from your parents and have absolutely no contact with them. Since Dad had been paying child support for me, I couldn't claim we were estranged, even though I didn't see him."

"That's crazy," Jack said.

Tara shrugged. "I suppose in most instances the system works. I doubt it happens very often that parents refuse to pay or kids refuse to let them."

Emily caught Lizzie's eye. "Do you think Scarlett was serious?"

"Yes," Lizzie said sadly.

"I wouldn't put it past her," Emily said. "And there was something odd about the way they interacted when he came to see her. As though they had a secret."

"What's he like?" Tara asked.

"Cute," Lizzie said automatically, then laughed at the look Emily gave her. "Oh, shut up! You thought so too."

"But I'm not old enough to be his mother!"

"You're so mean," Lizzie said.

"Have you been checking out young boys?" Tara asked with a grin.

Lizzie felt her cheeks heating up. "He seemed very polite and well-mannered."

"Now you sound like someone's grandma," Jack quipped. "Never mind his mother."

"Can everyone leave me alone." Lizzie leaned into Max. He'd gone quiet and didn't seem as amused by the conversation as everyone else. She gave him a gentle nudge to get his attention. "Are you okay?"

"Yeah, fine." He glanced around the room. "The pool table's free. Do you want a game?"

"Shall we have a tournament?" Tara said, jumping into the conversation. "Loser buys the shots?"

"There are always shots involved when you're around," Jack said.

Tara arched an eyebrow. "I've never heard you complaining about shots."

"I wasn't complaining," he said, grinning.

They picked up their drinks and headed across the room, taking up position around the pool table.

CHAPTER 34

The atmosphere in the pub was jovial, as it always was on Christmas Eve. Late in the evening, Lizzie noticed Max sitting alone and went to join him, sliding onto the bench beside him.

"You're being antisocial," she told him as he scrolled on his phone.

"Sorry." He met her gaze. "It's true about the student loan. The assessment is based on your parents' income unless you're married."

"You're still thinking about Scarlett?"

"If she really did marry this guy to get the loan, I'm worried about what she's got herself into."

"Scarlett will be fine. She's pretty streetwise."

"Is she?" Max asked seriously. "What's this guy like? Why did he go along with it? He must be getting something out of the arrangement."

Lizzie's stomach lurched. "Scarlett was adamant they weren't sleeping together if that's what you're thinking."

"Then why would he go along with it? It doesn't make

sense. You said he was well dressed? As though he has money?"

"Yes. But he also didn't seem like someone who'd need to use sinister tactics to get laid."

Max quirked an eyebrow. "Should I be worried that you seem to have a crush on this guy?"

"No!" Lizzie laughed. "I don't have a crush on him." She leaned closer and ran her fingers through Max's hair. "And you don't ever need to be jealous. I only have eyes for you."

Max rolled his eyes. "Are you sure you haven't been drinking?"

"No." Lizzie was confused by the fact that Max seemed irritated by what was supposed to be a compliment. "I just really love you."

"I know," he said flatly.

"Why do you seem annoyed with me?"

He shrugged. "Maybe you being so affectionate is starting to grate on my nerves."

"You don't like me being affectionate?" she asked as a flutter of anxiety hit deep in her stomach.

"I wouldn't mind if it was genuine." He finished his pint. "Let's not have this conversation now. I'm going to get another drink. Do you want something?"

She paused for a moment, stunned by his words. "I want to go home."

"It's not midnight yet. I thought we were staying to wish everyone happy Christmas."

"I really don't feel like being here any more."

"So now you're upset with me?"

"Yes. And I'm concerned that you think I'm being fake when I tell you I love you."

"That's not what I meant," Max said.

She glared at him. "It's what you said."

"Okay, fine. Let's go." He picked up his jacket from the

back of the chair and Lizzie followed as he went around their friends, saying goodbye and wishing everyone a merry Christmas.

By the time they got in the car, Lizzie was fuming. She switched the engine on, then turned it off again, sure she wasn't safe to drive in her frame of mind. Shifting in her seat, she looked squarely at Max.

"Do you want to explain why you're annoyed with me for being affectionate?"

He pushed his head back into the headrest, looking as though he regretted saying anything.

Lizzie struggled to keep her emotions under control. "I thought everything was great with us," she whispered. "What the heck is going on with you?"

He reached for her hand. "Everything *is* great. I shouldn't have said anything. I was just being grumpy."

"I'd like to know what you meant by it."

He blew out a long breath. "I know you're excited about the publishing company. I understand that. It's a new venture and it's exciting. But I keep thinking you could do that *and* have a baby …"

"What?"

"Just listen for a second," he said, not letting her say any more. "I told you I'd take paternity leave. And I meant it. Obviously you'd need to take a bit of time off work, but I'd do as much as I could so that you could go back to work as soon as you wanted."

Lizzie screwed her face up in confusion. "We already agreed to this."

"Yes, but you also fobbed me off. I don't want to wait to have a baby until some mystical time in the future when you decide it's the right time."

"I want a baby too," she said slowly. "I'm not sure why you think I fobbed you off."

He looked at her impatiently. "All that stuff about having to finish the cycle of your pill and that it might take a while to get back to a normal rhythm or whatever."

"That was the truth. I was warning you it might take some time because I didn't want you to get your hopes up too soon."

"You also said it was bad timing. That you couldn't set up the business *and* have a baby."

"Because I was worried it would be too much. Not because I didn't want a baby. And you told me we could handle both."

For a moment they fell into silence.

"So you want to have a baby?" Max asked eventually.

Lizzie caught a tear at the corner of her eye. "Yes."

"And we can start trying already?"

She glared at him, then let out a humourless laugh. "What exactly do you think we've been doing for the last two months?"

"What do you mean?"

"Well, what did you think all the sex was about?" She could almost see his brain working.

"I thought you were being nice to me because you'd fobbed me off about having another baby."

Lizzie put her hands over her face. "Are you serious?"

"I thought you felt guilty for putting your career first. You fall over yourself to be nice to me. If I say I'm going to do something – bath the girls or make dinner or whatever – you jump in to do it first. Or like tonight when I offered to drive and you insisted you would."

"I don't do those things because I feel guilty. I just see how much you do around the house and with the girls and I try to give you a break sometimes." Tears trickled down her cheeks. "Do you seriously think I'm so manipulative that I'd ignore the fact that you want to have a baby and try and placate you with sex?"

He closed his eyes briefly. "When you say it like that it sounds bad."

"I would never do that to you," she said, then sniffled. "I do actually love you, you know?"

"I'm sorry." He turned in his seat and took both her hands in his. "Am I the biggest idiot in the world?"

"Possibly," she said with a nod. "And I hope you enjoyed all the sex because there's a good chance we're never doing it again."

"I'm really sorry. I'll make it up to you, I promise."

She didn't resist when he pulled her to him, and she cried quietly on his shoulder.

"I love you so much," he whispered into her hair.

"You ruined everything," she said when she pulled away from him. "I thought our relationship was better than ever, but now it feels like a joke."

"It's just me who's the joke. I should have talked to you properly."

She nodded in agreement and wiped her hands across her cheeks. Taking a deep breath, she tried to compose herself enough to drive. After pulling her seatbelt around her, she turned the engine on again.

"Were we really trying to get pregnant all this time and I had no idea?" Max asked sheepishly.

Her mouth twitched to a reluctant smile. She was about to drive away but paused. "I didn't volunteer to drive tonight just to be nice to you. I didn't think I should be drinking."

"Should I cut out alcohol too?" Max asked in earnest. "It's supposed to make it easier to conceive, isn't it?"

"That wasn't really my point … I don't think I should drink because I think I might be pregnant."

His eyes widened. "Really?"

"I'm not sure," she said quickly. "Don't get too excited. I'm only a few days late."

"Why didn't you say anything?"

"I wanted to wait and be sure, so you weren't disappointed if I'm not."

He looked at her with a pained expression. "I feel like the worst person on the planet. I really don't deserve you."

Lizzie thought back over their conversations and could see why he'd got the wrong idea. "Maybe I wasn't very clear. I was definitely hesitant about the idea of having another baby at first. But once I got used to the idea, I loved it too."

"When can you take a pregnancy test?" he asked.

"Any time. I bought one already."

"So we could go home and take it now?" he said with a glimmer of excitement in his eyes.

"I was going to wait until after Christmas. I don't want to spend Christmas Day being disappointed if it's negative."

"Okay." He squeezed her hand. "Whatever you want."

They drove in silence for a while. Lizzie was fairly shocked by their conversation and was trying to get her head around it.

"Lizzie?" Max said, rolling his head on the headrest to look at her.

"Yeah?"

"Did you mean what you said about never having sex with me again?"

She had to laugh at the concern in his features. "No. I definitely didn't mean that."

Tara always enjoyed the atmosphere in the Bluebell Inn on Christmas Eve but that night felt extra special. Finding out their window display had won the contest had put her in a good mood before they'd even gone out, but it was having James with her that made everything feel perfect.

She'd been surprised to see her mum in the pub too. Tara and James had gone over for a quick chat when they'd arrived and had been introduced to the group of women Debbie was with, most of whom Tara knew by sight at least. Apparently they'd decided to extend the party after their afternoon at Sheila's house.

Throughout the evening, Tara glanced over at her mum, happy to see her laughing and chatting with her new friends. Once or twice, she'd caught her up at the bar talking to Andy.

The lively evening seemed to slow after Max and Lizzie left. Amber and Paul were talking to some friends at the other side of the pub, while Tara and James sat with Emily and Jack.

"I never thought I'd say this," Tara said, looking into her empty glass. "But I quite like the idea of not staying until midnight."

"Marriage has really changed you," Emily said. "But if you leave, we'll leave too. I'm not bothered about staying until midnight either."

Jack finished his pint. "So I'm not going to the bar?" he said to Tara.

"Not on my account," she said after a questioning glance at James. "I want to go home. I just need to nip to the toilet."

Her head was a little woozy when she pushed the door at the side of the room which led to a corridor, off which were the bathrooms. It was definitely a good idea to go home and limit her Christmas Day hangover. When she caught sight of a couple embracing at the end of the corridor she stopped dead, then slowly backtracked.

"What are you doing?" James asked.

"There's a queue." She forced a tight smile. "I can wait until I get home."

"A queue?" Emily said, standing. "I don't think I've ever known a queue for the ladies' in here. And I definitely can't wait until I get home."

Tara opened her mouth to protest as Emily headed for the ladies' but couldn't think of an excuse to stop her. She watched as Emily walked through the door, then slowly turned back and re-joined them. Her eyes were wide as she looked at Tara.

"Maybe I can wait," she said.

"Sneak into the gents," Jack suggested.

"How long is the queue?" James asked with a frown.

"Pretty long," Tara murmured, as Andy wandered through from the corridor.

"Any of you need a drink?" he asked.

"No," Tara said quickly. "We're just leaving. Thanks."

"Are you sure?" He raised his eyebrows. "They're on me …"

"No. We're fine. Thank you. Happy Christmas."

"Happy Christmas!" he called, smiling before heading back behind the bar.

James held out Tara's coat for her. "Did you just turn down free drinks?"

Before she could answer, her mum wandered through the side door, smoothing her hair down. "Are you leaving?" she asked when she noticed their coats.

Tara caught the look of amusement that passed between Jack and Emily, before Jack snorted a laugh. He covered his mouth and managed to make it sound like a cough.

"We'll see you in the morning," Tara said to her mum.

"Enjoy the rest of your evening," James said as Debbie wished them all goodnight.

Emily stifled a grin as she looked at Tara. "Did you know about them?"

"No! I had no idea. And I'd really like to know how old Andy is!"

"Fifty-three," a voice said.

Tara looked around until her eyes landed on Belinda, sitting with a crowd of people at a table nearby.

"Sorry," she said. "I overheard you. Andy's fifty-three. Why did you want to know?"

"No reason," Tara replied brightly. "Have a good Christmas!"

"You too. And congratulations again on winning the window display. I knew you would."

"Thanks." Tara smiled sheepishly. "We should get going," she said to James.

When they stepped outside, Jack beamed at her. "What exactly did you just catch your mum and Andy doing?"

"Kissing," she hissed. "Just kissing!"

CHAPTER 35

Lizzie shivered in the darkness of the bedroom and snuggled up to Max. They'd moved all the Christmas presents from their bedroom to the living room when they'd got home. The thought of the girls opening them in the morning filled Lizzie with anticipation.

"Your feet are like ice blocks," Max said, pulling her closer.

"I know. Thankfully your legs are nice and warm so they should thaw out soon."

"Always happy to be your hot-water bottle."

With her face nestled against his neck, she inhaled the lingering scent of his aftershave. "You want me to take the test now, don't you?"

"I didn't say anything," he said, a hint of laughter in his voice.

"You're thinking about it, though, aren't you?"

"I'm fairly sure *you* are."

"I can take it now if you really want me to?" She shivered against him. "I just don't like the thought of getting out of bed. I'm all cosy."

"Wait and take it after Christmas. I don't mind."

Lizzie sat up abruptly and reached to switch the lamp on. "You're going to spend all of tomorrow wondering. That's going to be annoying. I think I'm going to take it now. Then we'll know."

"Okay." Max squinted in the sudden light. "If you want to."

"I don't know if I do or not," she complained. "I want it to be positive."

"Take the test now," Max said, throwing the covers off him. "If it's negative, it's not a big deal. We haven't been trying for long. And I didn't even know we were trying." Walking around the bed, he took her hand and pulled her up.

"Where are you going?" she whispered as he followed her onto the landing.

"I'm coming with you."

"Wait here," she said, walking into the bathroom.

"No. Let me come in." Gently, he pushed the door to stop her closing it behind her.

"Do you understand how pregnancy tests work?" she asked.

He closed and locked the bathroom door. "Yes. But I watched you give birth to two babies, I don't think you need to be shy about going to the toilet in front of me."

"Fine." Taking his shoulders, she turned him to face the other way. "Don't look."

"Do you want me to sing too so I can't hear you?"

"Please don't." She took the test from the cupboard and removed it from the packaging. "Goodness knows what Scarlett will think if she gets woken by the sound of your out-of-tune singing, then finds us in the bathroom together."

"That's true."

Lizzie felt mildly self-conscious as she manoeuvred the stick into position.

"Can I turn around?" Max asked when she flushed the toilet.

"Yeah." She put the cap on the test before handing it to Max.

"How long does it take?" he asked as he looked at it.

"A couple of minutes." After washing her hands, she turned and looked at him sadly. "I wish I'd waited. I'm nervous now."

"Don't be." He sat on the edge of the bath and pulled her to sit on his knee. "I think it's going to be positive."

"I really want it to be," she said, resting her forehead against his. All of her initial worries about having another baby had vanished, and she loved the thought of expanding their family.

"If it's not, we'll just keep trying," he said quietly.

"I know." Time seemed to stand still as she looked at her watch.

"Remember the first time we were in this bathroom together?" Max said.

"Yes." She smiled, partly because she appreciated his attempt to distract her, and partly because the memory of catching Max in the shower after letting herself into the wrong cottage always made her smile. "I'm very happy I got the wrong cottage."

He kissed her softly. "Me too. I don't know what my life would be like if I hadn't met you. I hate the thought of it."

Lizzie felt the same. If the test was negative, it wasn't going to ruin her mood. She had Max and two gorgeous children. Spending Christmas with them couldn't ever be disappointing. "Is it two minutes yet?" she asked.

"I'd say so." He inhaled deeply, then turned the test over in his hand. They stared at it for a moment before Max spoke again. "Not bad considering I didn't even know we were trying!"

"Not bad at all," she said, laughing in delight, then kissing him deeply.

~

"Happy Christmas," Max said when Lizzie opened her eyes.

"Happy Christmas," she replied blearily, then checked the time. "Where are the girls?"

"Still asleep."

"They can't be. It's eight o'clock. Scarlett must have got up with them."

"Nope. I checked on them and they're fast asleep. Apparently they decided to give us the gift of sleep for Christmas."

"That was kind of them."

"Enjoy it. I guess next year won't be such a peaceful Christmas morning."

"I don't suppose it will," Lizzie said happily. "I still can't believe you didn't realise we were trying to get pregnant."

"I can't either. Now that I think about it, it's pretty obvious. I'm sorry for being so grumpy with you."

"It was a stupid misunderstanding." She rolled onto her side and kissed his shoulder. "And it was partly my fault for not being enthusiastic at the beginning."

"I think we have better things to think about now."

"I know." She brushed her fingers across his forehead. "What are all these worry lines for?"

Pushing her hand away he rubbed at the creases and made a conscious effort to relax his features. "I was thinking about Scarlett."

"I'm sure she knows what she's got herself into. I can't imagine any guy getting her to do something she's not comfortable with. I'm fairly certain they're not actually living together as husband and wife. They just got the paperwork."

"In order to get a loan," Max said on a sigh. "That's fraud."

It hadn't occurred to Lizzie that there could be legal ramifications, but with Max's legal background, of course that's where his mind would go.

"Could she get into trouble?"

"Yes. I'm not sure how much, but if she got caught there'd definitely be consequences." Max stood up and pulled on a pair of jogging bottoms and a T-shirt. "She's already up. I heard the coffee machine a while ago. I'm going to talk to her before the girls wake up. I'm still hoping she was joking."

"I hope so too." Lizzie followed him downstairs in her pyjamas.

"Happy Christmas!" Scarlett said when they walked into the living room. She was lying on the couch and settled a heavy book on her stomach as she greeted them.

They wished her a happy Christmas and sat on the armchair, Lizzie perching on the arm. The room felt wonderfully festive with the presents under the tree.

"I'm glad you're up before the girls," Scarlett said. "I was hoping to have a quick word with you about my babysitting rates. I've decided it makes sense for me to charge per child. So if you decide to have another kid, it'd obviously cost you more."

Lizzie looked at Max with wide eyes. He opened his mouth to speak, then clearly couldn't think what to say and kept quiet.

Scarlett snorted a laugh. "That was my weird way of saying congratulations."

"Thanks," Lizzie said.

"Were we talking really loudly last night?" Max asked.

"I didn't hear you come in. I have crazy detective skills, though, so it would be almost impossible for you to keep it from me."

"I'm confused," Lizzie said. "How could you know?"

Scarlett smirked. "You left the pregnancy test in the bathroom."

"Oh!" Lizzie said, feeling slightly stupid. "Oops."

"I presume it's a secret?"

"Yes." Max looked to Lizzie for confirmation.

"We'll probably wait a few weeks to tell people," she said.

"My lips are sealed." Scarlett swung her legs off the couch and sat up. "Can I go and nudge the girls? I want to watch them open their presents before I go to Verity and Bill's place."

"In a minute," Max said, glancing nervously at Lizzie. "I wanted to ask you something first. We were wondering about what you said yesterday. About being married."

Her features tensed. "What about it?"

"Is it true?"

"It would be a weird thing to joke about."

Max shook his head. "You joke about weird things all the time."

"True. But it wasn't a joke."

Lizzie shifted on the arm of the chair. "I understand why you did it, but what did he get out of it?"

"You're wondering why someone like Fraser would marry someone like me?"

"I didn't say that," Lizzie said. "I just don't understand his motivation. Unless he's in love with you?"

"No." She shook her head fiercely. "Definitely not. He seems to enjoy annoying me, but I'm sure he doesn't actually like me."

"So you're not …" Max trailed off.

"Spit it out," Scarlett said.

"Are you sleeping with him?"

"No. Not that it's any of your business."

"I know it's not," Max said. "We're only worried about what you've got yourself into. Just because you married the guy, doesn't mean you ever have to …"

"Please stop!" Scarlett said, shuddering dramatically. "I can't have a sex conversation with you. It's weird and creepy. But you don't have to worry, he's annoying but he's nicer than a lot of guys my age. He wouldn't try and sleep with me or anything."

Silence fell for a moment before Max spoke again. "So you're legally married?"

"Yes!" She threw her hands up. "This is why I didn't want to tell anyone. You're making a big deal out of it."

"Because a fake marriage is a criminal offence."

Scarlett's gaze flicked to Max. "What?"

"You could get into trouble."

"No." She swallowed hard. "I won't get into trouble because no one will ever know. It's not as though anyone's going to come and check. And as soon as we graduate, we'll get a divorce."

"But what if someone does check?" Max asked.

She gave a quick shrug. "I'll say I didn't know it was against the law."

"Except if you're intelligent enough to figure out how to game the system, you're intelligent enough to realise it's wrong."

"It's the system that's wrong," Scarlett said quickly.

"That doesn't mean you can just make up your own rules," Max said, exasperated.

"Don't look at me like that," she snapped. "You have no idea. You studied law and I bet you never even had to think about money. You probably didn't even have a part-time job while you were studying, so you don't get to sit and judge me." Her voice came out strangled and her eyes filled with tears.

"I'm sorry," Max said, holding up his hands as Scarlett shot off the couch.

"Wait," Lizzie said, sure that Scarlett was about to bolt. "Sit down and we can talk about it. Maybe we can help."

"No, you can't." She sniffed and sat down again. "You don't understand. Mum and Dad think I'm stupid. They don't want to waste their money on me. What else was I supposed to do? I don't want to work in a shop. That's what Mum thinks I should do."

Lizzie automatically moved to comfort Scarlett. She should have known better; Scarlett had never invited physical contact, and the fact that she moved further along the couch indicated that was no different just because she was upset. Lizzie remained at the other end of the couch and looked at her sympathetically.

"It's not fair," Scarlett said tearfully. "Why shouldn't I get a degree if I want to?"

"You should definitely be able to," Lizzie said. "And you're right that it's not fair."

"What will happen to me if we get found out?" she asked Max.

"I'm not sure. You'd get kicked out of uni. Possibly a fine and a criminal record. But I couldn't say for sure. That's just a guess."

"So you think I should quit my degree and divorce him?"

Max ran his hands through his hair, looking pained. "No."

"What should I do then?"

"Make sure no one finds out." He looked directly at her. "Like you said, it's likely that no one will ever look into it. But you definitely shouldn't be telling people it's a fake marriage. Who knows about it?"

"I only told you. Some of his friends know. They think it's funny."

"You need to get him to stop telling people. The fewer

people who know, the less chance that you'll get investigated. And if you do get investigated, it needs to look like a real marriage."

Scarlett pulled a face. "Are you saying I should have sex with him? Because I think I'd rather go to prison."

"No." Max shook his head. "Don't sleep with him. But don't tell people you've never slept with him and are disgusted by the thought."

"Do you really dislike him so much?" Lizzie asked.

"You met him!" Scarlett went slightly shrill. "Did you see his stupid floppy hair? He's constantly pushing it away from his eyes. I don't understand why he doesn't get it cut. And what's with his clothes? He's like a walking advert. And he leaves his underwear in the bathroom and dumps wet towels all over the place."

Lizzie caught Max's eye and they exchanged a small smile.

"Why are you looking at each other like that?" Scarlett demanded.

"No reason," Lizzie said. "He sounds awful."

"I don't know how I'm going to live with him for three years without killing him."

"Definitely don't kill him," Max said. "That would get you into a lot of trouble."

"I was joking. He's annoying, though."

Max leaned back in the chair. "Try and pretend you like him a little bit. It would be safer if you actually seemed to be in a relationship with him."

"I guess Fraser won't be very happy with that idea," Scarlett said.

"He should have thought about that before he married you," Max remarked.

Lizzie's mind wandered to the day he'd turned up at the

office. "When he came to the office that day, what was it he wanted to apologise for?"

Scarlett's gaze dropped to the floor. "He had some friends over. I overheard them talking about me and they weren't exactly complimentary. I guess he felt bad."

"Bad enough that he'd drive all the way here to apologise? Couldn't he have called or messaged you?"

"I was ignoring his calls and messages," she said quietly.

"He must like you if he was worried you were upset."

Scarlett threw her hands up. "I don't know."

"Sorry. It all seems a bit odd. I don't understand why he'd agree to marry you." Lizzie's brain worked frantically, trying to get it straight in her head. "Did he need to get married for the loan too?"

"I don't think so."

"And you haven't asked?"

"We don't speak much. Just ignore each other."

"Aren't you curious?"

"Not really." Her eyes darted around the room, and Lizzie had the feeling that she was much more interested than she was letting on.

"You should ask him."

Scarlett gave an exasperated shake of the head, signalling that she'd had enough of the conversation. "Can I wake the girls up now?"

"Yes." Lizzie wanted to be there when they woke up too, but she lingered for a moment when Scarlett left the room. "I feel so sorry for her," she whispered to Max.

He stood when she did and folded her in a hug. "Me too. She's right; I've never had to worry about money. My parents threw money at me while I was growing up. I can't imagine having to fight to get the education you want."

"Do you think she'll be okay?"

Gently, he stroked her hair. "Well, they're not having sex,

she hates his hair and wants to change the way he dresses. Sounds like a fairly convincing marriage to me."

"Max!" She stepped back and playfully slapped his arm.

"Come on! That was an obvious joke." He gave her a quick kiss. "Let's go and tell the girls that Santa's been."

CHAPTER 36

James volunteered to drive to Debbie's place on Christmas Day. Tara was happy to be in the passenger seat as her mind chewed over the events of the previous evening.

"So, do you think Mum's seeing Andy?" she asked James.

He smiled at the question, which she'd already asked several times. "Is it such a bad thing if she is?"

"I suppose not. It just feels really weird. And why didn't she mention it to me?"

"Probably because she didn't want your opinion on it."

"Why not?"

"In case you were disapproving?"

"I wouldn't be."

He kept his eyes on the road. "You were disapproving of Rupert."

"With good reason!"

He gave her a sidelong glance. "Maybe it was a Christmas kiss and nothing more."

"That would be very out of character." She sighed as they

pulled up outside her mum's house. "I'm just going to ask her what's going on."

"Try not to be judgemental."

She shot him a look as they got out of the car. "Of course I won't be."

"There are worse people to have as a stepdad." He dodged out of the way when Tara swiped at him. "Think of all the free drinks," he said cheekily.

She tipped her head to one side. "I hadn't thought about that."

There was a bustle of hugs and Christmas wishes when they walked inside.

"It smells amazing in here," James remarked as they followed Debbie to the kitchen.

"Lunch will be ready in about half an hour," she said. "I hope you're hungry. I made loads."

"I assumed we'd help you cook," Tara said.

"I thought I'd get on with it this morning. If we eat earlier, we could wander down to the pub this afternoon."

Tara exchanged a look with James. "We never go to the pub on Christmas Day," she said. "And you were in the pub last night. What's the sudden attraction?"

James rolled his eyes and took a seat at the kitchen table, which was covered in a festive tablecloth and set with a Christmas cracker at each place.

Debbie peered at the pans of veg bubbling away on the stove. "I just thought it might be fun to be sociable and see who's around. I'm sure there'll be a nice atmosphere with everyone in the Christmas spirit."

"So you haven't arranged to meet any of your new friends?"

"No. They'll all be busy with their families. Although Sheila mentioned that they sometimes go for a drink on Christmas Day."

"Right." Tara watched her mum open the oven for a quick glance at the turkey. She moved back as a waft of hot air hit her, then closed the oven again. "Have you made any new male friends since you've started being more sociable?"

Debbie's gaze flicked to Tara. "I get the feeling you know I have. Will you be getting to your point any time soon?"

"My point is, I saw you kissing Andy in the pub last night."

"Ah."

"Ah? What kind of an explanation is that?"

Debbie smiled sweetly. "You want me to explain why I was kissing Andy?"

"Well … I'd like to know the nature of your relationship with Andy."

"If you saw me kissing him, you already know the nature of our relationship. It involves kissing!"

"Mum!" Tara took a seat. "What's going on?"

James gave Debbie a reassuring look. "I think Andy's a nice guy."

"I think so too," Debbie replied happily, leaning against the counter.

"How long has this been going on for?" Tara asked. James gave her a quick kick under the table, and she realised she didn't have the most supportive tone. "Sorry. I'm just surprised."

"He was really nice to me after my disastrous date with Rupert. After he invited me out for a drink, he invited me out for a meal." Her cheeks pinked as she smiled. "He promised he'd pay and wouldn't make a fuss about the bill. Since then we've been seeing more and more of each other. I like spending time with him. That's about all I can tell you."

"I suppose that's good." Tara glared at James when he gave her another kick. "I mean, if you're happy, that's great."

"We're very happy for you," James said brightly.

"So we're going to have Christmas dinner and then go down to the pub to visit your boyfriend?" Tara asked.

"If that's okay?" Debbie flushed slightly but didn't refute that he was her boyfriend. She picked up her phone from the sideboard and her smile widened at the message she'd received.

"Oh my God. He's messaging you." Tara dropped her head to the table. "This is sickening. Can you please stop kicking me?" she said, laughing at James. "She's my mum – I don't have to watch what I say."

"Maybe you should!" James said, moving his legs when she attempted to kick him back.

"What are we drinking?" Tara asked, moving to the fridge. "I'm going to open the wine." When she turned, Debbie was looking at her intently.

"You don't mind me spending time with Andy, do you? Is it awkward for you?"

"No." Tara shook her head and set the chilled bottle of white aside. She wrapped her mum in a big hug. "It's not awkward for me. I'm glad you're happy."

It ended up being one of the best Christmases Tara could remember. They stuffed themselves with turkey and all the trimmings, then exchanged gifts before wandering down to the Bluebell Inn. Andy sat with them for a while. It felt a little odd at first. Previously, their conversations had always been brief exchanges across the bar. Having him sit and chat to them felt slightly awkward, but that was partly due to the fact that he and Debbie kept grinning at each other like lovesick teenagers.

Since the pub was reasonably busy, Andy kept having to go and serve customers, making the situation less intense. Tara felt pretty merry when they left the pub late in the afternoon – whether that was from the alcohol or the jovial atmosphere she wasn't sure.

"Why did Andy say he'd see you later?" she asked her mum as they set off up the road. "Actually, I don't think I want to know! But I guess you're not expecting us to stay too late."

"I presumed you wouldn't be staying all evening."

"Counting on it, more like." Tara's smile slipped. "Did you arrange a time to call Dad?" The video call with David was a Christmas tradition. Nat and Ben would always come on and say hello, and even Gillian would pop up to wish them a happy Christmas. It was awkward, but it was what they did.

"I sent him a message earlier. We agreed not to do the video call this year."

"Really? How come?"

"Because I hate it," Debbie said. "I always felt we had to do it because I thought you should speak to your dad on Christmas Day. Especially when you refused to have anything to do with him for the rest of the year. But you're an adult; if you want to talk to him, you can organise it yourself. And if you don't, then that's up to you. It puts a dampener on the day for me so I'm not doing it any more."

"Fair enough." Tara had always hated it too, but also felt a bit strange about not doing it. Maybe the issue was that it should never have included her mum. "I'll probably call him later. Nat's been messaging me a lot so she'll definitely want to call at some point."

"Good. You can go home to call them and leave me in peace!"

Tara laughed and slipped her arm through Debbie's. "I like seeing you so happy."

"I'm glad," she replied. "I like it too."

After getting home and calling her dad, and then James's parents, Christmas Day was finished off nicely with a couple of nostalgic films while the lights of the Christmas tree twinkled in the dimly lit room. By the time the credits rolled up on *Miracle on 34th Street*, James was fast asleep. Gently, Tara nudged him awake.

"Time for bed," she said and received a grunt in reply. He appeared to go back to sleep, and Tara sat watching his steady breaths. "I'm worried about Dad," she said, not sure whether she was talking to herself or James.

"Why?" James muttered, stretching as he sat up.

"He was quiet on the video call."

"Because no one can get a word in with Nat."

"She's really like me in some ways," Tara said with a grin. "People used to complain that I talk too much. Anyway, I think seeing Mum so happy made me wish Dad was too. Which is slightly ironic since I spent most of my life thinking he was blissfully happy and resenting him for it."

"I'm not sure there's much you can do if his marriage is in a mess." He stood and pulled Tara up.

"I know. But I also feel bad that I made him miserable for so many years when I refused to see him. And I wish I hadn't told him that I didn't always read his emails."

"Because it was a mean thing to say or because he stopped emailing you and you miss it?"

"Both." She pouted. "I do miss the emails. And there's no need for you to look so amused by that!"

"Sorry. But I think there's probably an easy fix."

"Swallowing my pride and apologising isn't easy."

He gave her a gentle smile and headed for bed. While he went straight back to sleep, Tara lay awake for ages, then seemed to spend most of the night tossing and turning until a shaft of sunlight streamed through a gap in the curtains. She crept out to the living room to fetch her laptop, then returned to the warmth of their bed. The click of the keyboard cut through the silence as she typed, but James didn't stir. It was almost an hour later when he rolled towards her and flicked his eyes open.

"What are you doing?" he asked, a husky rasp to his voice.

"I wrote an email to Dad."

"What does it say?"

"That I miss his emails. That even though I couldn't always bring myself to open them, I always liked that he sent them. And lots of stuff about how I feel and what I think. I spilled my guts." A lump formed in her throat and she blinked back tears. "I don't know if I should send it or not."

James looked up at her sympathetically. "I think it might be a good thing for him to know how you feel. He'll probably appreciate it."

She stared at the screen for a moment before hitting send. Immediately, she felt nerves flutter in her stomach. "That might have been a mistake," she said as she closed the laptop. Setting it aside, she lay down and pulled the duvet over her head. "I think I'm going to hide here forever."

"Mind if I join you?" James asked, burrowing under the covers with her and slipping his arms around her.

"I don't mind at all."

When his lips covered hers, she felt better immediately.

CHAPTER 37

Closing the shop between Christmas and New Year had felt like a good idea, but Tara soon felt restless. On the day after Boxing Day, she spent the morning pacing the flat.

"Why are you so stressed?" James asked. "Your dad's coming for lunch, that's all."

"I know, but I think he's coming alone. And it's because I sent that stupid waffly email." Her dad had called her the previous day, shortly after she'd emailed him. He hadn't said much about it on the phone – just thanked her for sending it and asked if she was free for lunch the following day as he'd be in the area. "Obviously he wants to talk about all that stuff I said to him in the email. I wish I hadn't sent it. I wanted him to know what was going on in my head, but I don't want to discuss it. And it's just my luck that he happens to be in the area today. I thought I'd send the email and then not see him for a month or two. There's no way I'd have sent it if I'd known I'd see him the next day."

"Can you stop pacing?" James said. "And stop talking – you're going around in circles. He's your dad and he's coming to take you out for lunch. You're making too much out of it."

"He's coming to take *us* out for lunch," Tara said forcefully. "You're coming too. I need you there."

"Can you please sit down, you're making me nervous."

She sank onto the couch beside him. "I'm a nervous wreck."

"I can see that."

The doorbell sounded and Tara jumped up to buzz David into the shop. When she opened the door to the flat for him, he kissed her cheek, then moved inside and shook James's hand.

"Are you hungry?" Tara asked. "Do you want to go straight out for lunch or have a coffee first?"

David shrugged. "I don't mind. We could go straight out?"

"Great. I don't think there are many places open today, so it might just have to be the pub. The food's good, though."

"That's fine with me," David said. "You choose the place and I'll pay."

"Thanks." Tara grabbed her coat from the hook, then glanced back at James.

"I've actually got some work I should be getting on with," he said, directing his words at David. "You don't mind if I leave you to it, do you?"

"Not at all."

"Great. Have fun." He kissed Tara's cheek when she glared at him.

"Let's go then," she said, forcing a smile for her dad. As they stepped outside, she pulled her hat down over her ears and took her gloves out of her pockets.

They walked in silence for a few minutes.

"I didn't realise you ever did business in Devon," Tara said eventually.

He gave her a sidelong glance. "I don't."

"Oh. I assumed when you said you'd be in the area today, it was a business thing."

"No." He glanced into the shops as they walked. "It was more of a 'having lunch with my daughter' thing."

Tara whipped her gaze to his face. "You came all the way here just to have lunch with me?"

"Yes. In your email you said it annoyed you that Nat always came along when we met up."

"I probably shouldn't have said that. I must've sounded like a petulant twelve-year-old."

"No. You were right. Nat always invited herself along. I think because she's insecure when it comes to you. But I have the feeling that me trying to keep everyone happy has had the opposite effect."

Tara didn't know what to say so they fell silent again until they were settled in a quiet corner of the Jolly Farmer.

"How are Ben and Nat?" she asked, for lack of anything else to say.

"They're fine." David smiled. "Same as always. It's a constant battle with Ben to get him away from his computer. And Nat keeps nagging us about some party she wants to go to."

"You should let her go to parties," Tara said, wiping condensation from the side of her glass. "She'll no doubt get drunk and do stupid things, but that's part of growing up. You can't lock her away because you're scared of letting her grow up."

His brows drew together. "I'm not sure you're the best person to give me advice. I might be an overprotective parent, but you let fear control your life far more than I do."

She stared at him for a moment, unblinking. "Because I choose not to have kids?"

David leaned back in his chair and squeezed the bridge of

his nose. "I'm sorry. I shouldn't have said that. I just wanted us to have lunch. I didn't mean to stir up more issues."

With great effort, Tara let her anger subside. She was sick of all the issues between them too. "It's okay," she finally said. "You might have a point."

"It's none of my business, and I shouldn't have commented on it."

Tara stared into her glass of coke. "After losing Reuben, weren't you terrified of having more kids?"

"Gillian wanted kids," he said slowly, his features softening.

"So you just went along with it for her?"

"No. I was happy at the chance to have more children. Losing Reuben was the worst pain in the world, but I wouldn't give up the time we had with him for anything." He hesitated, looking uncertain. "I know I've no right to comment on your choices, but I hate the thought of you missing out on anything in life."

Tara's chest felt tight and she scanned the pub in a bid to distract herself from the seriousness of the conversation.

"Do you always close the shop at this time of year?" David asked after a moment.

"No." Tara was thankful for the change of subject. "Previously we opened between Christmas and New Year, but we decided to have a break this year."

"Have you got any more authors lined up to visit the shop?"

"The next author event is at the end of January." Tara relaxed back into her seat. "He's from Cornwall and he writes murder mysteries. It's always interesting to meet the authors. Some of them have been quite surprising."

"Really?" he asked with a small smile.

She nodded and told him about the sweet old lady who wrote gruesome horror books, and the guy who wrote comedy fiction who was one of the dullest people she'd ever met. David coaxed more stories from her over lunch, and the conversation was light and easy. He talked about his job a little, but mostly the conversation revolved around Tara and her life.

When she glanced at her watch, three hours had passed with her barely noticing it.

"Thank you for coming to visit," Tara said when they ambled back home. The frozen pavement sparkled and a smattering of snowflakes fluttered on the icy breeze.

"I enjoyed it," David said.

They were approaching the bookshop, and Tara glanced up to see a warm glow of light seeping from the upstairs windows. "Do you want to come up for a coffee?"

"I think I'll get straight off." He pressed the button on his key fob and the lights on his car blinked as the doors unlocked. "Say bye to James for me. And tell your mum I said hi when you see her."

"I will. She's doing really well at the moment."

"I got that impression. I heard she's seeing someone?"

"Did she tell you that?"

"No. Nat mentioned something about some guy coming into the shop."

"That was Rupert. Thankfully she's not seeing *him*, but there is someone. It's early days but she seems happy."

David shifted his attention to the car key in his hand. "What's he like?"

"He's a really nice guy."

"Glad to hear it," he replied with a nod.

Tara hugged him tightly. "You don't have to worry about me and Mum. We're okay."

"I'm not sure it's possible for me not to worry about you," he said sadly.

"Try. Maybe that will make things easier for you. I'd feel

better if you were as happy as I always assumed you were. I'll talk to you soon," she said as they broke apart.

"Call me any time. And I'll email you," he said with a smile.

"I'd like that." She told him to drive safely.

As she watched him drive away, she didn't feel the same heaviness as she usually did. In fact, she felt surprisingly positive. Walking through the shop, she pondered Annette's comment about how much she'd achieved with the bookshop. It made her think of how rundown the place had been the first time she'd set foot inside. She felt an overwhelming sense of pride as she looked around. When her gaze landed on the photo wall, she walked over and stood in front of it. She and James looked so happy in the photos.

Inevitably, she landed on the picture of them with Josie and baby Annie. She smiled to herself as she stared at James laughing with the baby in his arms. Lost in thought, she almost jumped out of her skin when the door at the back of the shop opened.

"I thought I heard someone down here," James said. "Has your dad left?"

"Yes."

"How was it?"

She pursed her lips as she pondered the question. "Good, actually."

"You sound surprised."

"I was getting used to there being an issue or argument every time I see him, but it was pretty chilled out."

"Issues and arguments are normal with families," he said, putting an arm around her shoulders.

"It feels as though things are getting easier." She leaned into him. "And I'm very happy for you to say 'I told you so' in this instance."

"I wouldn't dare." He squeezed her tighter. "What are you doing skulking around down here?"

"Looking at the photos." Tears stung her eyes. "Every time I look at the photo of you with Annie, I feel as though I'm depriving you of something."

"You're not. But if the photo bothers you we can take it down."

She shook her head. "You just look so happy in the photo."

"Because I was having fun teasing Josie, not because having a baby in my arms makes my life complete." He raised an eyebrow. "If it makes you feel better, the next time I hold her I'll be sure to look miserable."

"Now you're being ridiculous."

He kissed the side of her head. "I don't know why we keep having the same conversation."

"Because it's something I worry about. I spoke to Annette about it the other day. I keep reminding myself that she and Wendy didn't have kids and they were perfectly content."

"We will be too," he said.

Tara paused, thinking about how Annette's house had always felt like a second home to her. "Wendy and Annette always seemed to have a busy house," she mused. "I spent a lot of my childhood at their place, as did Amber and Sam and Max. So they might not have had their own kids, but they always seemed to have other people's children around them."

James's gaze turned deadly serious and his lips parted as he started to say something, then stopped abruptly.

"What?" Tara asked.

"Nothing," he replied too quickly.

"You were about to say something."

His features relaxed. "Maybe it would be helpful if we started to look at the advantages of it only being the two of us… there are a lot of things people with kids can't do …"

The twinkle in his eye gave away the fact that he was trying to lighten the atmosphere.

"Such as?" she asked.

He pretended to mull it over. "Middle-of-the-day sex," he finally said.

She couldn't help but smile. "We hardly ever do that."

"I think we should," he said with a cheeky grin. "Just because we can."

"You're very obviously trying to change the subject," she managed before his lips covered hers, silencing her in an instant.

He kissed her deeply, pulling her body against his. "I'm doing a good job though, aren't I?" he finally murmured.

"Yes," she whispered. "Let's go upstairs."

CHAPTER 38

"You've changed," James said, when he woke on New Year's Day.

Tara had been awake for a while but had stayed in bed, watching him sleep. "In what way?"

"You always used to sleep until at least noon if you didn't have anything to get up for. Now you're always awake at the crack of dawn."

"That's because we were in bed before eleven last night," she pointed out.

"Exactly. Usually, you'd be the last to leave a party, but you wanted to leave the New Year's party at ten o'clock."

"Sorry," she said, entwining her legs with his and snuggling into his chest. "Did I ruin your night?"

"No. I would have happily left an hour earlier when my crazy sister insisted on games. Who really wants to walk around with the name of a celebrity stuck to their forehead?"

"It was quite entertaining," Tara said.

James kissed the side of her head and gazed into her eyes. "I'm worried about you," he said. "You've been so quiet the last few days. Whatever's going on in your head, you can talk to me about it."

She almost pointed out that she couldn't talk to him. There were some subjects which he brushed aside whenever she tried to speak about them. She ran a hand through his hair. "Can we go out somewhere?"

"I thought we were going over to Annette's house today?"

"Yes. But she said to come at any time. Can we go somewhere first, just the two of us?"

"Where?"

"I don't know. Just drive and find a beach somewhere? I feel like sitting and watching the waves. We could take a flask of hot chocolate …"

"Now you've really sold it to me," he said with a grin.

~

South Milton Sands was a favourite spot of theirs. The long sandy beach was almost deserted, the cold and damp weather clearly putting people off. Even wrapped up in thick coats and with hats, scarves and gloves, the cold wind bit at them. The hot chocolate had been a good call. Not that Tara cared much about the weather as she sat on a blanket on the sand with James.

"I want to talk to you about something," she said, leaning close to him. "But I need you to promise to be honest."

"What makes you think I wouldn't be?"

"Because I know you!"

A smile played at his lips. "And you think I'm a liar?"

"No." She looked at him seriously. "I think you'll say whatever you think I want to hear. And then you'll change the subject."

His gaze shifted out to sea. "Is this about kids again?"

"Yes."

He turned to face her. "As long as I have you in my life, I don't need anything else."

She rested a hand against his cheek. "You always say that."

"Because it's the truth."

She kissed him softly, then looked deep into his eyes. "When we decided to be together I needed you to know there was a possibility that we'd never have kids. And I needed to know that you'd never pressure me into it."

"I wouldn't—"

"I know you wouldn't," she said, taking his hand. "But somehow that's turned into us definitely not having kids and avoiding the subject entirely."

His brow creased. "I know how you feel about children, and I understand why you feel that way. I don't want to upset you by going on about it."

"You won't upset me. If anything, avoiding conversations about kids is upsetting me. We should be able to discuss it."

"Okay," he agreed, not looking at all convinced.

"Every time I see you with someone else's kids—"

He looked at her impatiently as he cut her off. "You need to stop feeling guilty, and stop worrying that you're depriving me of something when you're not."

"I don't feel guilty," she said calmly. "I was going to say that when I see you with other people's kids, it makes me sad to think it won't ever be our kids. And I don't worry that I'm depriving you of something . . . " Her voice became strangled by the lump in her throat and she paused to take a breath. "I worry I'm depriving *us* of something."

James opened his mouth to speak, then stopped himself, shifting his gaze out over the water.

"I'm not saying that I definitely want to have kids," she continued. "Just that I want us to talk about it." When she pulled his face to look at her, tears shone in his eyes.

"I don't know what to say," he whispered.

"Just tell me how you feel. Without worrying about saying the wrong thing and upsetting me."

He rubbed at his jaw. "I get the impression that you think I'm desperate to have children and I'm somehow tortured by the thought of not having kids. But it's honestly not something I think about much. I'm genuinely happy as we are."

"And what if I changed my mind about children?"

"Have you?"

It took a moment for her to formulate an answer. "I don't know," she said. "But I know I feel differently about it than I did a year ago. At one time I was adamant that I'd never have children to please someone else … but that's changed. If you wanted to have children, I would do it for you."

"You know I'd never want that."

"You wouldn't be pressuring me into it. I'd happily do it for you. And I would love our children and I know I'd be happy."

"That's not the same as wanting children."

Tara pushed a strand of hair from her face as the wind caught it. "Part of my problem is that I spent so many years telling myself I'd never have kids. To make it easier I focused on all the negatives … I told myself that being pregnant would be awful and childbirth would be horrific. I thought about sleepless nights and messed-up hormones and the lack of freedom. I don't have the romantic ideas about having a baby that other people have."

"We don't have to have a baby," James said.

She sighed in exasperation. "You're missing the point of the conversation. I don't want you to say whatever you think I want to hear. This isn't a test."

"No." He looked at her seriously. "I mean a baby's not the only option."

She stared at him until he kept speaking.

"If we want to expand our family, having a baby isn't the only choice. When you were talking about Annette the other day, you said she and Wendy always had a house full of kids. They ended up with a big family even though they didn't have children."

Tara opened her mouth, but wasn't sure what to say.

"I think it will be the same for us," he went on. "Even if we don't have our own kids, we'll be the cool aunt and uncle with the bookshop. Not just to Kate's kids but to Kieron and Maya and Phoebe and little Annie … and whoever else comes along. And you said yourself that you feel differently now about having children than you did a year ago. So a year from now – or five years – you might feel differently again. And if we decide we want children, there are other options besides having a baby…" His jaw tensed and he seemed unsure of himself. "We could adopt. Or foster … You were so great with Nat …"

"No, I wasn't," Tara protested weakly, her mind spinning at all he was saying.

"You were. Even when it was hard for you, you were patient and kind. When she was upset and struggling with her own issues, you helped her. You could do that for other kids too."

Tara's eyes welled up. "You've been thinking about this?"

"A little bit."

"Why didn't you say?"

"Because I thought you'd take it to mean that I wasn't happy as we are. And I am happy. But one way or another, I don't think our family will end up being just the two of us."

Tara pushed tears from her cheeks as she smiled at James. "I love you so much," she said, leaning in to kiss him.

He held her tightly as the wind swirled sand on the beach around them. "I love you too."

"I like the idea of fostering," she said.

"Yeah?"

She nodded. "When I was younger, I always knew I could go to Annette and Wendy's house when things weren't good at home. I like the thought of giving kids a safe place when they need it." Tara felt a rush of relief at the frankness of the conversation. "I think I always had it in my head that the choice was having a baby or not. I never considered anything else. And I always felt as though I needed to stick to my decision not to have kids, but things change, and you're right that things will probably be different again in a year or two."

"We have lots of options," James said. "And loads of time to decide what we want."

"What do you want?" Tara asked, gazing at him intently.

"I don't know." A small smile tugged at the corners of his mouth. "I never really let myself think about it."

"I'm sorry," she said, hit by a wave of guilt.

He shook his head, then kissed her lightly. "I already have everything I want. Anything more would just be a bonus."

CHAPTER 39

On the bitterly cold beach, Tara and James huddled together as the sun sank to the horizon, chatting about all their hopes and wishes for the future. The possibilities felt boundless. After spending so long being sure she knew what her life had in store, Tara was thrilled by the feeling that her future was a blank slate and she and James could make whatever they wanted with it.

When they finally left the beach, they were still no closer to deciding what exactly they wanted. There'd be plenty more conversations to come, but she was certain that whatever they decided on would be exactly right for them.

Tara's fingers and toes were icy by the time they got back in the car, and she didn't feel as though she thawed out much on the drive to Annette's place. James parked the car beside the house alongside the others.

"I guess we're the last to arrive," Tara remarked as they crunched across the frozen grass to the front door.

It opened before they reached it and Kieron came running out, all wrapped up in his winter gear.

"Happy New Year!" Tara called, opening her arms to him.

As he dodged around her, she just managed to ruffle his hair before he ran away down the garden.

"There you are!" Amber exclaimed, walking outside with Paul. "I thought you'd have been here ages ago."

"We got held up," Tara said, a smile pulling at her lips as she caught James's eye.

"We're just leaving." Amber wrapped Tara in a hug. "We've been here all afternoon."

"The shop is closed for a couple more days," Tara said. "How about we do something tomorrow?"

"Perfect." Amber touched the back of her hand to Tara's cheek. "You're freezing. Get inside and warm up."

The warmth of Annette's kitchen felt wonderful and the smell of freshly baked goods was divine.

"You two look half frozen," Annette said as she wandered in from the living room.

Tara rubbed her hands together and stamped her feet on the mat. "We are."

"I'll make some hot chocolate." Annette put a saucepan on the stove and poured milk into it. "Where've you been all day? Everyone else has been here for hours."

"We were at the beach," James told her, draping his coat over the back of a chair.

"No wonder you look like two blocks of ice then." She passed him a plate of biscuits. "Take those through and warm yourselves up by the fire."

In the living room there was a bustle of greetings and everyone wishing each other a happy new year.

Emily was on the couch with Josie and Sam beside her and little Annie nestled in her arms. By her feet, Jack sat with one of the twins on his lap, her arms and legs wrapped around him like a baby monkey.

Tara peered down to see her face, which was buried in his chest. "Is she asleep?"

"Fast asleep," Jack replied. "I'm not allowed to move."

"They're both worn out," Lizzie said. She'd been sitting on Max's lap on the armchair but stood and headed for the kitchen.

James said hello to Maya as he and Tara settled themselves on the floor in front of the fire. She ignored him and continued stroking the grey tabby sprawled beside Charlie in the middle of the rug.

"Where did the cat come from?" Tara asked.

"Just another stray," Annette said, handing Tara and James mugs of hot chocolate.

Tara blew on hers before taking a mouthful of the deliciously warm and creamy drink. She reached for a biscuit to dip in it. "I don't remember you ever taking in strays," she said.

Annette chuckled as she lowered herself into her chair. Then she looked pointedly at everyone in the room.

"Hey!" Max said, amidst a lot of laughter. "I'm your nephew, remember?"

"Yes, you're family. The rest of them are strays."

"I'm your nephew's wife," Lizzie called from the kitchen.

"I'm family too," Jack said. "I'm your nephew's wife's sister's ex-boyfriend. Can't get much more closely related than that!"

"I'll admit to being a stray," Tara said happily.

"I suppose I am too then," James said, looking up at Annette. "Sorry."

"You don't need to apologise," she replied. "Not with a face like that."

"Annette!" Tara snapped, slightly drowned out by the laughter around her. "Stop flirting!"

"You don't have to worry," Annette said. "I'm a lesbian. Otherwise you might have a fight on your hands."

Lizzie wandered in and handed Josie a cup of tea. She

smiled down at baby Annie and appeared to tickle her foot until Josie reached over and swatted her hand away.

"Can you stop pinching your niece!" she said. "You're the worst auntie in the world."

"Well if she won't cry, I have to resort to trying to make her cry. How on earth did you end up with such an angelic baby? It's not fair."

Max smiled lightly as Lizzie settled herself on his lap again. "Maybe this one will be an easy baby," he said, placing a hand on her stomach.

The room fell silent and all eyes turned to Lizzie.

She glared at Max. "I thought we weren't telling anyone yet?"

"Sorry," he said, shrinking back into the chair. "It slipped out."

"You're pregnant?" Josie shrieked.

"Congratulations," Emily said, beaming at Lizzie.

Josie gasped and turned to look squarely at Emily. "Did you already know? You did, didn't you? I can tell by your face." Her attention switched to Lizzie. "You realise I'm your sister? I can't believe you told my best friend before you told me. And don't start saying she's your best friend too. She's mine and you stole her!"

Sam patted Josie's leg and gave her a meaningful look.

"Congratulations!" she added brightly, making them all chuckle.

"I didn't know," Emily said. "Honestly."

"You better not have done," Josie said with mock annoyance.

"That's lovely news," Annette said. "It's a good job I've got a big house. I wonder how many kids there'll be running around here five years from now." She paused, and her eyes settled on Jack. "Oh, don't look at me like that!"

"Like what?" he asked in amusement.

"Like you don't think I'll be around in five years."

"I didn't," he insisted, laughing as Emily gave him a playful nudge with her foot.

"I'll be here," Annette said with a bright smile. "You all just keep turning up and I'll keep baking biscuits."

"Deal," Sam said, reaching for another biscuit from the table at the end of the couch. He passed the plate around and the room filled with chatter.

Tara felt emotional as her gaze swept around her friends. Annette might call them strays, but Tara knew that she considered each and every one of them family. She also knew that what James had said on the beach was true: whether they decided to have a baby one day, or to foster or adopt, or be the most amazing aunt and uncle to all their friends' kids, they would have the most wonderful family and always be surrounded by people they loved.

Tara blinked back tears as James shuffled close to her. "Are you okay?" he asked.

She rested her hand against his cheek as she kissed him.

"I've never been better," she whispered against his lips.

DON'T MISS THE NEXT BOOK IN THE HOPE COVE SERIES...

There's Something about Scarlett

(Hope Cove book 8)

Three years of marriage, then they'll go their separate ways...

Scarlett Mercer dreams of starting her own publishing company. But with no way to finance university, she might be stuck working in her aunt's café indefinitely.

When a chance encounter leads her to an extreme solution, she's desperate enough to go through with it. Even if it means marrying a guy she's only just met.

What she doesn't factor into her plans is how easily she gets overwhelmed. Soon, she's struggling to navigate university life while living with a guy she barely knows.

Meanwhile, **Fraser Graham** is trying to figure out what it is about Scarlett that mesmerised him so much that he agreed to marry her.

When he realises what it is that makes her so different to anyone he's ever met, the revelation leaves him reeling ...

Will Scarlett manage to fulfil her dreams? And as sparks begin to fly, will their marriage end up being more than just convenient?

ALSO BY HANNAH ELLIS

The Hope Cove Series

The Cottage at Hope Cove (Book 1)

Escape to Oakbrook Farm (Book 2)

Summer at The Old Boathouse (Book 3)

Whispers at the Bluebell Inn (Book 4)

The House on Lavender Lane (Book 5)

The Bookshop of Hopes and Dreams (Book 6)

Winter Wishes in Hope Cove (Book 7)

There's Something about Scarlett (Book 8)

The Loch Lannick Series

Coming Home to the Loch (Book 1)

The Castle by the Loch (Book 2)

Fireworks over the Loch (Book 3)

The Cafe at the Loch (Book 4)

Secrets at the Loch (Book 5)

Surprises at the Loch (Book 6)

Finding Hope at the Loch (Book 7)

Fragile Hearts by the Loch (Book 8)

Always With You (Standalone novel)

The Friends Like These Series

Friends Like These (Book 1)

Christmas with Friends (Book 2)

My Kind of Perfect (Book 3)

A Friend in Need (Book 4)

The Lucy Mitchell Series

Beyond the Lens (Book 1)

Beneath These Stars (Book 2)

Hannah has also written a series of children's books aimed at 5-9 year olds under the pen name, Hannah Sparks.

Books in the Land of Stars series:

Where Dragons Fly (Book 1)

Where Stars Fall (Book 2)

Where Penguins Party (Book 3)

ABOUT THE AUTHOR

When she's not writing, Hannah enjoys spending time with her husband and kids. She loves to read and also enjoys yoga and jogging. And tea … she really loves a good cup of tea!

Hannah can be found online at the following places:

Twitter: @BooksEllis

Facebook: @authorhannahellis

Instagram: @authorhannahellis

Website: www.authorhannahellis.com

Feel free to contact Hannah at any of the above or email her at this address:

authorhannahellis@gmail.com

If you'd like to be kept up to date with news about Hannah's books you can sign up to her mailing list through her website:

www.authorhannahellis.com/newsletter

Printed in Great Britain
by Amazon

38319350R00199